# A SOLO DANCE AND OTHER STORIES

BY MANNA LIU（嘉妮）
ENGLISH TRANSLATION
BY YINGRUI GONG / JICHENG SUN

1 Plus Books
San Francisco, 2025

**1 Plus Books**
https://1plusbooks.com

**Author:** Manna Liu
English Translation by Yingrui Gong and Jicheng Sun
**Title:** A Solo Dance and Other Stories
2025 1 Plus Books®
Paperback Edition
Published and Printed in the United States of America
**ISBN:** 978-1-966814-11-5
Library of Congress Control Number: 2025908323


**Publisher:** Yan Liu
**Book Design:** 1 Plus Books
**Price:** $24.99
San Francisco, USA, 2025
**https**://1plusbooks.com
**Email:** 1plus@1plusbooks.com

# Contents

# Xiaoxue in the Okanagan Valley

## I

Nelson, located in the province of British Columbia, Canada, is a multiracial town with a population of about ten thousand. The city has 350 buildings with different cultural influences, making it Canada's best-preserved folk culture city, like a pearl hidden deep in the Okanagan Valley. According to archaeological records, human history here dates back over five thousand years, and the first Europeans arrived in 1807. There is an airport in Castlegar, its neighboring town, and it only takes half an hour to reach Vancouver or Calgary.

The town attracts many tourists worldwide and is a haven for artisans, especially unrestrained artists. As you walk down the street, one folk-style building after another appears as if you are flipping through a historical album.

It was in this town that I met Xiaoxue for the first time, and I have not seen her for about eleven years now.

I remember Xiaoxue was an orphan, a tall and awkward Northern girl who was only devoted to others. After her divorce from her first Chinese husband, she, penniless, met her "Mr. Right," a handsome Swedish man named Hans, in Beijing. They fell in love at first sight and immigrated to Canada together to start a business. After enduring ten years of hardships, they finally opened their first clothing and handicraft store in Vancouver. Hans was responsible for sourcing goods from China, while Xiaoxue designed and made the clothing herself. Just when everything seemed to be going smoothly, however, Hans couldn't resist the temptation of another young and beautiful woman and kicked Xiaoxue out of the house with nothing. After the sadness, she settled in Nelson and isolated herself in this small town. Unexpectedly, she soon fell into the swamp of love again, incurably falling for a man named Bob who had moved from Newfoundland, and they barely got along together for nearly six years. Bob was lazy and indulgent, consuming her love immensely. The only thing that could make her happy was the sweet words that flowed effortlessly from the mouth on his fair-skinned face. It wasn't until Bob died in a car accident that a background investigation revealed to Xiaoxue that he was actually a wanted criminal.

As my car approached the destination, navigated by GPS, I saw a slender and vague figure standing under the shade of trees from afar. It quickly moved to the slightly dim streetlight as my car approached and stood there quietly.

It was not until I got out of the car that I recognized that the slender woman with long hair draped over her shoulders was Xiaoxue. The image of the "Northern tough girl" from before was completely gone.

A warm embrace made us both reluctant to let go of each other.

"I'm sorry for keeping you waiting for so long. The town seems to have changed slightly, and I forgot the route," I apologized to Xiaoxue.

She grabbed the bag from my shoulder with one hand and smiled as she pointed at the doorstep, "Yes, more and more tourists come here for vacation in summer. Hippies and tramps fill the streets, but artisans like us haven't increased in number."

"How are you? Where's Ah Qing? Why doesn't he come with you?" I opened the door and entered the house, and she asked hurriedly after handing me a pair of slippers.

Eleven years ago, Ah Qing and I came to Nelson in a second-hand Jeep to sell jewelry we had designed. It was here that I met Xiaoxue.

During the three months of summer selling, we were the only "Chinese hippies" among dozens of tents. Xiaoxue sold clothes, and I sold jewelry while Ah Qing cooked for us in front of the tent daily without complaint. Xiaoxue witnessed the love between Ah Qing and me, admiring our entrepreneurial spirit of sharing weal and woe in our mutual support. She regarded love as her eternal pursuit and described herself as a "thornbird", tirelessly pursuing love even if it meant getting hurt.

The three of us would occasionally sleep in the same tent or in the car. Meeting a confidant in a foreign land, I heard many of her love stories.

During the daytime in the Okanagan Mountains, the temperature had reached 36 degrees. Xiaoxue's house was a bit stuffy and messy, with a smell of Chinese medicine in the air. I looked around the room, trying to learn about her life from the details. Two silk skirts were being sewn on the sewing machine table against the wall. A slender metal pole supported by metal was in the corner of the room, on which there were beach skirts designed by herself like colorful flags. A huge floor-to-ceiling window ( 落 地 窗 ) was opposite the sofa, with several pots of succulent plants looking lifeless on the windowsill.

The clock on the wall showed that it was already 10:45 at night. The house was so quiet that you could hear the clock ticking. After the excitement of the reunion, we sat opposite each other on the sofa, and neither of us had anything to say for a moment. Although I originally felt like there was much to say, I didn't know how to start a conversation.

Xiaoxue's face was a little pale, and her slightly protruding belly gave the impression that she might be pregnant. Looking at her figure, I felt she had a hint of bitterness, but I didn't know whether to ask her for a moment.

"Your marriage is very successful. I've hardly ever seen such a loving couple like you two. Your love is genuine. I envy you so much!" Finally, she started a conversation.

She would collapse if she moved one of her hands. She put one hand against her belly and the other supporting her waist. Then, a bitter smile appeared on her pale face, tinged with a hint of helplessness.

"I actually miss you quite a bit. However, life is unpredictable, and I'm not the person I used to be. The happiness you envy no longer exists." I spoke a bit hesitantly. I knew she once envied my marriage so much, and I was afraid that the collapse of my marriage would be a heavy blow to her steadfast pursuit of love.

"Why is your inn empty?" I quickly changed the subject.

"It's been closed for almost a year. I've been through a lot of hardships these two years. I had a hysterectomy two years ago and lung and breast removal surgeries this year. I'm almost done for."

Seeing her condition, I had anticipated misfortune but didn't expect it to be so serious. Love is like a gorgeous poppy flower with a beautiful appearance; its fruit can cure diseases or harm people.

I stood up and walked over to sit beside her, grabbing one of her hands and gently patting it silently as if all the words I wanted to say were moving on my fingertips.

She withdrew her hand and patted my shoulder, saying, "My place is too messy, and the water heater broke down just now. How about we go to sleep at my boyfriend's house? There's a room for me and a spare guest room there."

Seeing my hesitation, she explained further: "Don't worry. I've been with my boyfriend for nine years already. When I was sick and in hospital, he took care of me all the time. He didn't eat Chinese food and couldn't cook it, so he ordered and delivered it to the hospital."

Her enthusiastic invitation made it hard to refuse. At the same time, I felt she really wanted me to meet her boyfriend. So, I followed her car, and luckily, we arrived about five minutes late.

This house looked much larger than Xiaoxue's from the outside. As she opened the garage door and we walked in, a man's voice came from upstairs, "Xue, is that you? Why are you coming over so late?"

"Yes, it's me. I brought a friend. My water heater doesn't work. Come and fix it tomorrow." Xiaoxue spoke in a commanding tone, quite casually.

"Nihao, 你好 !" As we entered the house, I saw an old gray man standing on the landing in his pajamas.

"His name is Frank. He can only say this sentence in Chinese," Xiaoxue explained with a smile.

"This is my friend, Maizi. We've known each other before I met you. I invited her to stay here for one night. You can go to bed now; everything's fine." Xiaoxue walked up to him, patting his shoulder gently with a sweet smile.

"Good night!" Frank called, walking straight into the room at the far end of the hallway and gently closing the door.

Compared to Xiaoxue's house, it was so clean here! The kitchen was neat and tidy, without any mess or smell. The cabinets on the walls were made of glass, so you could see the neatly arranged dishes. The unfolded quilt on the bed in the guest room was identical to the hotel's, and a cute little bear was holding a sign that said "Welcome" near the pillows. A pot of crimson hanging lobelia (fuchsia) bloomed vigorously on the bathroom countertop. There was a square transparent glass on the roof of the bathroom. After turning off the lights, the moonlight would pour through the glass and fill the floor. The bathtub showed signs of age, but there was not a single drop of water around it.

It was hard to imagine this house without a hostess on ordinary days.

## II

I had a great sleep that night and woke up at 9:30 in the morning. After tidying up the bed and dressing myself, I still didn't see Xiaoxue. Thinking she was still sleeping, I tiptoed into the living room. The solid wood floor was shining, and as I walked barefoot on it, I could feel its slight coolness from being cleaned.

"Good morning! Xiaoxue has gone to buy you breakfast, and there's hot coffee in the kitchen." The glass door of the kitchen led to a covered leisure platform. As soon as I entered, Frank saw me. He sat on a chair on the platform, holding a coffee cup.

"Thank you! I'm not used to drinking coffee because caffeine keeps me awake." I didn't sit down but leaned against the platform's railing, examining the surroundings and the man before me.

Frank looked almost seventy, about six feet tall. A large gold ring adorned the third finger of his left hand. His temples were gray, and a strand of hair lay on his bald head. He wore a neatly ironed white shirt and a pair of jeans. Gold-rimmed glasses sat on his high nose, indicating his fairness and cleanliness.

The ground of the platform, made of wooden planks, was about ten square meters in size and one meter above the ground, surrounded by a fence woven from wooden strips. Three bird nests hung in one corner. Frank explained that twelve recently hatched birds were chirping in the largest birdhouse.

Outside the platform lay a lush garden. Neatly trimmed green grass spread across the center of the yard. White lilies and red peonies bloomed beneath the west fence; two apple and pear trees, full of fruit, stood near the west fence, and a small patch of ripening tomatoes and peppers grew about two meters away. A squirrel jumped up and down on the pine tree in the corner of the yard, stuffing pine nuts into its mouth, already preparing food for the winter.

"Sitting on the rattan chair, you can see the distant mountains." Frank stood up and pointed to a tree stump under the fence in the distance, telling me there had been a tree there for over twenty years. He used to think that the tree, with its lush branches and leaves, acted as a barrier that blocked the view of the neighboring balcony. Frank liked to sit here every day after retiring but found that the tree blocked his view of the distant mountains. So, he had cut it down himself several days ago. It took him a week to cut the tree trunk into small pieces and then ask a friend to deliver them to a church.

I sat opposite Frank, separated by a coffee table. Sitting on the recliner, this was the vantage point for a panoramic view. In the distance, the undulating mountains seemed like the manes of fierce horses running side by side.

We began to chat.

"I am of French descent. I retired last year, and my wife has been dead for fourteen years. We have lived in this house I designed for over thirty years. I always maintain it; you see, it still looks new." Talking about his house, he showed immense pride as if admiring his treasure.

"Where did you move from to Nelson? Why did you come here?" I asked cautiously, not knowing if such questions would be offensive.

"I moved from Montreal. I initially lived in a small town nearby. I came here on vacation by chance and found this the ideal place to live after retirement. So, I moved here with my family thirty years ago, and we haven't moved since then." From his happy words and laughter, I could tell he was satisfied with his decision.

"Have you been to China? Where did you go? What impressed you the most?" I brought the topic to what I wanted to know most, starting the "interview" as a journalist.

"I've been to China three times, once with Xiaoxue and the other two times on my own. The most memorable experience was my first time in Anyang, Henan. It seemed like I was the only foreigner there, and people asked me to take photos with them all day, making me very tired." Although it sounded like a complaint, I could tell his words had a hint of pride.

"Xiaoxue mentioned that you didn't like Chinese food. What did you eat in China?" I had been curious since Xiaoxue mentioned it.

"I could only look for Western food, like McDonald's, KFC, and Starbucks. I found a delicious pizza in Beijing and would go there almost daily, walking dozens of li ( 里 , a unit of distance in China, 1 mile equals 3.2 li) back and forth. Fortunately, I enjoyed walking and could see many interesting things on the road. It was interesting that Chinese people don't like to initiate conversations. Still, if I greeted them first, they would respond enthusiastically, and young people even chatted with me in English."

"What is your favorite place?" I continued the interview.

"I like Beijing's hutong ('alley' in English) the most. I like the simple life there. Walking into the hutong feels like entering another world, but unfortunately, there aren't many." As he spoke, he spread his hands and frowned, showing a bit of regret.

"You've been to China, and your current girlfriend is Chinese. What is the biggest difference between Eastern and Western women?" I pressed on with a bit of momentum.

"Eastern women, um…" Perhaps my question caused some misunderstanding, so his face blushed slightly, seeming hesitant to continue.

"Oh, I mean the differences in mentality and culture," I added because I sensitively realized that my question wasn't very clear.

"Um, Western women are more independent and won't tie themselves to family and men. Eastern women are not independent and always hope to find a man to care for them. In fact, we should be independent and take care of ourselves unless we can't move anymore. For example, I can clean my house well, cook and care for myself. Xiaoxue's living habits are completely different from mine. She eats Chinese food, but I eat Western food. I like quietness, but she needs to use the sewing machine at home. So we respect each other and have our own house and independent space. We've known each other for nine years, and I admire her independence. We accept and tolerate our differences, so we've gotten along for a while."

After listening to his words, I contemplated and no longer asked questions.

He picked up the coffee cup on the table, took a sip, and continued, "Let me tell you a story."

The protagonist of the story was one of his friends named Kenbury. Frank had just returned from a trip to China and met him at a bar in the small town that year when Kenbury's wife had just divorced him. They had been married for four years without children. His wife, who had never worked a day, took half of his property according to legal procedures. Therefore, he was drinking in sorrow. Frank talked to him about his travel adventures in China, saying that the culture there was completely different, and the people were very enthusiastic, especially the Chinese women, many of whom wanted to go abroad. He suggested that Kenbury go to China for a vacation to relax.

Kenbury bought a plane ticket to China the next week and met a Chinese woman in Xi'an who wanted to marry him. This woman was wealthy with a daughter in college, and her only requirement was for him to marry her and take her to Canada. Kenbury quickly married this woman and used her money to buy a house in Vancouver. He also required both names to be written on the property ownership certificate. However, when the woman's daughter came to Canada for a visit, Kenbury didn't let her stay home, saying she was over eighteen and staying home would disturb his life. The couple divorced over this, and Kenbury took half of her property without spending a penny within two years after their marriage.

"I still feel guilty to this day. I shouldn't have told Kenbury about China. I look down on his actions, but I also want to say that many Chinese women don't understand foreign cultures and laws at all when they marry foreigners, so they are always cheated but unable to speak out about their grievances."

After speaking, his eyes stared at the distant sky as if he was self-reproaching or repenting. At the same time, I felt heavy and suffocated, as if falling into a quagmire. I felt sorry for such compatriots. Kenbury's Canadian ex-wife, who had never worked a day, took half of his property in the divorce. Kenbury's Chinese wife, who bought the house with her own money, had half of her property taken away by Kenbury because she didn't know the law. Was this the difference between Eastern and Western women?

### III

Xiaoxue returned, carrying soy milk and youtiao (fried dough sticks) from the farmers' market.

"Frank has already had breakfast, so don't worry about him," Xiaoxue told me as she opened the food container, noticing my intention to invite Frank for breakfast.

Seeing us speaking Chinese and getting ready to eat, Frank tactfully picked up the newspaper from the living room sofa and sat on the leisure platform again.

Last night, under the dim light, I could tell Xiaoxue was tired. This morning, having scrutinized her carefully, I found she had changed significantly over the past ten years. Her face was pale, with a few strands of white hair hanging disheveled. The high bridge of her nose looked more pronounced on her thin face. She wore a tight, short skirt with a black background and white flowers, accentuating her protruding belly. Her thin back was slightly hunched, and her once-tall figure seemed to have shrunk. She used to love dressing up, but now she was very casual, even a bit unkempt. The wounds inflicted by love left scars on this woman everywhere, inside and out. These scars had nurtured her, making her confident and brave, like a soldier on the battlefield, charging forward regardless of difficulties.

Last night, Xiaoxue and I talked until about three in the morning. Our conversation never strayed from love and my divorce from Ah Ching.

"How could a couple, once life and death companions, end their relationship so easily?" When I told her about my divorce, she furrowed her brow and squinted, unable to comprehend.

"Some couples aren't truly in love from the beginning. Their union is driven by ulterior motives, so such marriages won't last long. After enduring hardships together, some couples eventually split up when one feels tired and wants to rest. In contrast, the other wants to move forward."

"Yes, love is a brief chemical reaction between two people. If the balance is not maintained after the reaction, they will separate and go different ways. Marriage is identical to friendship, requiring both parties to be at the same equilibrium point for a permanent relationship. However, people change their minds constantly. A marriage certificate essentially chains and binds two people who love each other together for a lifetime. I've been through this, so Frank and I are free from marriage, making us cherish each other even more." From her explanation of love, she seemed less stubborn than before.

"Last night, I did most of the talking. Now, tell me about your story with Frank." I refilled her coffee cup while teasing her to chat with me.

"It's been almost ten years now. One day, I was selling clothes at a farmers' market stall. When I packed up the stall, it suddenly started raining heavily. Seeing me flustered, he came to help me tidy up. That's how we got to know each other."

"Your story is flat and featureless. It's just a black-and-white photo." I laughed while eating youtiao.

"So it is. In fact, I pursued love all my life, and I realized love is not passion until I met Frank. I used to love others deeply, even if there was no return, as I thought love cost a lot. But now, I feel tired and need a calm attitude to treat each other. Frank and I have no marriage or love, but we firmly believe in each other." Xiaoxue told her story calmly as if talking about the woman next door.

"You once described yourself as a thornbird, endlessly pursuing love despite being trapped in it and hurting yourself grievously. It seems your first three romances hurt you deeply, perhaps leading to the loss of passion to pursue love?" I tried to understand her.

"I still pursue and long for love, but in a different way. Previously, I thought that love equaled fearless efforts, never dreamed of rewards, or never thought women should love themselves first. A woman who does not love herself is difficult to get a man's love. It was not until I met Frank that I realized love cannot just be giving, but also rewarding, through his understanding, tolerance, and care for me during my illness." Xiaoxue spoke calmly, drinking soy milk with one hand supporting her waist.

"The water heater has been repaired, just a small snag." Xiaoxue and I chatted while eating, not even noticing when Frank left the house. When he returned with a cheerful smile to "report his work" to Xiaoxue, we had been eating breakfast for almost two hours.

Xiaoxue tried hard to persuade me to stay a few more days, and Frank chimed in, too, but I had to leave.

We walked out of the house together. Across the street lay a green lake where some people sat chatting on chairs while others played in the water with their children.

The garage door opened, and I noticed dozens of tools neatly arranged on the wall, lined up like soldiers. Several cardboard boxes were piled on a table, sent from India and containing clothing materials for Xiaoxue.

"You have a part-time job and need recuperation due to your bad condition, so you shouldn't go to the market stall on weekends." I expressed my concern for her health.

"I don't trade for money, don't you understand? Craftsmen like us don't work just for money but also for the love of art. This connection will never be broken except by death," she said, still patting my shoulder as she used to when talking.

Of course, I understood. I just didn't know how to comfort Xiaoxue. Ten years had passed, and Nelson had changed from a small town with only a few thousand people to a tourist city with over ten thousand residents. I had also changed from being part of a couple to being alone; Xiaoxue had changed physically, morally, and mentally. Only her love for art and her perseverance in love remained unchanged, undestroyed by several serious illnesses. She was indeed a thornbird! Although wounded and disabled, she still strove to fly and sing.

"I'll come to see you once a year from now on, okay?" I hugged her frail body, tears streaming down my face.

"That's great, and we finally reconnect. In this world, I have no attachments. You are my closest friend who understands me most. I'm so glad you came to see me. Maybe you'll see me again, or this is our last meeting." She choked up, tears filling her eyes.

I turned my head forcibly and got into my car. When I looked back at her, she was still standing by the road waving at me with the other hand supporting her slender waist, as slim as a willow.

Feeling too upset to drive, I stopped the car at a corner. When I looked back again, I couldn't see her figure anymore. My heart was aching as if it were bleeding. I lifted my head blankly and stared at the rearview mirror in front of the car window, where a pair of red eyes were shedding tears uncontrollably.

I said to myself, "Maizi, you must remember to come and see her every year, even if she is in her grave!"

# Nicholas V

## I

Nicholas V is about to celebrate his ninety-eighth birthday in two days and wears a red baseball cap. His snow-white hair peeks out from under the brim, and a barely noticeable smile on his wrinkled face gives him a slightly proud air. He wears a beige zip-up shirt and dark gray pants, with his feet tucked into a pair of faded, clean, brown, soft leather shoes without laces. He bends over, his head down, and his thin lips move slightly. He holds a cane in one hand and sways the other as he moves. He stumbles and moves forward slowly, his wooden cane tapping on the small gravel path, making a clattering sound.

His destination is the "Cuckoo Bakery," just a few dozen meters from the nursing home. The bakery is next to a nail salon run by Vietnamese owners. The bakery owner is from Hong Kong, and the shop only covers about ten square meters. You can see a variety of egg tarts, cookies, bread, and cakes inside through the glass window. As Nicholas V approaches the glass door of the bakery, he switches the cane to his other hand and focuses on the door handle. Just as he is about to reach for it, a delicate hand with the word "Love" tattooed on the wrist reaches out and pulls the door open ahead of him. The sudden gesture stuns him for a moment. As he looks up, he sees a young girl with black hair; even though she wears a mask with a big mouth pattern, her eyes reveal a smile. With one hand pulling the door, the other gestures for him to enter. Nicholas merely opens his mouth slightly courteously, bringing his snow-white teeth together, and his wrinkled face, full of age spots, shows a comical smile. He nods slightly and waves his retracting hand as if saying, "Thank you. I'm here to order a birthday cake for myself."

He orders a durian cake.

"It stinks; what on earth are you eating? Get it out quickly!" Sixty years ago, when Nicholas's mother, Fanny, opened the box containing the birthday cake she had ordered for herself, her husband angrily covered his nose and immediately turned away.

Feeling wronged and tearful, Fanny quickly closed the cake box. Since then, they had never seen a durian cake again. It wasn't until Fanny's seventy-sixth birthday, when she lay in bed, that her husband brought her a durian birthday cake and personally fed it. Tears flowed down her cheeks as she tasted the cream mixed with tears. She mumbled, "Durian? It's delicious! Tears taste sweet for the first time."

"This is your order." The masked waiter kindly awakens him from his reverie. Looking around, only Nicholas doesn't wear a mask among the few people in the room, which seems awkward. He takes the order and stands aside, putting his credit card back in his wallet with his trembling hand, then taking his presbyopic glasses from his pocket and carefully examining the order.

Customized Cake

Size: 2 inches

Fruit: Durian

Design: Make a small flag out of white chocolate, and write the words "Nicholas V, Ninety-Eight" on the flag with brown chocolate.

Order Date: September 12, 2021

Pickup Date: September 13, 2021

He folds the order neatly in satisfaction and stuffs it into his wallet. As he turns to leave, the girl has already bought the bread and opened the door for him again.

"Thank you!" Nicholas still doesn't look up; he just nods politely.

"Hello! My name is Chunyang. I am a sophomore living in the nearby apartment and a volunteer at the nursing home. Recently, we haven't been able to meet and chat with the elderly as before, so we can only draw some greeting cards to send to them." Stepping out the door, the girl initiates a conversation with him.

"Oh, thank you!" Nicholas turns his head slightly and nods at Chunyang out of politeness or perhaps out of gratitude for her twice opening the door for him. But he doesn't look at the girl. Instead, he continues to walk ahead.

"Can I ask you a question?"

"If I can answer it."

Nicholas becomes curious, stopping and looking at Chunyang with his eyes. He is serious this time. Chunyang has brown eyes and thick black hair and wears a jumper, denim shorts, and a pair of white sneakers. Chunyang, surrounded by a youthful aura, seems to inject a bit of vitality into Nicholas, causing the dopamine in his blood to surge.

"When you ordered the cake, you said your name was Nicholas V. That's interesting, which makes me wonder if your ancestors are royalty." Nicholas's scrutiny gives Chunyang a bit of courage, from which she feels there is a possibility of continuing the conversation.

"Royalty? No, just a degenerated aristocrat!" Nicholas V denies her suggestion decisively and resolutely, his pupils beginning to shrink.

"I study history and am very interested in Canadian history. Can we be friends? When you are free, we can make a phone call."

"Hmph, I never use a cellphone, let alone computers. If you have time and want to hear a story, we can sit in the park outside the nursing home for a while." Nicholas V doesn't expect to be interested in telling his story to a stranger, perhaps because he has been confined for a long time due to the recent epidemic.

The path to the park is lined with naturally formed dwarf tree clusters on one side and a group of high-voltage lines on the other. Recently, people worldwide have been staying indoors due to the pandemic, and there are almost no pedestrians on the road. Even when they occasionally encounter someone, no one smiles and greets each other as before. There is even a woman who seems to be going shopping, immediately covering her mouth with the mask hanging on her chin as if avoiding a plague when she sees them from afar.

II

Outside the nursing home walls, the park features a vast lawn. The wall comprises gray wooden planks, where two workers dismantle the decaying wood weathered by wind and rain. Several replaced wooden planks, the natural color of soil, stand out conspicuously against the gray planks, creating a stark contrast that feels discordant and depressing. Around the lawn are rows of wooden benches, each with an iron plate on the back bearing donors' names and birth and death dates. Most of them passed away in this nursing home.

"The nursing home records everyone's birthdays in a book. They give me a simple celebration on my birthday, but I still like to order a small cake for myself. This habit started when I turned twenty-two and left home," Nicholas V talks vividly, his voice tinged with stubbornness.

He enjoys sitting at his desk, placing the cake on a delicate saucer and using a special spoon engraved with the family badge to savor it little by little. He flips through or continues writing in his diary, tasting his life with every slow chew.

After being released from prison, Nicholas V moved to Firewood Town. He officially retired at the age of sixty-five. The day after retirement, he made himself a travel list excitedly. The first stop was the Canadian Vimy Memorial in France, a place his grandfather and father cherished. He vividly remembered his father often telling his two sisters and him that their great-grandfather was a member of the Canadian Expeditionary Force in World War I who sacrificed himself to defend Vimy Ridge in the early stage of the Battle of Arras. Therefore, he wanted to visit him.

He finally went there. The land covered with lush greenery and surrounded by serenity still holds wartime tunnels, trenches, bullet pits, and unexploded ammunition. As he approaches, he feels a heavy "smell of death" hitting him. He looks up at the twenty-seven-meter-high sculpture designed by the Canadian sculptor Walter Allward, desperately trying to find his great-grandfather's name among the names of the dead soldiers carved on the monument. The two pillars look like giants, while he feels like a small pebble or a speck of dust under their feet. He stands there silently as if hearing the thunderous roar of gunfire. The figure of his great-grandfather appears before him, bending over, holding a long rifle, and shuttling back and forth in the tunnels or hunkering down along the edge. He aimed ahead, ready to pull the trigger at any moment. Suddenly, he feels a bit of regret for breaking away from a family he should have been proud of.

Having returned to Canada, he unhesitatingly went to the municipal government. He submitted his application for a name change for the second time from Edward to Nicholas—a name abandoned by his father. So, he officially became the Nicholas V of this family.

### III

"Nicholas, I wasn't actually named Nicholas, but William. My father simply named me Nicholas. My mother married him because of this name. He was an outstanding businessman in our family. In the early 18th century, just after turning 20, he stationed himself with French missionaries in the Saint Lawrence River Valley near Montreal, Canada. Later, he followed some early settlers to the vicinity of Toronto and engaged in the fur trade with the local Hurons. At that time, a beaver pelt could increase in value by at least 100%, sometimes even yielding profits of over 200%."

Chunyang sat casually on the grass, listening to Nicholas V's storytelling. She stared at his face, trying hard to discern his definition of the family from the changing expressions as he spoke. But she found it to be a deeply mysterious and ever-changing expression. Pride? Contempt? Mockery? Sadness? She couldn't define it at the moment.

Lake Huron connects the State of Michigan in the United States and Ontario in Canada. To the west of the lake is the fertile triangle area, to the north are densely forested mountains, and to the east is the Gaspe Peninsula, surrounded by water. The region is connected to the famous Great Lakes (including Lake Superior, Lake Michigan, Lake Huron, Lake Erie, and Lake Ontario). It flows into the Atlantic Ocean through the Gulf of Saint Lawrence, making it an ideal waterway trade port. The French harvested not only gold here but also territory. Fur traders, centered around the Saint Lawrence River, gradually established a large-scale trading network deep into the forest while purchasing fur from Indigenous people, extending from Newfoundland in the east to Lake Superior in the west and from the State of Louisiana in the south to Hudson Bay in the north. At that time, the new Kingdom of France virtually controlled the heart of the entire North American continent.

After Nicholas I became wealthy, he returned to France. He married

Susanne, the 19-year-old daughter of a fur hat factory owner. When their daughter was three years old, he couldn't help but miss the excitement and adventure of making a fortune in North America every day, so he persuaded his wife to go with him to Canada.

"Darling, you know, I've told you that Canada is full of gold! We don't need to work as hard as we do now. We just need to carry empty bags!" Nicholas, I gestured with both hands, boiling his thoughts from days of preparation to just these few keywords: "picking gold."

"I have a bag! I want to pick gold." Their obedient daughter Elizabeth ran into her room, picked up a small cloth bag and spoke softly to her father, then turned to her mother, who was embroidering.

Nicholas I's persuasion finally succeeded. Two months later, in the autumn, their family of three, with several large suitcases and under the embraces of relatives, boarded an ocean liner at the Port of Brest in France to cross the Atlantic. After more than three months of sailing, they finally arrived in Saint Lawrence Bay. By then, Canada had started to snow.

"Mom, look! Dad said gold is yellow, which is not true; it's white." Elizabeth, who had never seen snow before, climbed up on a chair, pointing outside the window and shouting.

"Ha, ha, that's exactly what he said; even on my grandmother's seventieth birthday, the descendants still teased him." Nicholas V burst into laughter as he spoke. His laughter was a bit fierce, and he choked on his saliva. He raised his arm to cover his mouth and started coughing.

## IV

"Do you know Hudson Yards?"

"Yes, it's a huge commercial center. We still have it in our city."

"In the following years, they had a son, Nicholas the First, and two more daughters. From then on, the Nicholas family, a little sapling transplanted from France, flourished on the fertile land of Canada."

"Wow!" Chunyang's eyes widened in amazement.

"You see those rows of poplars in the distance. When I moved here more than twenty years ago, they were just saplings, but now they've grown tall. However, due to their old age and lack of proper maintenance, they've started to die off in batches."

They both looked at the distant trees in silence. The breeze blew on their cheeks, and Nicholas V's eyes were filled with sadness.

His words puzzled Chunyang, who ruminated over his words in her mind: "Is there any similarity or comparability between the trees in nature and their family 'tree'?"

"Ah, the love of money is the root of all evil."

Humanity on Earth is sick, and people wear masks like never before when going out. The air is filled with painful moans. The television broadcasts report on the number of infections and deaths every day, but nature pays no attention to the human world, continuing to run on its own track through the seasons. The autumn colors paint the sky and the earth, with flocks of swallows flying south and occasionally a few Canadian geese honking as they fly overhead. The grass on the ground quietly begins to change color, and the slightly yellowing leaves fall to the ground in the gentle breeze.

Nicholas V leaned back in his chair, resting against the back, and closed his eyes. His heavy breathing from his nostrils made Chunyang worry. She stood up, supporting herself on her thighs with her hands, and bent down to look at him, asking concernedly, "Are you okay?"

"I'm fine." A few seconds later, Nicholas V finally opened his eyes and shook his head.

Nicholas II inherited his father's legacy and expanded the fur business. He eventually became a shareholder in Canada's famous fur company, Hudson. Nicholas II's substantial assets enabled him to marry a banker's daughter who had migrated from London to Canada. Her dowry was close to five hundred pounds, but she was a bit impatient. She always carried around her beloved novel, Charles Dickens's Nicholas Nickleby, which had been published in 1839.

After marrying and having children, Nicholas II gradually lost interest in business. He began to reach some agreements with his missionary friends; they believed that conquering the land was useless and that they needed to completely conquer the hearts of the local people. So, even before his son was born, he abandoned his family and business to become a missionary, participating in various missionary activities and establishing churches and schools. They wanted the American Indians to speak French and English and believe in their God.

Mrs. Nicholas's mood became low and depressed. She always muttered about the opening passage of Dickens's novel, Nicholas Nickleby, which she had read to tatters since she was a young girl: "I can understand a person with a broken neck or a broken leg, but I can't understand a person with a broken heart."

For this, Nicholas II often teased his wife: "I can understand that your father gave you several men to choose from when you were young, and you married me just because of my name, right?!"

"You're not as stupid as you make yourself out to be, using peanut butter as sunscreen!" Mrs. Nicholas retorted without showing any weakness.

"When I was six, I accidentally swallowed a cherry seed for the first time. Our maid said the seed would sprout in my stomach. But I wasn't afraid; I looked forward to it sprouting daily. The first novel I read was Nicholas Nickleby, so this name, like the cherry seed I swallowed before, took root in my heart. All the boys in our family have to be named after this." Mrs. Nicholas couldn't remember how often she had said these words at the dinner table.

A few months later, their son was named Nicholas, and he was Nicholas III.

**V**

"God said, 'The wicked shall not go unpunished, and the lamp of the wicked shall be put out. Alas!'" Nicholas V sighed and closed his eyes again. His head involuntarily nodded slightly up and down.

Chunyang knew that Nicholas's emotions were getting a bit stirred up again. So, she didn't speak this time; she just quietly waited for his emotions to calm down.

"Great-grandfather and his companions built a Catholic church in the indigenous settlement and opened a boarding school. They forced the locals to send their children to school to learn English or French. The children were not allowed to speak their own language, celebrate their own festivals, or be visited by their parents. Some children missed their parents and ran home, only to be caught on the way and locked up in a small, dark room. Some were caught back and brutally beaten, but they still tried to escape, only to die tragically on the road."

"Just last year, near the residential schools in the Lake Manitoba area, about 104 children's bodies were found," Chunyang blurted out, never imagining that the news she saw on TV would be related to the person in front of her.

"That's all the sins of my ancestors." Nicholas V sat up straight, his head lowered and his hands clasped before his chest. His voice became weak, low, and muffled.

He looked like he was repenting, but Chunyang couldn't hear what he was saying.

Nicholas II ran away from home, which caused the family business to plummet and deprived the family of male heirs. Nicholas III hardly ever did anything against his mother's wishes. The only thing disappointing his mother was that he became an ordinary accountant, not a banker like her father.

To please his mother, Nicholas III, under his mother's arrangement, married his cousin, who, as his mother said, was a pure-blooded descendant of England. This pure-blooded descendant of England gave birth to five daughters until Nicholas III finally had a son, Nicholas IV, when he was nearly forty.

## VI

"My father was the eldest son of my great-grandmother, and since my great-grandfather died on the battlefield, my great-grandmother raised him to be quite precious. She indulged him in everything except for matters of marriage."

"A mama's boy?!" Chunyang's mind immediately flashed with these two modern terms.

"In 1914, Canada was still under British rule and was involved in the First World War, declaring war against Germany. In 1917, when my father Nicholas IV was thirteen, Nicholas III was called up and sacrificed on the battlefield." Nicholas V said this with a hint of indiscernible pride on his face.

Since Nicholas IV fell out with his mother over marriage, he moved with his wife from the east to a city in the west, becoming the first person in the family to leave the east. From then on, the Nicholas family began to fall apart, and his mother never forgave him.

Although Nicholas IV worked at a bank, he wasn't doing anything technical; he was just counting money. He dealt with money every day, seeing endless amounts of it. He said he seemed sensitive to money and that becoming rich was the scariest thing in his life. Whenever his wife got angry with him, she would leave with a sarcastic remark about buying a lottery ticket, knowing that he was afraid of winning the lottery.

As Nicholas V reached this point, he began coughing again. Seeing this, Chunyang quickly stood up again. "You must be tired. How about we continue our chat tomorrow?"

"Tomorrow? I don't know if I'll have a tomorrow," Nicholas V said with a worldly and relaxed smile.

"But aren't you going to pick up your cake tomorrow?"

"Oh, right, I almost forgot. Regardless, I have to live to see tomorrow. Ha, ha!" After saying this, Nicholas unconsciously touched his nose and picked up his cane so that he could stand.

"Then let's meet at Tim's Coffee Shop tomorrow at ten. I'll return and make a beautiful birthday card for you, wishing you a happy birthday." Seeing Nicholas V agree, Chunyang quickly made plans to meet the next day.

"Deal, see you tomorrow at Tim's Coffee Shop!" Nicholas V readily agreed. After speaking, he touched his nose again.

## VII

Outside the nursing home's gates lay a bustling commercial district. There were pizza shops, coffee shops, McDonald's, a Vietnamese rice noodle shop, nail salons, hair salons, gas stations, pharmacies, flower shops, libraries, gyms, a large supermarket, and the Cuckoo Bakery. Recently, an Indian restaurant had joined the mix. A Catholic church with stained glass windows and a large cross stood prominently nearby. Before the pandemic, this area was lively, with shops open until 8 p.m. and the supermarket until 11 p.m., even on Christmas, providing much convenience to the surrounding residents. Nowadays, however, the pandemic has turned it into a ghost town, with restaurants forced to close or limit the number of patrons and space tables two meters apart. Some restaurants received monthly over a thousand dollars in government subsidies if forced to close. The vast lanes and parking lots were empty, with exposed cracks in the asphalt freshly patched in the summer. From an aerial view, the neighborhood resembled a giant spider's web sprawling across the ground.

The next morning, the two met at Tim's Coffee Shop as planned. Chunyang carried a small paper bag containing a handmade birthday card she had crafted the night before and a small gift.

To their embarrassment, the coffee shop only provided coffee to go and didn't allow customers to stay. Worried about customers lingering, they kept the chairs locked to the tables.

"Hmph, unbelievable. This is my first time seeing a coffee shop greet customers like this!" Nicholas V said, shaking his head and leaning on his cane, looking somewhat helpless as he stood there motionless outside the shop.

"The outside is nice with fresh air, and we will not be infected by COVID. We can go to the park we visited yesterday," Chunyang suggested, holding two cups of coffee on a paper plate. She worried Nicholas might change his mind; older people often acted like children.

Chunyang wasn't wearing a mask today. Her round face, with slightly flattened features, reminded Nicholas V of his mother, Fanny.

Fanny was a gentle and refined woman of Chinese descent, studying to be a pharmacist. Their ancestors had come from China during the gold rush era to build railways. After Fanny's grandfather paid a $50 poll tax to bring his wife from Fujian to Canada, the family moved to a small town over 200 kilometers from Toronto, where they opened a Chinese restaurant.

In terms of bloodline, Fanny had no mixed heritage. Although her mother was a refugee from Vietnam to Canada, her grandparents had fled from Yunnan, China, to Vietnam. Fanny looked ordinary and was not tall, standing at least 1.6 meters. Perhaps influenced by her mother, Fanny tied two small braids behind her long bangs. Unlike many girls in her class who liked to wear jeans or shorts, she particularly liked wearing dresses. Although it looked a bit awkward, it added a touch of girlishness to her gentle face. The girls in her class didn't like her because they thought she looked rustic and unfashionable. The braids on her back were often pulled by a few mischievous boys.

Fanny was very sensible. She didn't go home or play with other kids after school but instead went directly to her parent's restaurant to help out. Her parents warned her to become a doctor, which would earn her respect. With patients, there would be doctors; with doctors, there would be prescriptions, and with prescriptions, there would be businesses and jobs, just like with their restaurant, where people needed to eat. However, becoming a doctor required a long study period and high tuition fees, so she eventually became a pharmacist.

Nicholas IV and Fanny were classmates in high school, and he especially loved the ginger beef at her restaurant, which made him appreciate this unique girl's shyness and gentleness.

However, Nicholas IV's mother had never liked Fanny, believing their social status was mismatched and that her Chinese ancestry would tarnish their noble bloodline.

"I absolutely forbid you to marry a Chinese woman unless you want to turn my heart to stone!" his mother roared angrily upon hearing his choice.

"Why? Is it just because she is Chinese?"

"Yes, just because she is Chinese, she will tarnish our noble bloodline!

Their family are uneducated. They don't believe in our God, and they have their own God on their table!"

"Noble bloodline? Which of us is nobler than her? I must marry her!"

Upon hearing these words from Nicholas IV, his mother fainted and was taken to the hospital, leading to their severed mother-son relationship.

## VIII

Last night, there was a light rain, leaving the freshly mowed lawn slightly damp. In the distance, two wild rabbits crouched under the chairs where they had sat yesterday. "Shh, don't disturb them," Nicholas V reached out and gently tugged at Chunyang's sleeve.

The two rabbits must have seen the newcomers as they pricked their ears alertly, ready to dash into the bushes at any moment.

They didn't approach the rabbits and chose another chair instead.

"Thank you! Come on, let's see what gift you have brought." After sitting down, Nicholas took the paper bag with a slight tremble and eagerly opened it.

Inside the bag was a hand-drawn card with the words: "On this special day, I wish a special old man a happy birthday! You have witnessed countless extraordinary moments. May this special birthday bring you even more wonderful memories."

"A Chinese knot!" Nicholas V exclaimed joyfully as he pulled out a purple Chinese knot from the bag, his face lighting up with a smile. "I know this is a gift that Chinese people use for blessings and good wishes. There was a larger red one in my parents' house, a gift from my grandparents to them. My mother once told me about the origin of Chinese knots, from keeping records by tying knots to symbolizing eternal love and harmony, representing auspiciousness, happiness, and blessing!" The purple knot was flipped back and forth in his hand, satisfaction evident in his expression.

"You're actually of Chinese descent! Then we must have been destined to meet!" Chunyang bounced on her feet in excitement, almost jumping up. Nicholas V also smiled and then inexplicably touched his nose with his hand again.

In 1927, a year after Nicholas IV and Fanny got married, they had a mixed-blood son who looked nothing like a Westerner, resembling the local indigenous people more. Nicholas IV refused to give his son the name Nicholas: "Since we have distanced ourselves from them, let's just cut off this root altogether."

After discussing it, the couple casually chose a Chinese name for their son, calling him Xiangshu because there happened to be an oak tree at the hospital where he was born. However, the son didn't like it and insisted on changing it, saying it sounded strange when his friends called him that.

His father stared at him and said, "No way! If you want to change it, do it yourself when you are eighteen!"

As stubborn as his father, the son went to the government on his eighteenth birthday to submit a name change application, giving himself a trendy name at the time -- Edward, now Nicholas V.

Nicholas's cousin's families all had successful careers, starting companies and making big money. However, Nicholas's family tree branch had veered off the family's course like a tottering little boat, gradually fading away in the vast ocean.

A paternal great-uncle once wrote a letter to Nicholas V's father, saying, "The ominous root of this is because your grandmother's grandmother insisted on using the name Nicholas, just like in that novel depicting the decline of the wealthy."

Does a name change one's fortune? Nonsense! Greed is one of the seven deadly sins. God gave the tenth commandment to the Israelites, emphasizing not to covet others' possessions, families, and properties.

"Although I don't believe it, sometimes I wonder if my paternal great-uncle's words aren't entirely without merit. What about this in Chinese culture?" Nicholas V paused, gazing at Chunyang, waiting quietly for an answer.

"In Chinese culture, naming is a very important tradition. In the past, many children from large families were named according to their generation. People believe a person's name is closely related to destiny, fortune, and misfortune.

Therefore, they usually hope to give their children a name conducive to their future development, hoping to change fate and bring good luck. Because of various bad events, some people wish to change their names for better luck. For example, my name is 春阳 (the two Chinese characters mean sunshine in spring in China). My parents hope I live like the sunshine in spring ...." Chunyang introduced Chinese culture with great interest.

"Chunyang -- the sunshine in spring? What a beautiful name!"

While Nicholas V not only deviated from the family's career path but also showed no interest in women and marriage. He became a music composer with no connection to making money and even befriended a homosexual. In the 1960s, homosexuality was considered madness and a crime. The two dared not openly date; they only met in private. However, after being discovered and reported, one was sent to a mental asylum, and the other was fired by the music company and spent two years in prison.

After his release, he moved to Firewood Town, rented an apartment, and found a job sorting mail at the post office. Besides work, he isolated himself from the outside world, with no electrical appliances in his home. Even as it later became common for every household to have a microwave oven, he still did not use one. He found joy in riding his bicycle and became an eccentric, individualistic, and conservative man to the people in the town. According to rumors spread by the gossiping women, a man who looked like an Indigenous person could be seen in his apartment from time to time. Of course, by that time, homosexuality was no longer seen as being as monstrous as it once was.

## IX

"I miss my mother. She was so gentle and deferential to my father," Nicholas V said, his eyes revealing a soft glow.

The second stop for Nicholas V after retirement was to fulfill the common Chinese saying told by his mother: "He who has never been to the Great Wall is not a true man!" His mother had explained this saying to him, "If a man never visits the Great Wall in his lifetime, he cannot be considered a real man!"

Of course, he is a man, a genuine man. How else can he have lived his life according to his own will? Even as a homosexual, he is still a man.

After Nicholas V went to Beijing, he didn't follow the crowd to Badaling or Jiayuguan, two famous sections of the Great Wall, because he disliked the hubbub. Instead, he rented a car and found a driver to take him to the Jinshanling section.

This section was near a small village. Because the local government hadn't promoted it to tourists yet, there were hardly any visitors. He asked the guide to wait at the foot of the mountain; he just wanted to be alone there for a while.

Nicholas V had seen the Great Wall on television in the coffee shop, the massive wall snaking along the ridges of the mountains, leaving him awestruck; he had never seen such a grand human construction before. Now, standing at the highest point and looking down the mountains, the red azaleas covering the slopes made him feel like he was in a painting—quiet, majestic, and magnificent, giving him a sense of satisfaction at the fresh experience he had never had before. Leaning against a broken wall, he looked at the crumbling brick walls. He remembered the Vimy Ridge Memorial in France, where similar traces of war remained. He contemplated himself, his family, and his own life. What did a person really want in their lifetime? What was the purpose of living? Oh, he remembered now. One of his father's younger male cousins once wrote to him a story: their great-grandmother once happily told a group of grandchildren surrounding her, "Canada is so good. There is gold everywhere, and we can pick it up casually." "But why do we need so much gold?" his father's younger male cousin, who was not yet ten, innocently asked. As a result, his father severely reprimanded him when he returned home, saying he lacked ambition.

In his great-grandmother's eyes, he was also a man without ambition. However, Nicholas V felt that he was living a dignified life. Why did they need so much gold anyway? The book of Exodus 20: 17 reads, "You shall not covet your neighbor's house. You shall not covet your neighbor's wife, his manservant or maidservant, his ox or donkey, or anything that belongs to your neighbor."

After this contemplation, he looked at the blue sky and shouted, "Mother, I'm at the Great Wall. I am a true man!" His voice carried far, far away, echoing back, startling the few scattered tourists. They couldn't understand what he was saying, and from afar, they thought they had encountered a lunatic who had escaped from the asylum.

The echo exhilarated him; he enjoyed listening to the distant reverberation as if celestial melodies were echoing back from heaven. Suddenly, he remembered his former lover, Treecut. Once, they went to the Rocky Mountains together, and one evening, they sang loudly, facing the majestic stone mountains. Their voices carried far and wide, reverberating after hitting the valleys and mountains as if the sounds of heaven were conversing with them.

**X**

"Exactly a year ago, a few of my relatives decided to come together to celebrate my birthday, but unfortunately, a deadly virus swept across the globe. Many elderly people died after being infected. The nursing home has advised everyone to stay indoors as much as possible and to wear masks if they have to go out. Hmph, if I get infected, then so be it. I've lived long enough anyway," Nicholas V said, his eyes reflecting a stubborn glint. His famously obstinate nature was not to be trifled with. He refused to wear a mask; breathing was already a bit difficult, and putting on that thing felt like it would suffocate him.

"Tomorrow is my birthday, and several people pass away every day in the nursing home due to the virus infection. I don't know if I'll live to see tomorrow, so I've decided to celebrate my birthday early."

"It's a pity I won't be able to share the birthday cake with you to wish you well," Chunyang said, sounding somewhat regretful.

"Thank you! As I'm about to meet God, I never expected that I would still be able to make a friend like you. When I meet my mother, I'll happily tell her I once had the chance to chat with a Chinese girl named Chunyang."

From Nicholas's words, it seemed like he had lived enough, and he even seemed somewhat looking forward to death. He didn't care about any virus, refused to wear a mask, and even hoped the virus would find him, but the virus simply ignored him.

"Just yesterday, the nursing home staff stopped me from going out, saying they could help me order a cake over the phone. I refused! Whether to wear a mask or not is my freedom! I have the freedom to go out and breathe the fresh air given to humanity by God. Then today, no one dares to stop me," Nicholas said, his tone tinged with a hint of cunning and pride in victory.

At that moment, Chunyang realized that she could now get the definition of this family from his weathered face. His face was like a history book, from which she read a passage of history, a history of Canada, a history of Canadian colonizers.

**XI**

On the way back to the nursing home, a father and his daughter rode their bikes towards him. The little girl greeted him with a cheerful "Hi." Then he heard her saying, "Daddy, I love this virus!"

The father turned to her in surprise, asking, "Why?"

"Because you used to leave for work early every day and come home late. Now, I don't have to go to kindergarten, and you don't have to go to work. You can play with me every day."

"It seems that this virus doesn't necessarily bring only bad things. From focusing on family living to pursuing independent and liberated modern marital lifestyles, humans have undergone a long journey toward self-realization. Suddenly, a virus that seems more authoritative than God has brought people back to the family-centered age. I wonder if it's a good or bad thing," Nicholas V murmured to himself, his face already devoid of fat and with sagging skin, trembling slightly. He felt like a philosopher. He was proud of his self-awareness, and his long and rich life had granted him a wealth of life experiences that many others lacked.

At the nursing home, people came and went incessantly, with someone dying from the virus every day. After meals, everyone hoped to return to their rooms as soon as possible and shut the door. Some couples would send one person to the dining hall to return food to their room. The nursing home didn't dare organize any communal activities. People refrained from going out, becoming hesitant to meet each other and even refusing visits from relatives. The nursing home even came up with a new way of visiting, using a plastic sheet with two holes in the middle to separate visitors. When people wearing masks hugged, their hands reached through the holes. People often waved through the glass doors and windows or blew kisses before leaving, making it look eerie, like a gathering from hell. None of Nicholas's relatives came to visit.

Nicholas V had long grown tired of these utterly boring birthday gatherings. Attended by people as aged as himself—some leaning on canes, some in wheelchairs, some with trembling steps and slouched shoulders, some with hearing aids dangling—a group of individuals teetering on the edge of death would come together, mechanically clap their hands, and sing "Happy birthday to you. We wish you health and longevity!" before sharing the cake, continuing with chats and so on. All the well-wishes were like old tunes played repeatedly, utterly lacking in novelty!

## XII

Today was the birthday of Nicholas V, and the nursing home regularly sent people to clean his room, wash his clothes, change his bedding, and help him bathe. This morning, these tasks were already completed as usual.

Nicholas V didn't come downstairs for dinner today. He locked himself in his room, eagerly took down the violin hanging on the wall, wiped it clean with a napkin, and tidied up the bookshelf; he never allowed anyone to touch it. Then, he comfortably sat on the single sofa, spooning cake into his mouth, lazily opening his diary and reading:

September 14, 1945, Rainy

There is heavy rain accompanied by thunder outside. The rain is heavy, dripping onto the roof. Lonely, who can hear the soliloquy in my heart? Only the sound of rain sliding down the glass, like the tears of sorrow, helped me cleanse the sadness in my heart.

I have no interest in women. In fact, I've known that I'm homosexual for a long time. Still, I dare not reveal it to others because homosexuality leads to imprisonment. My parents have noticed something but dare not think about it and won't ask. From their perspective, it's a shameful thing, better left unspoken. Especially my mother occasionally, when she looks at me, it's as if I'm a creature she has never seen before. So, I'll move out of the house...

September 14, 1959, In Prison

Today is my thirty-fourth birthday. The prison guard brings a specially made cake to celebrate for me. If my ancestors knew that I was spending my birthday in prison, they would probably be ashamed, maybe even kill me.

Ever since I was reported by the old couple next door about my relationship with Jason (Jiang Sen), Jason was sent to the mental hospital, and I was sent to this prison. My cellmates look at me with disgust. Compared to my "sin," their "crime" seems insignificant. "You are more disgusting than rapists! At least our sins are human, but yours is a sin only demons commit!" my cellmate Hamberny yelled at me.

I wonder how Jason is enduring his days in the mental hospital.

September 14, 1970, Hail

Hailstones bigger than chewing gum suddenly covered the balcony outside, banging against the glass as if trying to force their way into the room. I turned off the indoor lights and saw white balls falling in the streetlamp's light, like diagonal lines descending. I sit still at the table, quietly watching the lively scene outside the window.

My sister Ivy writes that she immigrated to Australia with her son. She says the climate there is much better than in Canada. She wonders why our ancestors didn't occupy the land in Australia. Australia has many rare minerals worth more than gold.

I can't help but think of what my father's younger male cousin said: "Why do people need so much gold?!"

September 14, 1977, Overcast

The Canadian Human Rights Act was approved by Parliament on July 14, explicitly stating equality for all and prohibiting discrimination on sexual orientation. Humanity is slowly progressing, but this slow pace is struggling to keep up with the changes happening or already happening in humanity.

It's been two years since my mother passed away. These past two years, I've missed her every time. Whenever I missed her, I would look up and pull my ears with my hands as if she was watching me from above, gently pulling my ears and making me listen to her words.

I still order a cake from the bakery for myself. Mother said eating cake on your birthday celebrates your birth and remembers the life your mother gave you.

September 14, 1989, Sunny

Treecut and I helplessly fell in love with each other: we "love at first sight."

At a street cultural festival in Firewood, I unexpectedly met Treecut, who was playing a bamboo flute. "She" was a handsome-looking but internally fragile "female" named Metti. Her tenderness stirred the hormones hidden deep within me, making me long to be entwined with her.

Treecut learned to make instruments from bamboo from her ancestors. We played a piece by composer John Winston Lennon called "Imagine" together, with lingering melodies as soothing as the sound of nature. Later, we collaborated on several good pieces of music, which became popular in her community. We also enjoyed humming our own composed songs. "Release the bonds in our hearts. Stride towards the journey of freedom. In the darkness, let us light up the stars of hope ...."

Treecut is a woman without a fixed abode. She says she needs to be close to nature to find creative inspiration, so she sometimes lives with me and returns to her ancestral home. Sometimes, she even brings some herbs and ganoderma lucidum she found in the mountains for me.

Although homosexuals still dare not appear in public, society seems to be more tolerant of homosexuality than before.

The townspeople turn a blind eye to us. I've even been to jail for this, so I don't care about those gossips.

September 14, 1995, Rainy

The rainy weather makes me gloomy and restless. The air is heavy and moist and seems to lack oxygen, permeated with an inescapable feeling, making it hard to breathe. Do I need to see a psychologist?

I received a letter from my distant relatives recently. Their family has become successful. After buying a lot of land, they are preparing to evict the indigenous people from the town to start oil exploration. Their industrial development has polluted the local water sources, sparking protests. But no one cares. Businessmen want to make money, and the government needs industrial and economic development!

Why has humanity become so greedy?!

September 14, 2005, Bright Sunshine

A heartwarming piece of news! It's also a day worth celebrating! On July 20, 2005, the Canadian Parliament passed the Civil Marriage Act, becoming the fourth country globally to allow same-sex couples to register for marriage nationwide and the first in North America to legalize same-sex marriage. This good news comes too late for me, but it's still worth rejoicing.

Last week, our provincial capital held a large "GBLT Pride" parade. The nursing home drove us to watch the parade. Like many others, I brought a chair and sat on the street to watch the excitement. Watching those who dressed strangely, wore colorful makeup, and were unafraid of certain onlookers celebrating with a sense of defiance, I couldn't help but feel a myriad of emotions and a sense of envy.

Alas, the world is changing in a way that even my running can't keep up with…

Five diaries are enough for him to read. He begins to feel dizzy and thirsty, and his body seems to be burning hot. He remembers the symptoms of COVID-19 distributed in literature by the nursing home, one of which is fever. Trembling, he removes a thermometer from the end of the drawer and places it under his armpit. With two beeps, he takes it out to look: 39 degrees! Afraid he might be mistaken, he leans closer to the desk lamp and places the thermometer under it. The red letters on the black background indeed display 39 degrees.

He sits there for a while, then picks up a pen and writes down these words on the last page of the diary:

September 13, 2021, Pandemic

I'm tired, going to sleep!

# Rose Valley

## I

The global greenhouse effect dramatically altered this western Canadian city during the summer. Normally, the locals were accustomed to winter temperatures around minus 20 degrees Celsius and relied solely on heating. They had to use electric fans and air conditioners in the summer. The surge in demand rendered these products in short supply in shopping malls.

Before noon, the sun blazed overhead like a gigantic fireball, its intensity causing the skin to tingle painfully. The window air conditioner hummed inside Mrs. Zhen's home, sending forth a refreshing breeze that whimsically stirred a red ribbon tied to the windowsill.

A pot of pale purple orchids rested on the windowsill, resembling butterflies perched on lush green branches from afar. To the left of the window stood a sofa with a half-height dresser beside it, a relic left behind by Mrs. Zhen's deceased in-laws. Adorned with photographs spanning five generations, the dresser held a cherished place in the room. Nearly half of the wall above the dresser was covered with various Chinese and English certificates and awards, among them a congratulatory letter from Canadian Prime Minister Stephen Harper to Mr. and Mrs. Zhen on their golden wedding anniversary.

The solid wood tea table before the sofa gleamed with an antique bronze-like shine. At the center, a thriving asparagus fern, a gift on her 80th birthday, sat graciously. It was purchased with money saved by her grandson, Jiamin, who was adopted from China by Mrs. Zhen's second daughter, Haizi.

Mrs. Zhen settled into the rocking chair cushioned with a red embroidered pad, her feet resting flatly on a small stool before her. A frugal woman, she and her husband had decided to sell their house a decade ago and move into a retirement home. While browsing through stores, she immediately liked this discounted chair.

Wearing a light green collarless blouse with floral patterns, Mrs. Zhen casually rested her hands on the chair's armrests, gently swaying back and forth with a contented expression. What is there to worry about in a country where one's right to information is guaranteed, everything requires an appointment, and even one's time of death is planned?

Like someone admiring natural scenery, she alternated between gazing at the photographs on the dresser, glancing up at the awards on the wall, and looking across the table at her husband, who was busy tinkering with the computer.

At 87, Mr. Zhen remained cheerful, optimistic, and active. His long, curved eyebrows resembled two half-moons resting on his temples. At the same time, the two bright red blushes on his high cheekbones added an extra radiance to his serene complexion.

In his youth, Mr. Zhen was fond of playing soccer. After retiring, he developed a passion for skating and photography. He had only ceased his weekly skating outings at the age of 82. Just two months before, he had undergone surgery to remove a cardiovascular tumor. Suppose his illness hadn't led to the suspension of his driver's license. In that case, he might have already been out with his camera, taking photographs.

At that moment, he was completely absorbed in the computer, much like a mischievous child. He busily searched for a photo for his wife's memorial portrait, occasionally glancing back at the old lady and emitting a chuckle.

II

Rose Valley Nursing Home is a private institution located in a western Canadian city, offering a picturesque view of a large supermarket from afar. The location boasts excellent shopping and transportation convenience, with a subway station just a five-minute walk away. A mere two streets over, a large hospital stands, and nearby, a funeral home completes the local infrastructure.

The nursing home comprises three six-story buildings arranged in a semicircle, with the ground floors of each building housing essential facilities like the kitchen, dining room, living room, and activity room. When viewed from above, these buildings resemble an open paper fan, with glass walkways connecting them akin to the ribs of the fan. Flanking these walkways, colorful roses bloom for nearly half the year, from April to the end of September. Even during the winter, when snowflakes dance in the air, the walkways remain adorned with clusters of flowers, emitting a fragrant warmth.

Legend has it that the owner who invested in this nursing home was nearing retirement age and conceived of investing in a nursing home to reside in. It's also rumored that the investor is a compassionate Christian, and his wife has a particular fondness for roses. Given that roses symbolize love, they bestowed an exceedingly romantic name upon the place — Rose Valley Nursing Home.

Inside the nursing home, the dining room boasts non-slip tiled flooring, ensuring safety for all residents. The rest of the areas are carpeted, providing comfort and warmth. Whether navigating with a cane or in a wheelchair, the elderly residents can move around securely without slipping. The hallways on each floor are as wide as a car, designed to facilitate emergency medical aid. Above the mirrors on each room's door are bronze-cast bouquets of roses, with the room number prominently displayed in the center. Despite these thoughtful details, some elderly residents still struggle to locate their rooms for various reasons. Therefore, the nursing home has installed small carved wooden platforms next to each door, allowing residents to place small handicrafts, flowers, or their names, making it easier to identify their own doors at a glance.

### III

The pager beeped from Mrs. Zhen's chest, making a "ring, ring, ring" sound. The device had been sent to her by the nursing home the day after she returned from the hospital. Both she and her husband understood that it must be news from the tumor hospital reaching the nursing home.

"Hello, Mrs. Zhen! This is Jessica speaking. May I ask if you need any special services?" The voice on the other end was sweet; just listening to it could make one feel the caller's friendly smile.

Mr. Zhen, sitting in front of the computer, turned his head to gaze at his wife, his eyes filled with concern.

"Hello, Jessica! Could you please start changing my sheets every day from today?" Mrs. Zhen's English pronunciation wasn't standard, but she spoke fluently.

"No problem. Is there anything else you need help with?" Jessica's voice on the phone remained gentle.

"Not for now, thank you, Jessica!" Mrs. Zhen made an effort to keep a smile on her face.

After hearing his wife's conversation, Mr. Zhen chuckled and remarked, "The average life expectancy of Canadians is eighty-four. You're eighty-five this year, and I'm eighty-eight. We've lived longer than most people. Look at Mao Zedong and Zhou Enlai; even the average lifespan of American presidents is seventy-three. The founding president, Washington, only lived to sixty-seven. We should be content!"

"Yes, reaching this age is something to be content about. But, deep down in my heart, there seems to be a slight regret. Our family has been passed down for five generations overseas, and we've continued our family lineage. After we pass away, we'll be buried in a foreign land. But I worry, will anyone continue to write the family genealogy? Will the roots of our family be cut off? Oh, Blessed Virgin Mary, thank you for your grace! You give us our daily bread, forgive our debts, and save us from danger. I praise you!" Mrs. Zhen took her feet off the small stool, reached for the nearby rosary, held it to her chest, gazed at the Blessed Virgin Mary on the wall, took a deep breath, and then exhaled gently and quietly as if the air had become stagnant.

## IV

Mrs. Zhen's original name was Liwei Liang. After immigrating to Canada, all her documents were changed to her husband's surname, Zhen, making her Liwei Liang Zhen. Her hometown was Shuichicun Village in Kaiping County, Guangdong Province, where her grandfather was a renowned and enlightened member of the local gentry. In the early years of the Republic of China, he sent his three sons and one daughter to private schools. The eldest son clandestinely entered the United States with fellow villagers. He settled there, later bringing his two younger brothers to join him. Surprisingly, the youngest son returned to Guangdong province after completing all his medical school courses and opening a private clinic. He also sponsored his younger sister to complete her studies, and she later became the county's first female medical doctor.

Mrs. Zhen's maternal ancestors were among the earliest Catholics in the region. She frequently reminded her daughter, "The Blessed Virgin Mary saved our souls, and we have to employ our medical expertise to do everything possible to heal the bodies of those unfortunate poor patients."

She knew she would soon journey to another world, yet her heart remained remarkably serene. Death held no fear for her. To her, life resembled a series of games. Winning the first round merely marked the onset of another, not the end. She often envisioned the world her soul would venture to, where she would be awaited by her parents, her in-laws, and her numerous siblings, old classmates, and friends from the church who had preceded her. Occasionally, a faint sense of anticipation stirred within her, longing to surmount her illness swiftly and confront the next challenge in the subsequent game. She traversed this journey with tranquility. Though the process appeared prolonged, it was devoid of agony for her, as she didn't experience discomfort until the advanced stage of her lymphoma. Thus, she often silently thanked heaven for its benevolence toward her.

The lymph node tumor in her neck had exerted pressure on her facial and brain nerves. The continuous sessions of radiotherapy and chemotherapy had scorched her skin, resulting in swelling and discoloration of her right neck, which had begun to ulcerate and discharge. Her right facial side was also significantly swollen, distorting her mouth and eyes and causing her glasses to hang unevenly on her ears.

During a recent follow-up appointment, she met with the attending physician in the oncology department. "Following our consultation, we have decided to proceed with another round of chemotherapy given the condition, though we cannot assure its success," conveyed the Indian female doctor, her tone laced with a touch of apology.

Unperturbed, she calmly inquired, "If I opt for chemotherapy, how much time do I have? And if I forgo treatment, how much time remains?"

At that moment, the weight of "time" bore down on both parties, inducing discomfort.

"If you choose not to undergo treatment, you likely have about six months left; with treatment, it may extend to another two to three months beyond the initial six," the Indian female doctor responded candidly.

As the dialogue concluded, silence enveloped the room as if their breath echoed in the stillness, leaving everyone at a loss for words.

"I choose to forgo treatment! Extending my life a few more months will only burden my loved ones with worry, prolong their anguish, and hold no significance or value." Mrs. Zhen's declaration shattered the silence. With a slight furrow on her brow but a resolute tone, she waved her hand as before.

She affixed her name to the document, unequivocally opting out of treatment without hesitation.

**V**

Mrs. Zhen adjusted her glasses with a gentle push of her hand before smoothing her hair behind her head with both palms. With a tilt of her head, she rose from her seat and leisurely ambled toward the bookshelf in the living room, her slippers making a soft "tap, tap, tap" against the floor.

"Oh, dear, what are you up to?" Mr. Zhen, immersed in sorting through photos, heard the sound and turned to inquire.

"I just want to look at the family genealogy. Go on with your business, don't mind me!" Mrs. Zhen waved dismissively, her voice retaining its vigor.

The glass cabinet in the living room was very ordinary, housing a white folder on the top shelf labeled "Zhen Family Genealogy" in brush strokes. Adjacent to the family genealogy rested a wooden frame enclosing a certificate from Mr. Zhen's grandfather, who had paid head taxes to the Canadian government in 1885.

Mr. Zhen's grandfather was among the pioneers who journeyed from Guangdong to San Francisco aboard a pig-trading vessel in the 19th century. Following the gold rush, he was dispatched to Canada to contribute to railway construction. Upon its completion, he transitioned to labor as a laundry worker. Every day, he propelled a makeshift wooden cart from door to door, gathering garments from Western households and washing them by hand. Residing in a dilapidated wooden abode, plagued by pervasive leaks and lacking heat during frigid forty-degree-below-zero winters, they relied on residual warmth from the iron to stave off the chill at night. He pinched pennies to remit funds to his parents and siblings in China and eventually brought his wife from China. However, the stringent Canadian immigration policies of the time prohibited Chinese immigrants from reuniting with their families. Only after policy amendments and the payment of head taxes were they able to sponsor their family's migration from China, establishing a Chinese restaurant and finding stability.

In the early 1970s, Mrs. Zhen and her husband, accompanied by their four children—Haiyan Zhen, Haizi Zhen, Haigao Zhen, and Haifei Zhen—bearing names of Hai (sea, in English) imbued with the spirit of "Swallows Soaring High," ventured to Canada to join their grandparents, marking the third generation of Zhen family immigrants.

The day after their arrival, Mrs. Zhen was interviewed at a Chinese clothing factory. Being a doctor in her homeland, she was clueless about operating a sewing machine.

"I heard she was a doctor in China, but she seems so inept. Can't even handle a sewing machine? Must be lazy," remarked two women gossiping in Cantonese. Wordlessly, Mrs. Zhen bowed her head and hurried into the toilet, tears streaming down her face as she turned on the tap, splashing water on her cheeks.

Mr. Zhen worked in his father's restaurant, couldn't even wash dishes properly, and was often scolded by his father. After over half a year of washing dishes, he couldn't see any hope. Zhen gritted his teeth and persisted in getting up early every day, intending to finish work on time for English lessons. A year later, he finally passed the English proficiency test and took out a loan to study pharmacy for two years. Upon graduation, he found a job at Red Deer Hospital in a small town in the west, and the whole family moved there from Montreal.

In the blink of an eye, all the children had graduated from university and gone their separate ways. Two became doctors, one became a department manager, and the youngest son became a construction engineer. Only the eldest daughter, Haiyan, lived in the same city as them.

Whenever she mentioned her nearly forty-year-old son still being single, Mrs. Zhen's face couldn't help but show a hint of embarrassment. However, recently, she began to secretly blame herself. Why did her son, born and raised in Canada, insist on finding a "Chinese wife"?!

Mrs. Zhen's stubbornness stemmed from her three daughters all marrying Westerners. Except for the two Chinese orphans adopted by Haiyan and Haizi, their children were all mixed race. Although she eventually accepted this fact, she still felt a strange sense of the family tree branching and the roots breaking from this fourth generation onward.

## VI

Seven years ago, when Mrs. Zhen found out she had breast cancer and needed to have one breast removed, she remained optimistic. She only informed her eldest daughter, Haiyan. She waited until after the surgery to call Haiyan in New York, Haigao in Vancouver, and Haifei in Ottawa.

After several follow-up examinations, everything seemed to be fine. But when it was discovered that the cancer cells had spread to Mrs. Zhen's neck lymph nodes and she needed to see the attending physician again, it was almost five years later.

After multiple rounds of radiation therapy with minimal effect, the lymph node tumor in her neck continued to grow. This time, the doctor presented two treatment options: continuing with traditional radiation therapy or reducing the number of radiation treatments and receiving intravenous injections twice a week. With some risks, this new cancer drug was under trial and data collection. If she chooses to use it, she must sign a disclaimer contract.

"Oh, we don't have any objections. You decide for yourself," Mr. Zhen said, smiling at his wife, with both hands resting on the back of the chair.

After contemplating for a moment, she waved her hand habitually. "I choose to adopt the new method! I am already of this age and used to be a doctor myself. I want to make a contribution to human medicine within my capacity. If this method fails, I will become an unsuccessful case recorded in the medical database. But if it succeeds, I will provide a successful data point. That's settled!"

The Indian female doctor, whose hair was turning gray, stood up, extended her hands, and looked at Mrs. Zhen with respectful eyes, saying, "Thank you, Mrs. Zhen. I wish you good luck!"

The treatment results came out, and the new technological therapy not only had no effect on Mrs. Zhen, but it also burned her neck skin. Both Mr. and Mrs. Zhen, medical professionals, knew this time was more likely to end badly than well. As soon as they left the hospital, Mrs. Zhen said to Mr. Zhen, "Call the children back from all over, find a lawyer, and prepare the will. Also, I want to talk to the people from the funeral home immediately."

**VII**

"May I ask what kind of service you need?" The meeting took place in a café not far from the nursing home. After some small talk, Steven, the funeral home staff member, got straight to the point.

"We would like to reserve an urn, a funeral service, and then cremation," Mrs. Zhen said calmly as if placing an order in a store.

"There are two things. Firstly, what price range are you looking for regarding the urn? Secondly, there are different forms of funeral services. If you opt for a religious service, your priest or pastor can conduct a mass, pray, recite scriptures, sing hymns, etc. The funeral home can also assist you in arranging for clergy members to be present. Please take a look at the prices first." Steven took out some pictures and price lists from his briefcase.

"What are the prices for the urns?" Mr. Zhen looked through the pictures and price lists while Mrs. Zhen cut to the chase.

"The most expensive one is two thousand five hundred, a high-quality carved oak urn," Steven said, pointing at a delicately crafted wooden box in the brochure.

"What's the price for the cheapest one?" Mr. Zhen inquired.

"Two hundred and fifty dollars, made of paper," Steven replied.

"Two hundred and fifty dollars? Great, I'll take that one!" Mr. Zhen paused momentarily, then became delighted as if he had found a treasure. "Do you know what 'two hundred and fifty' means in China?"

Mr. Zhen enthusiastically explained the meaning of "two hundred and fifty" to Steven. He ended with a cheerful remark, "In China, the numbers '250' are used to describe someone who is foolish or not very smart, but we don't mind the connotation of the number!" The old gentleman said this with a laugh, finding a bit of levity in the heavy topic.

"I understand," Steven said, giving a vague thumbs up.

In this way, the husband and wife ordered a 250-dollar urn for themselves.

## VIII

"Ring, ring, ring," Mrs. Zhen's chest-mounted communicator sounded for the second time.

A sweet female voice spoke: "Hello, Mrs. Zhen! My name is Anna, and I'm a nurse from the hospital. Starting tomorrow, I will visit your house daily to apply medicine to your neck. Is 9 o'clock in the morning convenient for you?"

"Hello, Anna! That's very convenient. I'll be waiting for you at home. Thank you!"

Mrs. Zhen's heart filled with gratitude. She silently replayed and savored the words of the caregiver Jessica and the nurse Anna in her mind countless times. Suddenly, she realized that Jessica's voice sounded very familiar. "Ah, it's been months since I last went downstairs to the dining hall for a meal. I must be getting forgetful. Jessica is the girl with black hair, isn't she?"

She recalled something that happened on the first day they moved into the nursing home and had lunch, the first time she saw Jessica.

That day, Mrs. Zhen and Mr. Zhen were sitting at a table. Diagonally across from Mrs. Zhen was an elderly man in a wheelchair with a thin face and white hair. He looked well over ninety years old, with a mauve napkin hanging around his neck.

She glanced at him unintentionally, and the old man grinned at her. Then, she witnessed a scene that surprised her so much that she forgot to bring the soup spoon to her mouth.

Like a mischievous child, she saw the old man deliberately tearing off the napkin around his neck and throwing it to the ground, shouting, "Help! Help!" Jessica quickly approached, picked up the napkin from the ground, and spoke to him with a smile as if coaxing a child. The old man's face lit up with childlike innocence, and he obediently let Jessica help him put the napkin back around his neck.

The same situation could be seen almost every day. Later, she heard from others that the old man might have done it deliberately out of loneliness, probably wanting to attract attention.

The old man had passed away many years ago, but Jessica left a deep impression on Mrs. Zhen because of this incident.

<h2 style="text-align:center">IX</h2>

"Hello, Mrs. Zhen! My name is Demi Terry; I'm the chef at the nursing home. The nutritionist has given me your food formula. Today, we have three options: mushroom chicken soup with salad, cheese with tomato sautéed pasta, and red bean soup with garlic bread. Which one would you like to have today?" This time, it was an Italian-accented male voice but still polite and courteous.

"Hello, Demi Terry! I would like the mushroom chicken soup with salad," Mrs. Zhen replied, feeling a slight trembling in the corners of her mouth.

"This is the third call today!" Mr. Zhen stood up and handed his wife a glass of water.

Since the tumor hospital had informed the nursing home about her condition, various special care services had poured in. Mrs. Zhen's eyes gradually moistened as she recalled her more than forty years in Canada. She realized she had been just an ordinary citizen who paid taxes to the government annually and hadn't made any special contributions to society. Yet the government had sent her so much care before her passing. Thinking of her deceased parents, she felt much luckier than them.

She turned to look at her parents' wedding photo on the dresser. Her mother wore a neat, short hairdo, sweet dimples on her delicate face, and a golden velvet cheongsam. The photo was black and white, but what flashed through her mind was the purple color that her mother had told her about. Her father wore a Zhongshan suit with round gold-rimmed glasses on his nose. In his youth, her father had followed Mr. Sun Yat-sen, raising funds overseas for the democratic revolution. Mr. Sun had offered him a government position. Still, he returned to his hometown to save people by opening a clinic and a pharmacy. He was used to drinking coffee, often receiving it as gifts from relatives in Hong Kong. After 1949, he donated his entire pharmacy to the government, leaving himself impoverished. His last words before passing away were, "I really want to have a cup of coffee!"

The first time Mr. and Mrs. Zhen returned to their hometown with their entire family, they placed a cup of Nestlé coffee, his favorite, on his father's grave.

X

"Ring, ring, ring."

"Hello, Mrs. Zhen! How are you feeling? I'm Dr. Sandton, the psychologist. I'd like to schedule a time to meet with you. When would be convenient for you?" The phone rang for the fourth time.

Mrs. Zhen paused for about thirty seconds, collecting her thoughts. She felt like there was nothing wrong with her that required psychological counseling.

She cleared her throat as if Dr. Sandton were sitting right before her. "Thank you, Dr. Sandton. I feel like I don't currently need any psychological therapy. Everyone will die eventually, and I don't feel afraid of death. My mind is at peace. I don't want to waste your time. Please go help those who need it."

"Ha, ha, it seems like you don't need my care at all, given that the government has taken care of everything," Mr. Zhen chuckled, waving his hand at her, then continuing to fiddle with his photos.

Suddenly, hail began to fall outside, tapping on the glass windows. The power went out, and the air conditioner in the window fell silent. The room became quiet all of a sudden.

After several phone calls, Mrs. Zhen felt a bit tired and confused. She didn't have the strength to rock her chair anymore. She lay quietly in the chair, feeling somewhat dazed. "How could a terminal cancer patient sentenced to death attract so much attention? Why do I suddenly feel like a child overwhelmed by an unexpected favor?!"

Her throat felt choked up. She reached for a tissue from the box, folded it, and gently wiped her eyes. Her right eye was swollen shut, making it impossible to open it. She could only use her hand to lift her eyelid.

Then, she gently caressed her swollen face with her hand, closed her eyes, and ran the rosary through her fingers, silently saying in her heart, "Hail Mary, full of grace."

## XI

"Look, there are several cards placed at the door. They must be from others. Hurry to open them and take a look."

Mr. Zhen had just opened the door when he saw his second daughter, Haiyan, holding several cards in one hand and carrying a pot of chicken soup prepared at her elder sister's house. Her son, Jiamin, and Haiyan's daughter, Yangyang, followed behind.

Three cards were placed in envelopes without being sealed. Mrs. Zhen opened them; indeed, they were from several old friends from the nursing home. She handed the papers to Yangyang, standing next to her, and asked her to read them aloud.

The first card was handmade by 92-year-old Mrs. Daisy. She painted a colorful bouquet of roses with watercolor on the white card. She wrote: "Dear Mrs. Zhen, the enemy of illness is a good mood, and the best medicine is having friends who care about you. I hope you recover soon and continue to teach me Chinese, the most beautiful writing in the world!"

The second card was from 83-year-old Mrs. Flora: "Dear Mrs. Zhen, our writing group enjoys listening to your stories!" The third card was written by

Mr. Brooks, a 79-year-old. It read, "Dear Mrs. Zhen, wishing you a speedy recovery. Let's continue dancing!"

"Ah, I can't bear to leave my old friends here!" Mrs. Zhen sighed deeply.

"Grandma, my mom, elder sister, and I have cooked some delicious chicken soup for you." Jiamin gently shook his grandma's arm, showing maturity beyond his age.

"Jiamin is so sensible. Your father and mother didn't raise you in vain," Mrs. Zhen said, taking Jiamin's hand in hers and gently stroking it with her other one.

"My mom said that when I get a little older, she'll take me back to China to find my real dad and mom." Jiamin's voice was filled with innocent joy.

"Don't go. I went back last year, and it was all in vain. I went to the orphanage, and the people there were very hospitable. Still, in the end, I didn't find my biological dad and mom," said Yangyang, who was adopted by Haiyan from China.

"Why didn't you listen to me? Jiamin is still so young; what does he understand?" Mr. Zhen reproached Haiyan after hearing the conversation between the two grandchildren.

"Yes, don't mention it until the time is right. You're too open-minded. You've adopted a child, but you're urging him to find his biological parents," Mrs. Zhen said to Haiyan, a little upset as well.

"Grandma, my mom said that as long as I want to, she can take me to China to find my biological dad and mom anytime," said Jiamin, still with a scar on his upper jaw from the surgery.

The sight of the two well-behaved grandchildren standing in front of her reminded Mrs. Zhen of what Haiyan had said over the phone ten years ago when she decided to adopt the disabled child: "Mom, I indeed can still have my own children, but what's the difference between my own and adopted? The responsibility of parents is to raise a life into a qualified citizen, isn't it? Also, I'm a doctor. I want to bring hope to his life!"

"Both your parents and I are blessed to have you," Mrs. Zhen said as she reached out and hugged the two grandchildren.

"Grandma, are you going to die?" Jiamin suddenly blurted out, startling

Haiyan. She grabbed Jiamin's arm, saying, "Shut up, Jiamin!"

The air was filled with tension. Yangyang was scared and covered her mouth with her hand, wide-eyed, hurriedly running to the side.

"Oh dear, it's okay. It's a fact. Everyone is going to die. God has reserved a time for everyone," Mr. Zhen broke the awkward silence with a smile, hands behind his back.

"We have an appointment to visit the funeral home tomorrow morning at nine. It's only a ten-minute walk from here for your father and me. You don't need to drive to pick us up," Mrs. Zhen quietly told Haiyan, her voice calm as if she were talking about someone else's business.

## XII

The Kenli-Maru Funeral Home has over a century's history, making it one of the city's oldest and most reputable. The two-story building, constructed with cement and gravel walls, features a flat roof, a spacious parking lot at the entrance, and several towering cypress trees flanking both sides.

Dim yellow lights illuminated the entrance, and the walls transitioned from light green to dark green as one moved further inside. Several large halls lined each side of the corridor. Contrary to the somber image typically associated with funeral homes, people were diligently working at their computers in the office.

The hall that Mrs. Zhen had reserved was designated for Catholic funeral ceremonies. The room's windows were adorned with colorful stained glass, and a large picture of the Virgin Mary hung above a platform. At the center was a substantial marble surface intended for placing the coffin. The overall layout closely resembled that of a church.

"Our church priest will come to perform the mass and prayers for me," Mrs. Zhen explained to Steven. "The choir members will also come to sing hymns."

"If we both leave on the same day, everything remains the same, just the price doubles," Mr. Zhen humorously interjected, attempting to lighten the mood.

No one spoke. The children's hearts weighed heavily as they watched their parents. It felt as if they were accompanying them on a shopping trip, unsure of what to say, their emotions tangled and overwhelming.

Everything was arranged perfectly. As they were about to leave, the diligent Steven didn't forget to make one last pitch. He casually took a few brochures from the wooden rack at the entrance and said, "We've recently launched a new plan. You can pre-book your funeral or purchase a burial plot based on your finances. You only need to pay a small monthly amount, just like a mortgage. The biggest advantage of this plan is that if the buyer dies anywhere in the world, we will airlift them back for free and take care of the funeral arrangements. The younger you are when you buy, the more favorable the price."

After speaking, he handed Haoyan, Haiyan, Haigao, and Haifei his "Death Plan" booklets featuring an angel with wings on the cover.

"That's funny. You have to plan for death while you're alive. Why do people live anyway?" Haifei muttered with a confused and bitter smile on the way back.

"I recently read a book, Being and Time, by the German philosopher Heidegger. A sentence in it enlightened me: 'Only when you approach death can you truly understand the meaning of life.' Alas! Living is about exploring the meaning of life and accepting the fact of death at any time! Of course, you need to live to a certain age to have such an understanding," Mr. Zhen remarked, refusing assistance to walk despite his white hair and stooped posture.

"I'm all set, just waiting to bid farewell to life, to end this life, and thank the audience!" Mrs. Zhen leaned on a cane with her right hand while Haiyan supported her left. She didn't raise her head, and her low voice seemed more like she was speaking to herself or perhaps to her Virgin Mary.

In the distance, the sun was setting, casting a radiant glow and tinting the horizon red.

# Miraculous

Xiaoxin reclined comfortably in the dentist's chair, with the television screen in clear view. It displayed scenes of Hong Kong submerged by the heaviest rainfall in 139 years. Unable to understand Cantonese, her gaze drifted along the distressing images. Watching streets flooding and cars getting swept away, she felt a knot form in her stomach. Such news always left her feeling despondent and sorrowful. Whenever she saw or heard about natural disasters, she silently gave thanks for having immigrated to a country with fewer such calamities.

The visuals on the television troubled her, and she wished to stop watching. She asked the nurse to change the channel, but to her surprise, the next scene depicted wildfires in Canada.

She closed her eyes helplessly and sighed. The pandemic had claimed millions of lives over the past three years. There were over six hundred wildfires in a single year in Canada, monsoon rains in Pakistan lasting for over a month, earthquakes in Turkey and Syria, the Russia-Ukraine war raging for nearly a year without respite, while conflicts in the Middle East were stirring up again. There were shooting incidents in German churches, dozens, even hundreds, of people in the United States collectively robbing malls, and the recklessness of a BMW driver in Dalian. Ah, human consumption exceeded the Earth's capacity to bear, and the direct consequences fell heavily on humanity. Since she couldn't change it, she decided to lie flat. It had almost become a consensus among young people not to get married or have children.

"Do you want me to turn off the TV?" the nurse asked concernedly, seeing Xiaoxin closing her eyes in silence.

"Yes, please. Turn it off," Xiaoxin lazily replied without even opening her eyes.

"Do you need sunglasses?" the nurse asked thoughtfully after turning off the TV.

"Yes, please. Thank you!" replied Xiaoxin as she immediately took off her glasses and handed them.

The nurse took her glasses and carefully placed them on a tissue from the box. She then turned around and retrieved a large pair of sunglasses from the cabinet, handing them to Xiaoxin. Shielding her eyes under the black lenses provided her a sense of security. As she donned the sunglasses, the phrase "burying one's head in the sand" suddenly came to her mind, and a barely noticeable self-deprecating smile appeared on her lips.

The dentist, checking Xiaoxin's information on the nearby computer, was a Hong Kong native who had immigrated to Canada with her parents at a young age. Sensing Xiaoxin's mood, she lamented the recent strings of disasters. Xiaoxin couldn't see her masked face, but she could feel the bitterness in her tone: "Look, the world is deteriorating, and it's an undeniable reality. Not even God can save it. I don't believe in my children getting married and having children; there's no point in bringing the next generation into this world to suffer!"

The dentist's words struck Xiaoxin like thunder. How reminiscent they were of what her son had said: "Life is tough for everyone. Since it's so tough, why should I get married and have children only to let them suffer in this world?!" Her son, raised in Canada, never grasped the nuances of euphemism, always bluntly catching people off guard.

Xiaoxin never expected that the younger generation and some of their elders harbored such sentiments. "Is this world still worth our efforts?" they might ask. "Where is the God people believe in? Who can save humanity?" After hearing the dentist's words, Xiaoxin lapsed into silence. Now, she began to harbor doubts about life.

Exiting the dentist's office and finding it still early with pleasant weather, Xiaoxin felt it might be a good idea to take a solitary walk and ponder the questions in her mind.

The outdoor sunlight felt warm and gentle. As Xiaoxin walked, she thought, "One falling leaf is indicative of the coming of autumn" because the summer heat had quietly disappeared with the changing seasons. The poplar leaves on both sides of the street were transitioning to yellow, and as the breeze rustled through, they shimmered in the sunlight like countless Buddha's hands. Occasionally, a few young people jogged past, their presence akin to a passing breeze, urging one to move along with them. Across the street, two seniors stood hand in hand, waiting for the green light. They exchanged smiles and whispered to each other. Although Xiaoxin couldn't hear their conversation, she could sense the warm aura of love enveloping them. It reminded her of a survey conducted by a research company on couples over eighty years old, posing the question, "If there were another life, would you still choose to marry him or her?" The vast majority answered, "Yes!"

"That's a truly high-quality marriage! If a couple wants to spend their entire lives together and even beyond, it's a sign of true love. How beautiful this world should be is their point of view." Xiaoxin's face betrayed an indescribable look of envy. However, her marriage was far from such bliss—it was shrouded in perpetual darkness. On the voyage of her marriage, she found herself adrift with no clear destination in sight. Lost amidst thick fog, she drifted aimlessly, unsure where she would ultimately land. At times, she even wished for the ship to capsize and sink to the ocean floor, taking her with it.

Several meters away, a stone bridge spanned the Wendemir River, with an iron bicycle lane sign on the side of the sidewalk at the bridgehead. The top of the sign was slightly crooked, apparently not due to the wind, for only a drunk person could have the strength to bend the iron pole, or perhaps it had been knocked askew by a passing car. In any case, its presence went largely unnoticed by passersby.

Xiaoxin had never been here before and wasn't familiar with the surrounding scenery. Glancing at the sign, she reasoned that since there was a bicycle lane indicated, it must be passable. Moreover, walking along the riverbank with the flowing water might be conducive to contemplation. Intrigued, she followed the sign onward. Soon, a dim forest path emerged, flanked by towering Colorado spruce and larch trees. The dark green branches were covered with brown pinecones, and some dried pine needles and cones were under the trees. Several squirrels scurried about, diligently gathering fruit from the ground for the winter. At the base of a tree lay a glossy black feather. Xiaoxin bent down and picked it up, pondering if it belonged to a crow, either shed during preening or the aftermath of a fierce bird skirmish.

"Survival of the fittest; wars don't just happen among humans," Xiaoxin mused as she examined the feather in her hand. Later, she felt that likening animal conflicts to human ones might be a bit of an exaggeration. "But if aliens were observing Earth from other planets, wouldn't they perceive human conflict much like animal territorial disputes? Perhaps the distinction lies in that animal battles are driven solely by survival, while human conflicts, besides survival, also involve existential struggles," she mused further.

The further along the path she went, the taller the surrounding trees grew. From the flora, it was evident that this community had been established for at least a century. The path led to a T-shaped pedestrian walkway. Crossing it, one could see houses looming in the lush bushes. However, there was no way to the left. Xiaoxin stood there feeling frustrated and embarrassed. To the left was the river, and she wanted to stroll along the riverside. Just as she hesitated, a man in a plain blue work suit got off a truck loaded with building materials. Xiaoxin glanced back at a house under renovation on the roadside, then smiled as she approached, inquiring about the path ahead. He shook his head and pointed to a warning sign in the distance, saying it was the end. Disappointed, Xiaoxin thanked him and turned to walk in another direction.

As she meandered along, she couldn't help but admire the quaint courtyards adorning the houses lining the road, and the beautiful scenery momentarily swept away her original purpose for taking a walk.

The first courtyard left a lasting impression on Xiaoxin. Though not expansive, it was neatly arranged. A clump of golden chrysanthemums greeted visitors at the door, while walls were adorned with purple and light green hydrangeas. Even in the corners, long hyacinth beans flourished. Seeing the vibrant emerald-green beans made her mouth water, and she couldn't help but feel a pang of greed. Pausing for a moment, she wondered whether the occupants of this home might be Chinese. Whenever she spotted vegetables growing in someone's yard, her mind instinctively gravitated towards the possibility. Her son always teased her, saying that her first thought on encountering any plant or animal was whether it was edible.

"Food is the first necessity of the people!" Xiaoxin recalled her second day in Canada, which happened to be a Saturday. Her family had curiously wandered around the neighborhood, seeing a sign on the roadside that read

"Yard Sale." Puzzled, they wondered, "Why is this family selling only the yard and not the house? What could they possibly do with the yard?" Unable to decipher the mystery, Xiaoxin felt a surge of cleverness and explained, "Stop guessing. Buying a yard must be for planting vegetables!"

As the thought crossed her mind, Xiaoxin couldn't help but blush with embarrassment. Turning her head, she noticed two men in suits sitting in a black car parked on the side of the road, staring at her. Lowering her head, she felt her cheeks warm. Standing alone and giggling while being seen by others could be embarrassing. Suddenly, she became alert, recalling the recent incident of a Chinese woman being criticized online for trespassing on someone else's yard to pick vegetables. "Oh, God, please don't think I'm here to steal vegetables," she silently pleaded, hastening her steps away from their gaze.

The front yards of the houses along the road grew increasingly beautiful, each meticulously decorated as if for a beauty pageant. The front yards and houses' design indicated this was an upscale community. Xiaoxin estimated one yard as at least 2,000 chi, a unit of length of approximately 0.33 meters, featuring a grand fountain at its center surrounded by lush greenery. The autumn sunlight bathed the two tall windows, while two large pillars at the front door exuded warmth and dignity. At the top of the steps, Xiaoxin noticed two ember-red metal doors. In another house, an abstract metal sculpture adorned the front yard, comprised of three metal pieces of different colors— bronze, white, and black—interlocked at the top. She naturally assumed that it represented the integration of multiculturalism. After all, Canada is a multicultural country, and the three colors might symbolize different human skin tones.

Then, in the blink of an eye, the quaint and snug house next door stood out among the "luxury homes," catching Xiaoxin's notice. With its black pointed roof, white walls, greenish-blue doors and lattice windows, the yard, adorned with pink African daisies and clusters of light gray sea holly, emitted a tranquil atmosphere. Three elderly women stood in the yard chatting with gentle smiles. The woman who appeared to be the homeowner still cradled a watering can, its nozzle dripping onto the ground. Xiaoxin's pace slowed, her gaze lingering on the scene, captivated by its uniqueness. She even fantasized that one of the three women would turn around and greet her. An urge to join their conversation, to share in their smiles, tugged at her.

Right in front of Xiaoxin, a man wearing a baseball cap, a blue tracksuit, and sneakers was pushing a stroller. With one hand on the stroller and the other holding a small dog, he smiled and greeted her as they neared, proudly saying, "Hi" in a way that embodied the contentment of a family man.

"Life is so cozy! Isn't this what God created for mankind?" Xiaoxin couldn't help but sigh to herself. These captivating sights delighted her, making her stroll a truly rewarding experience.

At the end of the next T-junction, a solitary black iron bench sat on the perpendicular roadside. "A meandering path cuts through a serene patch. Monks' quarters are deep in vegetation growths," Xiaoxin continued musing, feeling upbeat, firmly believing that brighter moments lay ahead.

The road gradually widened, devoid of any pedestrians. The poplar and birch trees lined the sides, their dense growth creating an impression of being enveloped. Xiaoxin began to fret, wondering if she had indeed lost her way. She knew herself as someone with no innate sense of direction, her curiosity about everything and everyone often overriding her navigational skills. She relied on landmarks like trees, billboards, or buildings to find her way, realizing later that she was a visual learner. Her science geek husband often chided her for her lack of navigation skills. Every time they wanted to go somewhere, she couldn't give a specific address, but she always said she could guide them and assured him that she could find the way by turning and turning. Their disagreements on this matter were frequent. Amid her uncertainty, she spotted a blue road sign ahead. Hastily, she produced her phone and took a picture, feeling a sudden surge of security, convincing herself she wouldn't get lost.

A row of beautifully crafted sandy-brown townhouses stretched before them, adorned with green roofs, brownish-red doors, and garages, echoing a touch of 18th-century architectural style. In Canada, it's a requirement for communities to encompass a blend of detached houses, townhouses, and apartments, fostering a mix of high and low-income residents for community stability and mutual support. Although the townhouses' yards were notably smaller than the detached houses, they maintained a tidy and beautiful appearance. The front lawn of the first house had just been freshly trimmed, emanating a distant, sweet scent of grass. Purple irises, white miniature roses, and a large cluster of blue hydrangeas were in full bloom in the yard. Under a plum tree, a man who appeared to be of Middle Eastern descent was squatting, engaged in conversation with two identical Shar Pei dogs. They lounged lazily on the grass, unmoving, only lifting their heads to glance at passersby while seeming indifferent.

"Hi," Xiaoxin suddenly transformed into an innocent young girl, unable to resist waving in their direction. Lost in a moment of self-forgetfulness, she didn't even realize if she was greeting the dogs or the man.

"Hi," the man turned around, offering a polite wave in response.

"Are they twins?" Xiaoxin stood at the edge of the lawn, pressing her hands against her knees and leaning forward with evident curiosity toward the two dogs.

"Yes," the man replied politely without rising from his squatting position. He turned his head again and replied equally politely, showing no inclination to prolong the conversation. He caressed the heads of the two dogs with gentle strokes, who lay contentedly with closed eyes, relishing their owner's affection.

Ahead, the path was obscured by clusters of yellowing bushes, and glimpses of the bustling main road on the other side of the river peeked through intermittent trees. Xiaoxin felt she had traversed a circular route, finding herself back in the valley where the trees indicated that the Wendermir River was nearby.

Xiaoxin felt a little disappointed because there seemed to be no way forward. To stave off her ennui, she began scrutinizing the dwellings in the vicinity. Many older homes had been completely demolished and renovated because of their age. One cluster of houses was currently undergoing demolition, marked by two sizable dumpsters stationed in front. With the weekend upon them, the site was devoid of any laborers. The newly rebuilt houses for these antiquated structures tended towards the abstract, employing stone, brick, and concrete in lieu of their original wood frames. A "For Sale" sign was in front of a freshly refurbished house along the roadside. Black marble adorned its exterior walls, while even the windows boasted black glass, giving the entire structure a rectangular, angled shape. The somber hues imparted a chilly aura to the structure, prompting Xiaoxin to remark that it resembled less a residential home and more an industrial laboratory. She had encountered and critiqued a similar structure in Calgary before. Her friends teased her for being out of touch with contemporary tastes.

Across the street, a man and a woman stood by a BMW, conversing. Donned in a cycling helmet, the man perched on his bike with one foot firmly planted on the ground. The woman, clad in a casual white ensemble, held the car key as if preparing to depart. Xiaoxin approached them, hoping to inquire about a shortcut to the main road and spare herself the trouble of retracing her steps. As Xiaoxin neared, the man pedaled away. The woman kindly informed Xiaoxin that there was no direct route to the main road from this spot, gesturing back at Xiaoxin's coming path. Xiaoxin instantly understood what she meant. It was uncommon for strangers to wander into this area, prompting the woman to introduce the community to Xiaoxin warmly. Revealing its century-old history, the neighborhood boasted towering poplar trees lining the street, one of which appeared so substantial that it would likely require three individuals linking hands to encircle it. Pointing across the street, the woman enthusiastically highlighted a recently constructed house for sale. Xiaoxin followed her finger and glanced sideways, then turned her eyes back to ask about the price. However, she had no real intention of purchasing—she was typical of many Chinese individuals, keen on exploring investment opportunities. Indeed, discussions about real estate remained a popular and engaging topic, regardless of location. The woman disclosed that the house was selling for over one million five hundred thousand. Though taken aback, Xiaoxin maintained her composure, offering a nod in response. Then, the woman gestured behind Xiaoxin, indicating another property priced at six hundred and thirty thousand. Turning to observe, Xiaoxin discovered a century-old, dilapidated house. She smiled, opting to remain silent.

After bidding farewell to the woman, Xiaoxin retraced her steps along the familiar path. Grateful for the woman's warmth and friendliness, she couldn't help but feel a twinge of guilt, thinking, "I had no intention of buying a house, yet I allowed myself to indulge in her hospitality." Later, she reasoned, "Perhaps the woman works in real estate; it's only natural for her to passionately showcase properties." With this realization, she felt much lighter in her heart.

Relying on her memory, Xiaoxin carefully navigated the road, observing the trees and buildings lining her route. However, she saw a man seated on the black iron chair. Surrounding him were scattered plastic bags and a bundled sleeping bag, and his attire was rumpled and disheveled, resembling that of a vagrant. Instantly on edge, Xiaoxin felt a surge of apprehension, fearing a potential threat. Despite keeping her gaze lowered, her senses remained sharply attuned to any movement from him, preparing her to flee at a moment's notice.

"Good morning!" His unexpected politeness immediately caused her guard to drop. She halted, ready to approach him and chat. She was curious about the lives of individuals like him, always eager to glean insights from diverse strata to enrich her life experience.

"How are you?"

"Not bad, thank you!" the man replied, stooping slightly as he spoke, rummaging in his bag to retrieve a book. With its cover facing her, Xiaoxin identified it as The Adventures of Augie March, by Saul Bellow, published in 1953. He seemed to be in a good mood, but his facial expression seemed a bit indifferent. He delved into his book without further ado, signaling his disinclination to continue the conversation.

Xiaoxin resigned herself to departing, retracing her steps back to the original road. She understood that everyone has their privacy, and not everyone is willing to reveal what it conceals, especially if it comes with scars.

As she walked, Xiaoxin noticed a squirrel by the roadside, poised to gather fallen beech nuts. At her approach, it initially recoiled instinctively, poised to flee. Yet, sensing no threat from Xiaoxin, it relaxed and proceeded to forage without fear, its fluffy tail swaying with each movement. At this moment,

Xiaoxin heard chatter. Turning her gaze, she spotted two women descending the steps of a large house, completely oblivious to Xiaoxin on the sidewalk. The ground before the yard was covered with fallen pears while a pair of magpies hopped around. Xiaoxin speculated that the two women were the house's inhabitants, observing them as they approached another residence. With a "clang," they deposited something into the mailbox before continuing their journey toward the next house.

"Seems like they're distributing advertisements to residents. What a peaceful and leisurely community!" Xiaoxin reflected, her mind consumed by the serenity of the moment. She had momentarily forgotten the purpose of her stroll and had pushed aside thoughts of the world's darker aspects.

Returning to the community entrance, Xiaoxin spotted the two suited men who had emerged from the black car earlier. They stood beside the vehicle on the pathway, their gazes fixed upon her with the same expressions. One tall, one short, with one of them being black, they were dressed smartly, looking like businesspeople. As Xiaoxin approached, they greeted her with smiles, calling out, "Good morning!"

"Good morning!" Xiaoxin replied politely.

"Have you ever pondered the whereabouts of God?" the shorter man tentatively inquired after a brief pause.

Xiaoxin was momentarily taken aback. "Where is God?" The question jolted her back to the purpose of her stroll. With a subtle tilt of her head, she offered a gentle smile, casting her gaze downwards, her hands clasped together, and didn't rush to answer.

Xiaoxin wasn't a devout Christian, but she had attended church services with friends, listening to sermons about God's role in creating and saving humanity. But, she wondered: "Where is God in the face of natural disasters? Where is God in times of war? Where is God as humanity succumbs to greed?"

"Many times, even I find myself perplexed. I often wonder where God is, especially amidst humanity's trials and tribulations," she calmly offered as her answer after a brief pause.

The tall man exuded confidence as he handed Xiaoxin a vibrant brochure with both hands, declaring, "God is here!"

Xiaoxin glanced at the brochure and realized it was a Christian evangelical flyer. The colorful pages were filled with phrases like, "God loves the world," "Believe in Jesus, and you will have eternal life," "The disasters of humanity are caused by human selfishness and greed," and "Disasters are a test of faith, an opportunity for God to test and strengthen the faith of believers. Through difficulties and disasters, people can experience faith more deeply, learn to rely on God, and cultivate strong faith." While these words were familiar to Xiaoxin, she often doubted such explanations or preaching. She couldn't help but wonder, "Isn't God supposed to be the ultimate architect of humanity? Didn't everything come into existence through God? Doesn't God love us? Then why would he design so many disasters for humanity?" It felt akin to a designer intentionally creating an unattractive and impractical house, making it hard for people to comprehend the purpose. Why couldn't God have fashioned a flawless human world right from the start? Of course, Christians argue that the human world's calamities are not God's handiwork. However, many human systems still require refinement rather than the consequence of human actions because humans are imperfect.

"So, does humanity need more patience and faith in this world? Will God destroy humanity, as stated in the Bible, and let someone who believes in Him build a new Noah's Ark and then recreate a brand new world?" These sorts of questions perpetually swirled in Xiaoxin's mind, perplexing her. Over the years, numerous friends encouraged her to embrace religion, dragging her to various church activities. Yet, she remained steadfast in her resolve, insisting she wouldn't fully commit until she found definitive answers.

As she boarded the bus home, the clock had already struck noon. Despite the sparse occupancy, she conscientiously donned her mask. It had become second nature to her; this concealment, as if shrouding herself, offered an unparalleled sense of security. Seated by the window, she observed the pale blue sky adorned with drifting white clouds as the bus rumbled along its route. Pedestrians continued their leisurely strolls, accompanied by their canine companions, while the houses lining the streets, though lacking in grandeur compared to those she had passed earlier, each possessed a distinct architectural charm, their front yards abloom with a myriad of colorful flowers. Vehicles passed by in the opposite direction, with no honking outside the car and no voices inside. She turned her gaze back to the window, closed her eyes, and reminisced about the devastation she had witnessed on TV, reproaching herself once more for failing to appreciate such beauty in the past. Everything beautiful seemed so natural to her. Reflecting on the suited men's words about humanity's trials, she sighed, acknowledging that the serenity before her might only be fleeting, one-sided, or even temporary, for no one could guarantee perpetual peace and tranquility nor predict the world's end. Lost in thought, her eyes narrowed, and she was startled by a sudden realization—she had encountered those suited gentlemen again as she traversed from the starting point to the ending point, then back to the starting point. Their unexpected query echoed her own ponderings. It seemed like a plan was in place: "Could they have divined the purpose of my stroll today and awaited my arrival to pose this profound question and illuminate its answer? Is this the will of God? Is God truly omniscient, capable of discerning the innermost thoughts of mortals?"

At that moment, Xiaoxin's countenance, obscured by the mask, took on an eerie quality. It was as if she had stumbled upon a revelation. Emitting a long, winding "Hmm" sound through her nostrils, which seemed to originate from the depths of her being yet remain confined within her heart, stifled and unexpressed, she exclaimed: "Incredible, absolutely miraculous!"

# A Solo Dance

## I

With a resounding "bang," the door was closed by the black police officer who was last to leave.

As Ah Sang hurried to the window, peering through the white tulle curtains, she caught a faint glimpse of her husband, Carlo, walking toward the police car parked by the roadside. He was accompanied by two officers—one black, one white, one tall, one short—each adorned with various objects hanging from his waist.

Carlo seemed to intentionally veer to the left of the police car, affording him a view of their home's windows. Just as he reached for the car door, one foot already inside, his head dipped momentarily as his eyes darted toward their window.

His gaze struck her like a lightning bolt, causing her heart to flutter as if it had been shocked. Instinctively, she stepped back as tears began to flow down her cheeks.

As the police car started, Ah Sang's nose tingled, and tears streamed down her cheeks.

With a "whoosh," the car gradually faded into the distance. Ah Sang felt hollow, her heart sinking, her chest tight with anguish as if she might suffocate. Her mind went blank.

Outside, the cawing of crows intensified as they approached, mocking her. Then, a deathly silence descended, so profound that even the airflow became audible.

She sank onto the sofa, hands covering her face, tears streaming unchecked. It had been years since she had wept like this, so they were reminiscent only of her childhood when she cried freely in her mother's embrace after being bullied by older children. She even felt a bit reckless, deliberately wailing as if a torrent needed to rush through a dangerous pass before finding serenity.

After several minutes, the sobs subsided, leaving her with tear-stained cheeks and quivering nostrils. Leaning her chin on her hand, her eyes reddened and swollen, she surveyed her surroundings with a vacant stare.

In front of the sofa sat a coffee table crafted from two rotating round glass panels resting atop a black circular base. She recalled first laying eyes on it in the furniture store. Initially, she had found the opened glass pieces resembled cheerful smiles, but they resembled a full moon while closed. However, now they seemed more akin to two large horseshoes, with one cradling a white porcelain basin containing an aloe vera plant. She had a habit of crushing a piece of aloe vera and mixing it with honey, egg whites, and milk to make a face mask. Carlo would playfully tease her whenever he watered it, saying it was the secret of Ah Sang's beauty. But neglected for some time, the plant appeared wilted, its pinched edges as ugly as a curled-up knife edge.

Across from the sofa stood an elegant fireplace adorned with a wooden shelf displaying several ceramic dolls. Suspended from the top of the shelf hung a rectangular clock encased within two crimson wooden frames, each about an inch wide, adorned with a dragon and a phoenix, respectively. Carlo was born in the year of the Dragon, and Ah Sang in the year of the Rooster--a perfect match! When Ah Sang proudly elucidated the symbolism to Carlo, she received a warm kiss.

Ah Sang's parents had just arrived for a visit. As they stepped into the house, her mother puckered her lips and exclaimed in her Yunnanese dialect, "What did you buy? It looks just like an urn!" Ah Sang angrily reached out to cover her mother's mouth, scolding her superstitious remarks, likening her words to the crow's beak, which is believed to bring bad luck in China.

Now, gazing at the object, she couldn't deny its resemblance to an urn, whose surface seemingly reflected her tears.

Adorning the wall behind the sofa, framed in gold, a wedding photo brimming with tenderness hung. With his gem-like blue eyes, high nose bridge, and golden hair, Carlo stood clad in a white suit, while Ah Sang, adorned in a pristine white wedding gown, wore a pink rose wreath atop her head. Together, they clasped hands to form a large heart shape. A bouquet of green lilies perched at its apex, and the youthful and carefree faces of the newlyweds exuded boundless happiness.

Ah Sang vividly recalled Carlo's friend, Steven, standing before their wedding photo, one hand grazing his chin stubble, the other crossed over his chest, shaking his head as he said, "Oh my God, I can't imagine how breathtaking your offspring will be with this perfect fusion of East and West. If it's a daughter, she'll inherit Carlo's French curls and Ah Sang's cherry lips …."

Ah Sang also remembered her father gazing at the photo, his expression contemplative. "Marriage," he said, his voice carrying the weight of wisdom, "is like that golden frame; your bond is securely nestled within it. But the frame itself is most susceptible to collecting dust. Remember to dust it off regularly."

II

The red roses she purchased yesterday still graced the ceramic vase on the windowsill, a petal drifting onto the light-colored carpet, resembling a drop of crimson blood.

Memories of her arrival at the Canadian airport flickered in Ah Sang's mind.

Carlo's towering height of 1.85 meters allowed her to spy the vibrant bouquet of roses swaying high above his head in the departure hall as soon as she entered.

With a massive hug, Carlo enveloped her, kissing her warmly as he said, "Welcome home!"

Ah Sang, playfully clinging to her husband's arm as they navigated the luggage cart through the hall, perhaps feeling a tad weary, rested her face against his arm, moving forward in sync with his steps. Her gypsy-like full skirt swayed from side to side with the "click-clack" of her high-heeled shoes.

Later, she skillfully removed a few hairpins from her hair, letting her jet-black locks cascade like a waterfall. With glossy shoulder-length hair and a round, cherubic face adorned with cherry lips, she chattered away like a bird. Her proud posture boasted a slightly balletic gait.

Ah Sang appeared lost in a dream until Carlo affectionately leaned over and kissed her hair. She blushed faintly but proudly smiled at him.

They exchanged smiles, lost in their own world, oblivious to the bustling airport surroundings.

Stepping through the revolving glass doors, Ah Sang came to a halt. Scenes once confined to movies and television now unfolded before her eyes—English letters everywhere, familiar Chinese absent from the airwaves; various people whose skin tones ranged from white to black to brown, and the fresh air carrying a hint of plant fragrance, reminiscent of a stroll through a pristine forest.

For a moment, she experienced a surreal sensation of weightlessness. She blinked forcefully, stood on her tiptoes, feet aligned, and drew in a deep breath.

Ah Sang gazed up at the flawless blue sky devoid of clouds. Two jet planes soared overhead, their trails resembling giant pens sketching a double arc across a pristine azure canvas, forming a shape reminiscent of an equal sign.

"What lies beyond that equals sign?" she mused to herself.

Tomorrow marked her second anniversary in Canada, a day meant for celebration. Although she had contemplated calling friends to celebrate over the past two days, she dialed 911 and called the police.

### III

Carlo sat in the back seat of the police car, his head still spinning. A subconscious feeling nagged at him that he had glimpsed Ah Sang in tears behind the window.

Last night, he had drunk a bit too much, the combination of the alcohol with marijuana having made it difficult to control himself.

Only two years into their marriage, everything seemed to be unraveling. It was because of this marriage, or rather because of Ah Sang, that he had returned to marijuana six months ago after two years of abstinence.

Leaning his head against the seatback, Carlo glanced sideways, watching a dense poplar tree smoothly recede as the police car advanced like soldiers in a parade. The orange leaves rustled in the breeze, glimmering like countless golden fish frolicking and jumping in the sunlight.

The police car's radio broadcasted the ongoing hockey game, in which the Yuson team lost to the Harris team.

Engrossed in their conversation, the two officers in the front seemed to have forgotten about the passenger in the back.

The chubby officer lamented the Yuson team's failure, pounding the steering wheel in frustration.

Carlo abruptly cut in with a gritted-teeth remark, "Those damn Yuson guys, they made me lose all the money I bet on them."

Hockey held a special place in Carlo's heart, shown in his purchasing season tickets for games online for over a decade.

He reminisced about the game two years ago when he splurged nearly three hundred Canadian dollars on a premium ticket for Ah Sang.

Ah Sang, however, bemoaned the expense, nearly two thousand RMB. "What's so special about it?" she demanded. "It's ridiculously pricey, and I don't get it. I'd rather stay at home watching TV and chatting online." She grumbled, furrowing her brows, but was dragged out reluctant by Carlo.

"Hockey is thrilling; it's Canada's national sport. I can teach you the rules if you don't understand. Watching TV is dull in comparison," Carlo said enthusiastically.

## VI

"Please leave the car and come with us to the office for a statement." The chubby officer had already opened the door next to Carlo.

The police station building was a square three-story structure, with a queue of people standing in line in the ground-floor lobby.

This was Carlo's second visit to the police station.

The previous incident had occurred when Carlo's truck skidded on snow and collided with a tree. An elderly man clearing snow nearby rushed over, checking the tree's condition before ensuring Carlo was unharmed. Finally, after inspecting the damaged vehicle, he reminded Carlo of the necessity to report to the police station if he intended to continue using it.

Accompanied by two officers, Carlo rode the elevator to the third floor and entered a large room. The atmosphere was far from tranquil; in the corner against the wall, a rectangular wooden table hosted a man and a woman engaged in a heated discussion with the officers across from them. The woman's voice carried a hint of anger as she spoke, while the young male officer she addressed appeared somewhat bashful. Meanwhile, a female officer occupied another corner chair, multitasking—engaged in a phone conversation while jotting down notes on paper.

After the trio entered, the short officer departed, leaving Carlo with the tall one at the service counter. From a file cabinet, the officer retrieved a form and handed it to Carlo, saying, "I'm sorry, but your wife reported domestic violence, and we have to handle this matter impartially."

"Though I may have had a bit too much to drink, I didn't lay a hand on her," Carlo said. "I merely grabbed her hand and asked why she had rearranged my belongings." What irked Carlo the most was Ah Sang's habit of moving his drinks from the fridge's top shelf to the bottom—putting them on the top shelf was a habit he had had since childhood. Every day upon returning home, his first action was to retrieve a can of his favorite cola from the fridge. It was a reachable position for him, yet Ah Sang persisted in relocating them to the bottom, forcing him to bend over each time.

He had repeatedly voiced his discontent to Ah Sang. Still, she always seemed to disregard his concerns, inevitably resulting in his drinks being returned to the bottom shelf the next day. Carlo couldn't understand why Ah Sang persistently acted according to her preferences, disregarding his habits and requests.

"But her wrist is injured," the officer interjected.

"That's from her struggling," Carlo argued.

"From now on, you must maintain a distance of at least three hundred meters from her. You are prohibited from returning home or contacting her by phone. The court's decision will determine the duration of these restrictions."

"Damn it, that's my house," Carlo exclaimed, nearly leaping up in anger.

The tall officer tilted his head, mouth pursed, hands spread out, and shrugged, looking helpless.

**V**

Ah Sang awoke nearly at noon, the harsh North American morning light already seeping through the unshielded edges of the bedroom curtains. After two years in Canada, she had grown accustomed to waking up alone, her heart still burdened with the memory of Carlo being taken away by the police the day before.

Too lethargic to get up and draw the curtains, she lazily switched on the bedside lamp.

Across from her stood a dressing table with an oval-shaped mirror. The two orange lights from the pale green glass hood above the headboard cast a particularly enchanting glow on her beautiful face, reflected through the misty light of the mirror.

"Clang," the mailman outside the door put mail into the mailbox by it.

She opened the door, retrieving a stack of items. Most were miscellaneous advertisements, but an envelope containing this month's bill was nestled among them.

Ah Sang had never handled online bill payments herself. Upon arriving in Canada, Carlo had taken her to the bank to open a joint account, leaving her solely responsible for spending.

Despite Carlo's lucrative self-employment, their bank account always seemed empty; it appeared he had little regard for saving money. Their home would inevitably fill with unnecessary items whenever the account was flush.

Ah Sang couldn't openly complain about the overflowing storage room because she earned no money. She could only hint at the situation.

In the following days, Ah Sang found the storage room cleared out. Upon inquiry, she learned that he had loaded the lightly used or unopened boxes into his little truck and deposited them into the donation bin near the mall.

Infuriated by this, Ah Sang angrily berated him in Chinese as a spendthrift. Fortunately, he couldn't understand, so her anger was evident only from her expression.

Following that incident, Ah Sang learned to curse in Chinese when she needed to scold someone.

## VI

Ah Sang recalled that their first argument had also revolved around money.

"This city is at its most vibrant now. I'll take you for a drive to revel in its beauty and charm you," Carlo declared eagerly the day after Ah Sang arrived in Canada. He roused her from bed with a playful pinch on her nose.

Pointing towards distant skyscrapers spaced elegantly, Carlo said, "That's downtown."

Once Ah Sang settled into the car, Carlo teased, "Hey, I knew you wouldn't bother with a seatbelt. Sweetheart, this is Canada, not China."

With a playful pout, Ah Sang quickly fastened her seatbelt.

Carlo opened the sunroof, letting the refreshing breeze in. Justin Bieber's upbeat track "Somebody to Love" filled the car, prompting Carlo to nod his head to the rhythm, his face lit up with joy. He sang along intermittently, stealing glances at Ah Sang and occasionally reaching out to pat her head.

On both sides of the road, trees burst with blooms of red or white flowers, while others boasted burgundy leaves weighed down with fruits. Several wild rabbits bounded away into the distance. At the same time, a solitary black crow stood its ground in the middle of the road. Carlo began to decelerate, but the crow remained unmoved, lifting its head defiantly, its gaze fixed on the approaching car.

Carlo laughed as the car rolled directly over the crow, which hadn't budged yet. Ah Sang looked back through the rear window to see the crow already gone, having fled in a panic.

The verdant grass was dotted with golden dandelions, while wisps of white dandelion seeds occasionally drifted in through the open window. Surrounding the low-rise buildings were trees and flowers. The car cruised along the road, occasionally passing a high-rise building, which appeared somewhat isolated. Some structures proudly displayed Canadian flags atop their rooftops or windows, the bright red maple leaves fluttering in the breeze.

As the car drew near the downtown skyscrapers, they seemed perpetually out of reach. Ah Sang grew increasingly anxious and impatient, her gaze fixed on the distant skyline of towering buildings.

Carlo had clearly told her that downtown was at most a half-hour drive away from home, but the imagined metropolis had yet to appear. Several times, she interrupted Carlo's intoxicated singing, anxiously questioning, "When will we arrive downtown? How much longer?"

Carlo gently stroked her long hair and quipped, "Darling, this is downtown. What kind of downtown were you expecting?"

Ah Sang's eyes widened in disbelief, a wave of disappointment washing over her. She covered her mouth with both hands, tears welling up as she exclaimed, "You lied to me! You said this is the fourth largest city in Canada, but what kind of city is this? There's nothing here, no skyscrapers. Even the high-rises in our small county surpass this. It is obvious it is the countryside!"

"Hey, I didn't know the city you wanted must have skyscrapers." Carlo chuckled, realizing Ah Sang had envisioned a different metropolis than the one he described.

Ah Sang's complaints didn't dampen Carlo's excitement. He was still thrilled because he had secretly arranged a fantastic itinerary for them.

Carlo was still buzzing with excitement about his plan. He wanted his bride to experience a romantic and cozy wedding night with him in the city's most luxurious hotel.

"Where is this?" Standing at the hotel entrance, Ah Sang looked bewildered.

"Darling, stop asking and be patient. You'll find out in a moment." Carlo kissed her on top of the head and led her towards the entrance.

As they stepped into the hotel and approached the front desk to get the keys, Ah Sang understood.

"Why are you wasting money like this?" Ah Sang couldn't understand. Their home was in this city, just a half-hour drive away. Why spend so much money on a hotel?

"You only know how to save money. I earn it, and I can spend it however I please."

Carlo glanced at Ah Sang, who had gone from hysterical tears during the journey to bitterly complaining, leaving him immensely disappointed. All his excitement evaporated in an instant.

Ah Sang lay on the enormous bed, still sobbing. After fourteen hours of flying, the jet lag hadn't faded. Soon, she drifted into a dazed sleep.

Carlo's heart was gripped by a sense of panic whose cause he could not pinpoint. Feeling bored, he called for the waiter to bring two bottles of champagne and some beer.

He got himself drunk.

## VII

Ah Sang lowered her head, raised her hands, and rotated her arms, inspecting the purplish bruises on her wrists, feeling an overwhelming bitterness welling up in her heart.

As an only child, she had never experienced any injustices from childhood to adulthood. It had only been two years since she arrived in Canada, and her relationship with Carlo had shifted from initial affection to the current rapid decline, leaving her somewhat unprepared.

A faded rubber chicken was hanging above the dining table, its belly embedded with a ticking clock.

It was nearly four o'clock, and soon, the children would arrive for their dance class after school. She took a long breath, exhaling sharply, then turned before heading to the bedroom to change into a long-sleeved T-shirt.

The dance studio was converted from the basement, with a large mirror facing the staircase.

Ah Sang stood expressionless before the mirror, using her jade-colored fingernails to tuck her long hair, which had fallen on her chest, behind her ears and tying it up with a rubber band.

Then, she switched on the stereo and selected her favorite dance song, "Loneliness." With her legs pressed together, head held high, and hands raised to the soft music, she executed a graceful turn, her face revealing a faint, melancholic, and elusive gaze. Swaying slowly to the rhythm, memories began to flood back to her.

That evening after dinner, Carlo called out to Ah Sang, who was engrossed in watching a Korean drama, "Darling, the snow outside has melted; let's go for a walk. You haven't been out for a week."

Ah Sang was somewhat reluctant to leave her Korean drama, especially since it was an exciting part.

Carlo sat down beside her and gently blew into her ear.

This breath stirred up Ah Sang's tenderness and broke down her reserve. She playfully muttered, "You're so annoying."

At first, Carlo didn't quite understand. But he knew she had given in every time he heard Ah Sang say these two words. He enjoyed hearing her utter them.

He once asked Ah Sang what these two words meant, but her explanation had only left him puzzled: "When someone likes the other person, why use 'hate'? Isn't 'hate' the opposite of 'like'?" He shook his head vigorously, still unable to comprehend.

Outside, the bare branches began to sprout green buds, and occasional patches of new green appeared on the grass. The melted snow trickled into the drainage ditch on both sides of the road with a gentle gurgle.

The glow of the setting sun had not completely faded, and a massive moon hung in the distance.

Suddenly, Carlo reached out and hugged her waist, saying, "Darling, you can't just stay at home and rely on me. You need a job; you need independence."

"I'll try to find a job. But why the rush?! I just finished studying English, didn't I?"

Carlo's words made Ah Sang feel abrupt, cold, and uncomfortable.

"Darling, you don't have to go out. You can continue teaching dance. I love watching you dance; that's when I'm most proud of you."

Carlo's words injected a surge of excitement into Ah Sang.

"Yes, why didn't I think of that? I was a dance teacher back in China, and I could do the same here."

Ah Sang jumped up, wrapped her arms around Carlo's neck, and kissed him, saying, "My sweetie", elongating the letter "e."

"Stop it; I don't want to hear that childish tone. Ugh, it gives me goosebumps, look."

Carlo raised his arm to show Ah Sang. The golden hairs shimmered like autumn reeds in the sunlight.

That weekend, Carlo drove his small truck to the building materials store, bought a load of renovation materials and tools, and worked tirelessly for two months. A simple dance studio was constructed.

On the day of completion, Carlo proudly said to her, "You see, I told you. There are fewer people in Canada, so you must rely on yourself for everything, right?"

Looking at the dance studio Carlo built for her, Ah Sang felt touched but somewhat disheartened. She cherished her dance career, and Carlo finally allowed her to rediscover herself. Yet, she couldn't help but wonder why, as her husband, he earned so much money every year and could easily support her, yet he was so eager for her to start earning money. Did he truly understand his responsibility as a husband?

Deep down, she felt a twinge of disappointment in this marriage.

## VIII

Ah Sang couldn't pinpoint when Carlo had resumed using marijuana and alcohol. Each time he indulged, he would forcefully engage in sexual acts with her.

Last year, he had even resorted to violence, but she never considered calling the police. So, if it hadn't been for the menacing look in his eyes this morning, as if he might kill her, she wouldn't have dialed the police.

When the police arrived to take her statement, they inquired if Ah Sang wished to press charges against Carlo. Their encouragement resonated: "If he mistreats you like this frequently, you should pursue legal action. Let him face the consequences. He needs to pay the price for his actions. Otherwise, he'll never understand the severity of his behavior."

The policeman's words sent shivers down Ah Sang's spine, and she hastily shook her head in fear, vehemently refusing. She was afraid that everyone would think she was truly a shrew, a bad woman who went abroad just for her husband's money.

She even regretted her impulsive decision to involve the police.

Recollections of the night before she departed overseas flooded her mind when her mother slept with her in the same bed and shared countless insights on being a devoted wife.

"A wife must embody virtue. She must master household chores, cook delicious meals, efficiently manage the home and family finances, and learn to manage her husband ...."

She had diligently adhered to all her mother's teachings.

Carlo always stored an abundance of drinks and alcohol in the top compartment of the refrigerator. Those bottles and cans were heavy. Concerned that the weight might damage the plastic shelf, she relocated them to the lower shelf. This action sparked a quarrel with Carlo, who insisted she refrain from interfering with his possessions.

In a household where husband and wife lived together, if the wife tidied up the house, that was virtuous. So, how could moving his things be seen as messing with them?

She enjoyed watching Korean dramas. The girls in them were so adorable, and the boys took such good care of their loved ones. But Carlo always mocked her, asking why those girls couldn't speak normally and why they always spoke in a cutesy way. He found it disgusting to watch.

The dishwasher was energy-consuming and water-consuming, so she washed it by hand. But he didn't appreciate it, insisting that hand washing wasn't clean enough.

She wanted to manage this home well, but he always complained that she was too controlling. He was an independent person.

As time went by, they slept together every night, but she felt like she couldn't get close to him or grasp him.

Yesterday was Sunday. They bought two bottles of champagne at a hotel. Carlo also bought a bouquet of bright red roses, planning to invite friends for a drink the next day to celebrate their two-year reunion.

Ah Sang also started to get busy, planning to prepare some food. Somehow, when she opened the refrigerator door, the bottle of wine fell from the top and shattered on the floor.

Carlo seemed to have just smoked marijuana, and when he heard the sound of glass breaking, he ran to the kitchen and immediately got angry. He grabbed her hand and shook it hard, his eyes wide open.

"Why? Why did you touch my things?!"

Carlo's distorted face frightened Ah Sang. She tried to twist her hand out of his grip, but the more she tried to pull away, the tighter his grip became. He shook her back and forth, and finally, he pushed her to the ground.

Terrified, Ah Sang dialed 911.

## IX

When the doorbell rang, ah Sang had just thrown those newspapers into the trash can.

Three police officers followed Carlo into the house, accompanying him to collect his daily necessities. Carlo didn't even glance at her. His expression was cold as he walked straight to the bedroom. The three police officers didn't take off their shoes. They just stood on the doormat, waiting. After Carlo had gathered what he needed, they all got into the police car and left.

Ah Sang could feel hatred burning in her husband's heart. At that moment, a sense of guilt welled up within her. She wanted to approach him and apologize, but she couldn't. They had to keep their distance, and communication had to go through their respective lawyers.

She couldn't understand why, in a country like Canada that respected individual privacy so much, marital conflicts were taken so seriously.

Ah Sang still hadn't figured out what had really happened between them. What was the key to their problems? They were like two people walking side by side toward the same goal but always colliding, sometimes even stepping on each other's heels.

She remembered the giant equal sign she saw at the airport on the first day she arrived as if she could have already seen a huge question mark looming behind it.

# X

"I really hate this woman now. She's disgusting. I don't want to see her again. Maybe my sister is right. She married me just for the status and hid it well. I'm such an idiot, playing the fool. I need to end this damn marriage as soon as possible; the sooner the better!"

Since Carlo couldn't go home, he stayed with his friend Steven. The surround sound system played "Under My Skin" by the famous Canadian rock singer Avril Lavigne. Carlo sat on the carpet in front of the sofa, drinking and venting to Steven.

In fact, just half a year into their marriage, Carlo began to feel like it was a tie pulled too tight, making his neck stiff and breathing difficult.

Since high school, he had been smoking marijuana and drinking with a group of classmates. For the sake of drinking, he and his buddies didn't hesitate to bribe older classmates, who were happy to make some money off the kids. During his senior year, he had his first girlfriend and several more, but he never considered getting married. When he turned eighteen, barely graduating from high school, his parents kicked him out of the house, refusing to give him a penny. They made him work every month to earn his own money. Their relationship became very tense. When he traveled to China and met Ah Sang, he felt like he had met a saint. This saint changed his worldview and values, forcing him to painfully give up his smoking and drinking habits.

When his parents heard the news of his marriage, it struck them like a thunderbolt. Then came unprecedented excitement. They believed that a woman who could change their son's original nature must be extraordinary, and they gave their heartfelt blessings without hesitation.

But, accustomed to wearing jeans and casual clothing, he felt an almost comic discomfort navigating life in the formal attire of marriage. Since he first mentioned "divorce," Ah Sang's saintly image was completely shattered in his mind. He even felt a sense of relief, like a bird released from its cage.

## XI

"How could you call the police? How could you send your own husband to the police station? Regardless of how wrong he may be, he is still your husband. Family matters should not be aired in public, don't you know that?"

A week later, Ah Sang couldn't hold back anymore. She called her parents, who were far away in Kunming and cried as her mother mercilessly scolded her.

"Mom, have you forgotten how he treated you when you visited a year ago?"

She tried to rally her mother to her side.

"Ah Sang did the right thing by calling the police, teaching him a lesson. Otherwise, he'll never know he's wrong."

Her father's words brought some comfort to Ah Sang.

A year ago, Ah Sang begged Carlo to guarantee her parents' visit. When Ah Sang's parents saw their daughter living in such a big house with a car, their worries dissipated, and their exhaustion from the long flight faded into excitement.

They put down their luggage and inspected the house, finding chaos everywhere.

"Let's quickly tidy up before our son-in-law gets back so they can be happy," Ah Sang's mother said, rolling up her sleeves and getting to work.

Her mother tackled the bedroom while her father tidied the garage. Afterward, they even organized the refrigerator.

"Mom, Dad, welcome!" Carlo came back, speaking the Chinese he had just learned with difficulty. He hugged them, then walked into the bedroom and closed the door.

Ah Sang's parents exchanged proud glances, thinking their son-in-law would be pleased with the tidy bedroom.

Less than five minutes later, Carlo stormed out with a furious expression, shouting, "Who moved my stuff? I can't find anything."

Ah Sang's parents couldn't understand what he was saying, but from his angry expression, they sensed trouble. Nervously sitting on the sofa watching

TV, they stood up together, unsure of what to say since they couldn't speak English and felt even more embarrassed and anxious.

Carlo didn't even look at them and went straight to the fridge, opened it to get a drink, and found it unfamiliar. Almost everything had been moved, and he couldn't find what he wanted.

He slammed the fridge door shut, turned around, walked into the bedroom, and slammed that door shut, too. A few minutes later, he came out with a bag, announcing he was moving out.

Seeing their Western son-in-law so agitated, Ah Sang's parents were nervous and at a loss for words. They could only apologize repeatedly with Ah Sang translating.

After persuasion, they convinced Carlo to stay, but the encounter left everyone with a lump in their throats.

Dinner was very quiet, with hardly anyone speaking. Only the sound of chopsticks hitting the bowls broke the silence.

Ah Sang's parents didn't dare to look up, quietly eating the food in their bowls, and refrained from offering dishes to their son-in-law as they would in China. Carlo kept frowning; even his favorite spicy chicken couldn't satisfy his appetite.

Ah Sang was extremely disappointed, feeling that Carlo's behavior was humiliating. That night, she slept in another guest room.

Despite their fear and trepidation, Ah Sang's parents still wanted to do more for their daughter and son-in-law. In their eyes, if they weren't family, they wouldn't be under the same roof. No matter how difficult their Western son-in-law was, they believed being more considerate would change him. So they always thought of ways to help Carlo and arrange things for him. However, they didn't realize that this only increased Carlo's resentment towards them.

About a month later, Carlo wouldn't listen to any explanation from Ah Sang. He bluntly told her, "Why can't you tell your parents to keep quiet while eating? Why do they have to be so loud? Please tell them to lower their voices and speak softly in public."

That night, Carlo walked into the bedroom with a scowl and said to

Ah Sang, "You said Chinese people don't close their mouths when they eat. When I walked by the living room, your parents were watching a TV drama. Why did the Chinese women in the drama eat with their mouths closed?"

Carlo's tone was full of contempt.

## XII

A week later, Ah Sang received a call from Steven asking if she needed help and informing her that Carlo was already living with his cousin. They had only been apart for a week, and Carlo had already done such a thing! It seemed that divorce was inevitable now.

Ah Sang called friends for advice, and almost everyone told her that in a legal society like this, friends couldn't help, and it was different from seeking personal connections in China. She needed to find a lawyer.

She walked to the government department specifically for low-income families, where the staff helped her find a free legal service lawyer.

The room was spacious and bright, with a black translucent desk holding a pure white telephone and a metal pen holder, while two photographs of lotus flowers were on the wall with a swinging pendulum clock.

The lawyer was a small Italian, somewhat balding man wearing a sharp suit with a red tie. His face was wrinkled with smiles, giving off a friendly vibe.

After the introductions, they got straight to the point.

"I have received the documents from your husband Carlo's lawyer proposing some basic property division conditions. Let's look at them together and see if you can accept these conditions."

"I have no conditions. Whatever he proposes, I accept." Ah Sang said, tears streaming down her face. When it came to divorce, all Ah Sang could think of were the good times she had with Carlo.

The lawyer quickly pushed the tissue box on the table toward her, saying, "No, that won't do. You have your rights. I'm here to help you protect those rights. I think there are some unreasonable aspects in this document. Although you've only been married to him for two and a half years, the increase in family property should be considered joint property. I plan to draft a new document based on this one to fight for the most reasonable property division for you."

**XIII**

Carlo hired a renowned local lawyer, and even though the fee was three hundred dollars per hour, he spared no expense. He was utterly disgusted with Ah Sang and just wanted to get out of this marriage as soon as possible. However, he still admitted that he had loved her at first, at least during the first one and a half years of their marriage.

The lawyer had already drafted a document concerning property divisions, which would soon be handed over to Ah Sang's lawyer. It included:

1. Ah Sang had been in Canada for less than three years. Carlo was still her guarantor, responsible for all living expenses for the remaining eight months, totaling ten thousand dollars.

2. The sports car purchased two years ago for forty-five thousand dollars, now worth twenty-five thousand dollars, would belong to Ah Sang.

3. The house was Carlo's pre-marital property. During their two and a half years of marriage, the appreciated part of the house could be divided equally. Carlo would give Ah Sang ten thousand dollars in cash at once.

4. After Ah Sang received all the above properties, she would move out immediately.

......

A few months later, when Ah Sang's lawyer handed her this now-official document, she didn't hesitate and signed it. Since this marriage failed, she wanted to end it immediately and start her new life. Her dance studio awaited her, and the students looked forward to her return.

As she walked out of the lawyer's office, a line from the novel Gone with the Wind suddenly came to her mind:

"Tomorrow is another day!"

# What a Good Fall

## I

She sensed her soul fluttering like a little winged angel out of her body and hovering over the room. Several figures surrounded the operating table below, meticulously resetting the fractured bones in her leg.

Later, she felt herself drifting through a deep blue circular tunnel. The hue was captivating, reminiscent of aquamarine, a shade that danced between blue and green. Smooth and transparent ice walls, like those in Elsa's ice palace from the film Frozen, flanked both sides of the tunnel. She sang a cheerful tune, joyfully tracing the smooth walls with her hand, unaffected by any chill.

As the anesthesia took effect, she slipped into a brief, dreamlike state. Upon regaining partial consciousness, her hearing remained intact, though she felt no sensation. Amidst the haze, she could hear the voices of people around her—male, female, laughter, chatter. Unable to fully grasp their words, she remained unaware of the presence of two sturdy male doctors, seemingly engaged in a tug-of-war to realign her fractured leg.

When she fully regained awareness, she found herself alone in the operating room, feeling a slight chill. Her fractured leg was already snugly wrapped in bandages.

"Are you alright?" asked a nurse who entered, standing beside her bed with a gentle smile.

"I'm okay, just a bit cold."

"Please wait; I'll fetch you a warm blanket."

"Oh, my goodness, this feels incredible!" As the nurse draped a soft blanket over her, a wave of warmth enveloped her entire body, momentarily rendering her blissfully faint.

## II

What serenity enveloped her! She found herself in a pristine world in the tranquility of a snow-covered meadow. Snowflakes had gently fallen the night before, but now the sky stretched azure and cloudless. No airplanes were streaking through the vastness and no flocks of geese crossing the horizon. The expansive grassland, devoid of the usual sounds of children at play or the scurrying of wild rabbits and squirrels, resembled a scene from a fairy tale, silent as if in deep hibernation.

The snow blanketed the ground, its thickness reaching half a foot high. Walking alone across this vast expanse, her face as pale as the snow beneath her, she felt weary. Sleep had eluded her the night before, and she had undergone a stomach endoscopy that very morning after fasting.

These past two years had been a relentless onslaught of challenges. It felt as if a lifetime's worth of misfortune had descended upon her all at once: the loss of her job and car, the passing of her father, the divorce of her brother, the departure of her lover, and the torment of stomach problems. Adding to her despair was the incident earlier that morning. While waiting for the bus and engrossed in conversation on her phone, she had been distracted, which caused her phone to slip from her grasp. It bounced onto the main road, only to be crushed by the wheels of an approaching bus.

"What rotten luck!" she cursed inwardly. "Life seems devoid of meaning; perhaps death would be preferable." With her hands tucked into her pockets, she sighed as she walked.

Suddenly, her foot sank into a pile of thick snow, causing her body, wrapped in a long down jacket and a backpack, to lose balance and collapse onto the snow with a sharp "crack!" that resonated through the air as intense pain shot up from her ankle, signaling a bone fracture.

A buzzing filled her ears, akin to adjusting the volume on a radio. Her vision dimmed, and cold sweat drenched her body. Looking upward, she saw the sun hanging overhead, encircled by a ring of black light, emitting a piercing glare. Despite going without food for fifteen hours, her unprecedented desire for life surged! Panicked, she reached out to the sky, calling for help as if beseeching the heavens: "Help! Help!"

However, there was no response, only a chilling silence.

A sense of dread enveloped her. "Am I going to die?" she asked herself. Her weakened body made her breathing increasingly difficult. She seemed to see an eagle circling above, waiting for her last gasp.

"I can't die! I must crawl to where there are people. Even if it means crawling!" The notion of death vanished as quickly as it had come.

"If only I had a phone, I could call 911, and an ambulance would arrive swiftly," she thought, staring hopelessly, on the brink of fainting, at the vast expanse of snow, trembling all over, her stomach gnawing at her.

Deep despair consumed her, unlike any she had ever known since entering the world. For the first time, she truly understood the depths of despair.

Shaking her head vigorously, she admonished herself: "I cannot fall asleep and remain here. If no one finds me, I will freeze to death. I must crawl out!"

Not far ahead, she spotted the fence of a residential community, behind which stood houses with closed doors and windows, cars parked like silent sentinels. In this sparsely populated part of Canada, there were no signs of life save for the vehicles in nearly minus twenty-degree weather. She resolved to crawl in that direction, dragging her body through the snow.

A swoosh sounded as a car zoomed past in the distance, followed by an eerie silence.

She had one thought alone: "I must not close my eyes; I must stay awake!"

No longer able to reach out, she inched step by step with her hands clutching the ground. Her eyelids drooped, on the brink of closure, while her lips weakly murmured, "Help! Help!" Yet, the world seemed eerily silent, devoid of any signs of life.

She struggled step by step. Tears, snot, and melted snow mingled on her face, her bare hands now swollen and numb, the initial pain from the fracture giving way to no feeling. With her broken left leg trailing behind, she weakly continued to call for help, her voice barely audible to herself.

Finally, she reached the pathway of the residential community. Before she lay, parked cars and houses lined either side of the road. Nearly all the vehicles were buried under thick snow, and the weight of it bowed the tree branches.

Resting her face on her arms for a moment, and her nose nearly touching the icy ground, she hesitated before turning her head, contemplating to herself: "If I crawl to the doorstep of the first house along the road, it's probably about ten meters away, and there are steps. If no one is there, I'll have to crawl back onto the road, which will drain more of my energy. It's better to crawl straight to the main road, where cars pass regularly."

Deciding to conserve her dwindling energy, she pressed on toward the main road as best she could.

With a clang, she was jolted awake from what felt like a dream. A glimmer of hope flickered as she thought someone was emerging from a nearby house. She was only disappointed when the noise continued with a crashing sound as a chunk of snow fell from a tree branch like an avalanche.

Despair washed over her again, each step she took requiring a gasp for air. Her exposed hands were now lacerated by the small, slippery stones on the road, blood oozing out. She felt herself growing drowsy, the sun seemingly mocking her from above as it gazed down upon her: "How she longed for death, but now she demonstrates a fierce will to survive amidst despair."

Her eyes could not stay open, the agony of her broken bones tormenting her deeply. She closed her eyes, and her body continued to move forward intentionally. No sound escaped her lips as her trembling mouth moved silently.

A clang rang out as a man in shorts emerged from a nearby house, accompanied by the barking of a dog. The sound pierced through her foggy consciousness, her heart sinking as she realized help was near.

Turning her head toward the approaching figure, she raised one hand with all her remaining strength and whispered, "Help! Help!"

She remembered nothing after that brief moment of faintness.

The man, clad in shorts and slippers, rushed out of his house, followed by the little dog wagging its tail and barking excitedly. He tried to squat down to assist her but found it futile.

When she regained consciousness, she informed him of her broken leg and inability to stand.

Still in his shorts, the man returned to his house to don shoes before gently lifting and carrying her inside. Slowly, he walked her to the sofa, where he laid her down, the little dog faithfully following behind, barking all the while.

The man in the house, Gio, saved her life.

### III

"I'm sorry this might cause you some discomfort. We've confirmed that your leg is broken, and now we need to lift you into the ambulance. The painkillers we have on board will help ease your discomfort." Tearfully, she met the gaze of Nari, a young man in an ambulance uniform, speaking softly and smiling kindly at her.

Nari and his female colleague wrapped her in a blanket and gingerly moved her onto the waiting ambulance outside. Each step they took sent waves of intense pain through her leg. She could sense their cautiousness, as if they were handling a delicate explosive that could detonate at any moment.

Inside the ambulance, Nari apologized, "The road conditions aren't great, but we'll do our best to drive smoothly. You'll need to endure a bit, okay?"

"Here, put this in your mouth and inhale gently. It will help alleviate the pain," Nari said, inserting a plastic tube into her mouth.

After a few breaths, the pain began to subside significantly. As the female paramedic began driving, Nari turned to her, asking for some personal information: "Can I have your phone number?"

"I don't have a phone at the moment. Mine broke this morning," she replied.

"I'm sorry, but I need to change you into a hospital gown and cut off your pants, socks, and shoes for bandaging," Nari said gently.

Reluctantly, she nodded, enduring the pain with each movement. Despite the discomfort, she felt an unparalleled sense of security and relief at being cared for by Nari and his colleagues.

Upon arriving at the hospital, she was wheeled out of the ambulance. Nari assisted her with the admission procedures and carefully packed her belongings into a bag under the stretcher. When a nurse took over, she was wheeled into the operating room.

Nari's task was complete, and as he bid her farewell, he said warmly, "Goodbye, and I wish you a speedy recovery!"

## IV

Lying on the operating table beneath the surgical lights, she felt vulnerable, akin to a helpless child. Yet, the knowledge that she was saved and wouldn't perish dispelled any lingering panic.

"What language do you speak? Can you speak English? Do you need a translator?" A nurse's kind inquiry broke through her thoughts as she entered the room.

"My mother tongue is Chinese, but I can manage some English," she replied, warmth blooming in her heart.

Soon after, she was wheeled into the X-ray room, where the orthopedic doctor carefully examined her images. After assessing the situation, he decided to forgo immediate surgery and opted instead for external force reduction therapy.

Upon awakening from partial anesthesia, she found herself back in the X-ray room. "Unfortunately, your leg is severely injured and requires surgery," the orthopedic doctor regretfully informed her, holding the examination results.

A nurse escorted her to wait in the corridor outside the operating room. Though her leg throbbed with pain, her heart remained surprisingly tranquil. She closed her eyes, listening to the soft murmur of nurses conversing nearby.

About thirty minutes later, someone approached her bedside. "Hello, could you please provide your name and date of birth?"

After confirming the information, the individual continued, "I'm the doctor's assistant. Your leg requires surgery, and you'll be staying in the hospital tonight. However, I can't give a precise time for the operation. Your bed has been arranged on this floor, and a nurse will escort you shortly. Additionally, I've reviewed your health records in our system and arranged for your prescribed medications. The nurse will deliver them to your ward."

The nurse wheeled her upstairs and settled her into a four-bed room. Two patients were already present—one asleep, the other an elderly lady reading with a pillow propped behind her.

Seeing another patient with a leg injury enter, the elderly lady offered a sympathetic greeting, "Hello, I broke my bones slipping on ice, and I've been here for ten days."

"Hello," she responded, a bitter smile gracing her face.

As the nurse hung an IV drip for her, she lay on the hospital bed, helpless and uncertain of when her surgery would take place. Nurses checked her blood pressure and heart rate throughout the night and administered pain relief. Unable to eat or drink, she relied on a call button to request assistance to use the bathroom.

After hours of waiting, she was informed that the surgery would occur the following day.

That night, the pain tormented her relentlessly. She repeatedly pressed the call button by her bedside, urgently informing the incoming nurses that her pain level was at a "ten."

Several nurses responded one after another. After being summoned twice, a young black male nurse took the time to explain, "You seem to have a low tolerance for pain. This painkiller only provides relief for four hours and takes about an hour to take effect. So, you should wait until three hours after taking the medicine before calling, and we will have enough time to retrieve the medication from the pharmacy."

She couldn't help but feel like the most troublesome patient, keeping the nurses busy throughout the night.

V

As dawn broke, the elderly lady's family arrived to take her home, and another patient who had slipped on the ice was admitted to the ward. The night's challenges had provided the nurses with valuable experience, and they were prepared with painkillers for administration. Gradually, her pain level decreased from a "ten" to a more manageable "three."

By noon, a nurse handed her a box of heated disposable washcloths, and the head nurse and the doctor's assistant entered the room with smiles. "Are you ready? The doctor will be operating on your leg soon."

"Of course!" Shortly after, the nurse injected anesthetic into her IV drip, and she was wheeled into the operating room by a tall male nurse.

After the harrowing experience between life and death, her heart gradually found peace and clarity. The worries and pains of the past seemed to fade away, and melancholic thoughts became transient.

She was still somewhat awake as she was wheeled into the operating room. Coincidentally, she crossed paths with a patient being wheeled out. She smiled, greeting him, "Hello, wishing you a speedy recovery. Goodbye!"

"You're so sweet! I've never seen a patient bid farewell to another in the operating room!" chuckled the nurse pushing her bed.

Under the effects of general anesthesia this time, she drifted into a dreamless sleep. When she finally awoke, more than four hours had passed. Two nurses stood by her bedside, patiently waiting for her to regain consciousness.

"You slept quite soundly! Dear, would you like some water?" the nurse beside her asked with a warm smile.

Groggily, she opened her eyes, taking in the unfamiliar surroundings. Her gaze landed on the crucifix hanging opposite the wall—confirming that, indeed, she was in a Catholic hospital!

Struggling to lift her head, she caught sight of her bandaged leg, and tears welled up in her eyes. Overwhelmed with gratitude, she realized that from her fall to the completion of her surgery, she hadn't incurred any expenses or personal worries—everything had been impeccably arranged.

The nurse, noticing her tears, reached for a tissue, gently wiping it away before offering her a cup of water with a straw.

"Dear, you'll need to rest in bed for two to three months to fully recover. But don't worry, everything will be fine," reassured the nurse, her face radiating kindness. Speaking with such gentleness, she remained unaware of the patient's inner thoughts, assuming the emotional response was due to the injury.

"Rest for two to three months?" she silently repeated in her heart, a strange sense of joy enveloping her. "Perfect! I'm exhausted. It's time to prioritize caring for my body and mind, to retreat for a while. Everything is perfectly arranged; this fall has become a blessing in disguise!"

After sipping the water, she turned her head, softly expressing her gratitude to the nurse before drifting into contemplation or perhaps another well-deserved sleep.

# Ah Lin's Bet

## I

Recently, Ah Lin had been feeling somewhat irked. The company's headquarters had just appointed Suha, a young man from the Middle East, as the project manager. Rumor had it that Suha had taken nearly five years to complete his master's degree, spending most of his earnings on travel and sightseeing. Despite being barely thirty, he had already journeyed across half the globe, yet he had never set foot in China. In his mind, this ancient East Asian country was a realm of strange and exotic wonders. Ah Lin couldn't quite fathom the source of his arrogance; Suha always seemed to display a hint of disdain for the Chinese. This irrational attitude only compounded Ah Lin's frustrations.

What grated on Ah Lin even more was listening to Suha speak. It was as if Suha's tongue was a smooth ball, bouncing around his mouth, making incomprehensible sounds. Every time Suha spoke, Ah Lin felt like a little white rabbit with two ears standing on end. When Ah Lin didn't understand, he always said, "Pardon." After a few instances, Suha began to show signs of impatience. He would pivot on his heel and wave dismissively, saying, "I'll email you." Of course, he knew that Ah Lin was better at reading and writing English than speaking it.

Typically, technical immigrants from mainland China met the English proficiency requirements set by the Canadian Immigration Department but often only learned a "mute" form of English in the classroom, and Ah Lin was no exception. However, those who knew Ah Lin always said his limited English proficiency was accompanied by good fortune.

In the early 2000s, Ah Lin immigrated to Canada's western oil city with his wife and son. It was a time when the global economy was slowly recovering from a downturn. Ah Lin observed that many of his university classmates who had immigrated years earlier were still grappling with challenges outside their chosen professional fields, struggling to establish themselves. Some found opportunities in Saudi Arabia, while others worked in restaurant delivery or washing dishes.

After much contemplation, several individuals decided to adapt to the prevailing trend. They shifted their academic focus to the burgeoning field of computers. During this period, it became evident that the most sought-after professions for immigrant families were husbands working in IT and wives in accounting.

To everyone's surprise, Ah Lin landed a job with an oil company within three months of arriving. News of his swift success quickly spread throughout the city, sparking discussions among acquaintances and friends, especially among fellow new immigrants. Ah Lin's achievement served as a source of inspiration for those still in search of employment, boosting their confidence during a challenging time. During this period, Ah Lin was inundated with daily calls, mostly from friends eager to learn the secret behind his job hunt.

Ah Lin knew his success wasn't due to special tricks; it was simply a stroke of luck. However, his background as a graduate of an oil university in the 1980s and his work experience at the China National Petroleum Corporation undoubtedly provided him with the solid technical foundation and support that contributed to his rapid employment.

## II

Ah Lin's background in petroleum naturally led him to settle in Canada's largest oil city. On the afternoon of his arrival, his classmate, Old Lan, picked him up from the airport. Upon entering Old Lan's house, Ah Lin couldn't help but wander around several times, admiring it with envy, nodding and approvingly drooling. Though not expansive, it was a cozy abode for Old Lan's family of three, a stark contrast to Ah Lin's own situation with just six large boxes as their sole possessions.

During the welcoming dinner, Old Lan imparted valuable advice: "From now on, finding a job will be your profession." Ah Lin held onto these words as if they were precious treasures. By day, he diligently revised his resume. He gathered information at the community immigrant service center while spending his nights scouring online job listings until midnight.

One weekend evening as Ah Lin opened his computer, his eyes landed on a job posting on KG Petroleum Drilling Company's website. This position seemed tailor-made for his expertise and experience back home. Excitement coursing through him, he swiftly tweaked his resume and submitted it. To his delight, he received an interview invitation on Monday from the department manager, Bill. Interestingly, KG Petroleum Drilling Company was in another oil-rich city. Bill would travel to Ah Lin's city for the interview.

Bill, a tall foreigner with a distinctive nose, was barely in his fifties, yet his hair had already turned completely white. Nevertheless, with his piercing blue Norwegian eyes and towering height of 1.90 meters, he appeared very handsome.

On the interview day, Ah Lin grappled with nerves, causing his English to falter even more than usual. He felt as though he were on the verge of vomiting, desperate to articulate the knowledge locked in his mind to impress Bill. Yet Bill remained patient and encouraging, his warm smile never faltering. Finally, Ah Lin resorted to sketching and jotting down explanations on paper, detailing various application methods and statistical formulas used in oil drilling. To his relief, bearded Bill appeared impressed by his efforts, breaking into a satisfied grin.

After the interview, Bill wasted no time and instructed Ah Lin to await an email. True to his word, the next day, Ah Lin found an offer letter from Bill in his inbox, accompanied by a note inviting him to negotiate if he wasn't satisfied with the salary.

Confused by the English email titled "offer," Ah Lin sought assistance from Xiong Wei, a fellow resident in his building who held a Ph.D. from the United States but was currently working as a pizza delivery person. Xiong Wei's excitement was palpable as he exclaimed, "This is an offer! It's a job contract—you got the job!" This remarkable tale spread like wildfire among the new immigrants in no time.

Ah Lin later realized that, in addition to finding a boss who understood him, he had also experienced another stroke of luck. On his first day reporting to Bill's office, Ah Lin learned a crucial detail: "Mr. Lin, your predecessor was Chinese, and he did an excellent job. I have a good impression of Chinese people; they work diligently and have strong technical skills. So, I hired you without hesitation. I believe you won't let us down."

At that moment, Ah Lin felt emotion sweep over him, his eyes growing moist. He keenly understood that every Chinese individual abroad represented China in the eyes of other nationalities. A surge of pride filled him, and from that point onward, he always reminded himself never to bring shame to his fellow countrymen.

Bill held Ah Lin in high regard, recognizing his depth of knowledge despite his struggles with expression. Interestingly, Ah Lin found that he could comprehend most of Bill's English, and even when he spoke in Chinglish, Bill could still grasp the essence. Whenever they discussed work, if Ah Lin had to ask "pardon" twice, Bill would earnestly, sometimes even sheepishly, say, "I'm sorry, my English isn't the best. Please email me." This often left Ah Lin feeling a tinge of embarrassment.

### III

Eighty-five percent of the world's oil sands were concentrated in the northern region of Alberta. Ah Lin's project team was tasked with conducting reserve analysis based on field data of oil sands in a specific formation, utilizing relevant instruments and equipment.

As an immigrant country, Canada boasts a diverse workforce. Yet, Ah Lin was the sole Chinese individual among more than ten employees on the project team.

Aside from Bill's warm welcome, the reception from others on his first-day reporting was lukewarm at best. Morning greetings usually amounted to a mere "hi" out of courtesy, with minimal language exchange thereafter. To his colleagues, Ah Lin appeared unable to comprehend English, akin to being deaf and mute. Consequently, during casual conversations or jokes, they hardly acknowledged his presence as a fully participating member. However, one day, during a discussion about power struggles within the company, Ah Lin unexpectedly interjected, "So, these things happen everywhere, huh?" This remark left his colleagues stunned, exchanging puzzled glances. Following this incident, they refrained from engaging in casual conversations around him altogether.

As the project progressed, Ah Lin's technical prowess became increasingly evident. Even Suha reluctantly acknowledged Ah Lin's importance within the project team. Yet his acceptance of Ah Lin remained influenced by his disdain for the stuttering Chinese man.

During one afternoon's discussion on the analysis report concerning the oil sands characteristics of region S, Suha used a laser pointer to elucidate his findings projected on the screen.

Having meticulously prepared beforehand, Ah Lin intended to apply the probability statistics method he had successfully employed in oil field work in China to analyze the geological parameters of the oil sands. As he stood to share his insights, Suha's visible impatience and disdainful shrug signaled his reluctance to entertain Ah Lin's contribution, as if he would leave at any moment. This gesture infuriated Ah Lin. In anger, he approached Suha, seizing his sleeve and loudly exclaiming in Chinese, "Why can't you understand my English? Do you even comprehend English? Damn!"

Suha was taken aback. While he couldn't understand Ah Lin's words, the intensity of Ah Lin's anger was palpable from his contorted expression. Suha had never anticipated the situation would escalate to this extent.

A heavy silence descended upon the meeting room, so profound that everyone's breathing seemed amplified.

Bill's displeasure was evident as he addressed Suha: "You should learn to respect others!"

Suha, now flushed with embarrassment, stood awkwardly for over ten seconds before forcefully extricating himself from Ah Lin's grip on his sleeve. "I'm sorry," he muttered before hastily exiting the room.

Still reeling from the outburst, Ah Lin was stunned by his uncontrollable anger. In a moment of panic, Chinese words had erupted from his lips. Turning around, he found that a colleague offered him a thumbs-up in support. At the same time, another couldn't resist making a mocking face.

The atmosphere grew tense after the incident, and the discussion was concluded on a sour note.

Following the altercation, Suha's interactions with Ah Lin became noticeably more reserved, though his underlying prejudice against China remained palpable.

Those who were familiar with Ah Lin described him as fiercely patriotic and something of a narrow-minded nationalist. During gatherings with his friends, they would discuss life in Canada and China, occasionally venting frustrations about corrupt businesses, tainted food, and dishonest officials back home. Ah Lin harbored deep resentment toward individuals who engaged in unethical behavior, betrayed their Chinese identity, or failed to understand China's complexities. He couldn't bear the criticism of his homeland from those foreigners who lacked a genuine understanding of its culture and history. Once, during a conversation with a friend who expressed a desire for his child to assimilate fully into Canadian culture—speaking flawless North American English, befriending foreigners, and embracing Western cuisine—Ah Lin's temper flared, the situation nearly escalating into a physical confrontation before his friend could finish speaking.

**IV**

As the project encountered a setback with the project team unable to reach a definitive conclusion regarding the reserve estimation of the oil sands in region S, Ah Lin took the initiative to visit Bill's office. He shared his previous involvement in the technical analysis of reservoir oil sand content in China, highlighting international technological advancements. Ah Lin suggested the project team contact China National Petroleum Corporation for potential collaboration.

However, when Suha caught wind of Ah Lin's proposal, he swiftly sought out Bill, engaging him in a lengthy discussion that lasted nearly an hour. Suha repeatedly emphasized the need to exercise caution and not place trust in Chinese individuals or their technology. He painted China as a country where deception was rampant, insinuating that everything could be falsified.

As the Beijing Olympics approached, the lounge buzzed with activity. CTV on the wall-mounted television was broadcasting scenes of Beijing, China, gearing up to welcome the prestigious event. As everyone enjoyed their lunch and coffee, they engaged in casual conversation.

Hailing from the Philippines, Jamie raised his coffee cup and gestured towards the TV. "They say Beijing has invested heavily in improving the environment for the Olympics," he remarked.

Brown, an Indian immigrant, was savoring his curry rice as he pondered aloud, "I wonder if Beijing truly possesses the capability to host such a large number of people."

Suha stood up and walked over to the coffee machine, grabbing a paper cup. As he poured his coffee, his tone took on a peculiar edge. "Do Chinese people still have braids? I heard they're so skinny because of eating with chopsticks. Do they even have buildings taller than ten floors?" His question hung heavily, casting a palpable tension over the room. As each person bowed their head to their meal or drink, the atmosphere seemed poised to erupt, laden with an impending sense of conflict.

At the end of the long table, Ah Lin sat with clenched fists and gritted teeth, his frustration simmering beneath the surface. Across from him, Sam subtly shook his head, silently urging Ah Lin to exercise restraint.

Summoning all his willpower, Ah Lin took a deep breath, exhaling slowly to quell his rising anger. He picked up his teacup and took a sip. Turning to face Suha, who stood by the coffee machine, he spoke calmly, "Actually, what China is like isn't up to me to decide, nor is it up to you or what's on TV or in newspapers. You have to experience it firsthand to truly understand. So, I'll offer you a ticket to Beijing. Upon arrival, my friend will be there to guide you. If your perception aligns with reality, consider the ticket a gift. However, listen carefully; if your experience differs significantly from your preconceptions, you'll need to reimburse me for the ticket and treat everyone here to drinks. What do you say?"

"Okay, deal! It's a deal, then!"

It felt like a stroke of luck; a deal couldn't have been sweeter. Suha, a travel enthusiast, was thrilled and instantly excitedly leaped up.

V

As Ah Lin calculated that it was Suha's third day in Beijing, he couldn't shake off the nagging feeling that he should have received an email from Suha by now.

"Even with the time difference, he should have settled in by now," Ah Lin mused. "Surely, he can't spend the entire week cooped up in his hotel room, can he?"

As Ah Lin stepped into the office that morning, a sense of unease settled over him. It had been the fifth day since Suha's departure, yet he still had no word. Doubt began to creep into Ah Lin's mind, regretting his impulsive decision to offer Suha the ticket. If Suha turned out to be someone who had taken advantage of him by lying, Ah Lin's hard-earned money would go to waste. However, upon reflection, Ah Lin found solace in the idea that even if Suha had deceived him, it would still be a small price to pay for the chance to showcase the reality of China and counter any misinformation spread by foreigners.

As Ah Lin settled into his desk, he was drawn to a ladder propped up in the corner, with a worker in a yellow uniform inspecting something on the roof. However, his irritation peaked when he noticed this maintenance worker placing a dirty toolbox on his desk without regard for cleanliness or etiquette. Reacting instinctively, Ah Lin slammed the box onto the ground with a resounding "bang" before taking his seat and turning on his computer.

Finding it difficult to focus on work, Ah Lin checked the latest medal standings online. To his delight, China remained in first place. Additionally, he learned that Canada had clinched its first-ever Olympic gold medal courtesy of a Chinese-Canadian athlete. This news filled him with pride, almost like he had won the gold medal. With his spirits lifted, Ah Lin found his mood improving as his mind cleared.

There were dozens of internal emails flooding Ah Lin's inbox. Among them, there was a particularly noteworthy message. It was a response to the letter he had drafted on behalf of the project team addressed to the Xinjiang Oilfield Company, seeking their cooperation. The sender was none other than his former colleague, Old Wang. In the email, Old Wang relayed the encouraging news that following discussions at the Xinjiang Oilfield Company's higher echelons, they had agreed to delve deeper into potential cooperation.

Despite the late hour—11:30 p.m. Beijing time—a new email notification suddenly appeared in Ah Lin's inbox. With a mixture of surprise and anticipation, he opened the message, only to find it was from Suha in Beijing, complete with an attachment. Suha seemed to stay on the other side of the world even in the late hours.

With mounting excitement, Ah Lin eagerly opened the email from Suha, revealing a collection of photos capturing the essence of Beijing. From the iconic Great Wall to the majestic Forbidden City and the serene Summer Palace, Suha's images painted a vivid picture of his experiences in the bustling city. There were snapshots from the Olympic Village, including one featuring the Canadian champion—a testament to Suha's remarkable journey.

The email was quite long, and Ah Lin found it almost like a beautiful piece of prose. This guy seemed to be treating Ah Lin as if he were a foreigner who had never visited China before, meticulously describing his own observations and experiences:

"Ah Lin, my dear friend. I had the incredible fortune of crossing paths with my graduate school mentor in Beijing! These past few days have been nothing short of surreal. Amidst the whirlwind of activities, I only found a moment to write to you today—please forgive my delay! I want to express my deepest gratitude for affording me this opportunity to truly immerse myself in your country's culture. Beijing has unfolded before my eyes as a city teeming with vitality, adorned with towering skyscrapers and pristine streets, graced by the presence of beautiful locals and warm-hearted citizens. And the spectacle of the Olympic opening ceremony truly left me in awe. In an instant, the negative stereotypes and misconceptions I once held about China and its people were shattered ...."

The email's closing remarks stated that the ticket cost would be fully reimbursed, cementing the bond between Suha's friend and Ah Lin. Suha also expressed his desire to visit China again, specifically craving Sichuan hotpot.

Upon returning to Canada, he promised to treat everyone to drinks.

"A+! 100 points!" Ah Lin exclaimed, his relief evident in his demeanor.

Standing up from his desk, Ah Lin smiled warmly at the maintenance worker in the yellow uniform descending the stairs. Whistling lightly, he swayed his head in contentment as he approached the bathroom.

# Struggle for Masks

## I

Wei Xinguan has been grappling with the mask situation lately.

Wuhan was already under lockdown two weeks after China's domestic epidemic outbreak began. It was reported that the situation in Wei Xinguan's hometown in Sichuan was relatively controlled and manageable. Some online voices even attributed this success to having a provincial governor who was a medical doctor.

As more cities implemented quarantine measures, those in Sichuan Province also mandated residents wear masks outside. Early this morning, Wei Xinguan's sister had messaged his wife, urging her to purchase masks in Canada and send them over, as their local supply had been depleted.

Upon receiving the urgent request, Wei Xinguan swiftly turned to his computer, scouring online pharmacies and retail giants like Wal-Mart, Shoppers, Rexall, Canadian Tire, London Drugs, Safeway, and Save-On-Foods. Each call yielded the same disheartening response: "Out of stock!" Wei Xinguan started to feel anxious. Now in his fifties, he had been working night shifts lately. During the day, he found it hard to stay awake, and his wife hesitated to disturb him. With little attention to the news recently, he hadn't grasped the severity of the situation. The epidemic was spreading rapidly, and even in Canada, masks were in short supply.

Unconsciously, he stepped onto the balcony, peering through the glass door at the sidewalk below.

"Hmm, nobody's wearing masks," he observed aloud.

"What's caught your eye? I ride the subway daily and haven't seen a soul wearing masks!" Wei Xinguan's wife interjected upon noticing his distress.

"Well, that's odd. Every store around seems to be out of masks!" Wei Xinguan said, scratching his bald head in bewilderment.

"I've heard whispers about some Chinese individuals hoarding masks at home or shipping them back to relatives and friends in China. And organizations are buying them up to donate to China," his wife added.

"Why didn't you mention this earlier?" Wei Xinguan complained.

"Do you think I'd dare bring you anything related to China?"

His usually gentle wife finally seized an opportunity to express her pent-up frustration with him.

"Let's put that aside for now. We've got two days off—let's make the most of them and rush out to hunt for masks!"

Wei Xinguan couldn't stand his wife's constant nagging about family matters in China. Ever since they had immigrated to Canada, his father back in the countryside seemed to think Wei was swimming in gold overseas, always finding reasons to ask for money, not for himself, but for various relatives, whether it was his brother's daughter's wedding, his brother's son buying a house, or his sister's son searching for a job. It weighed heavily on him.

"Where do we even find them? Seems like every store is sold out, huh?"

Seeing Wei visibly bothered, his wife's tone softened a bit.

**II**

"Hey, Old Wu, do you know where I can get some masks?"

Wei Xinguan recalled that his college classmate Old Wu worked as a buyer for a medical equipment company.

"Xinguan, you're only thinking about masks now? Did your folks in China ask you to snag some for them? I've already shipped two batches back to my hometown in Zhejiang."

"Ah, the outbreak wasn't too bad back home at first. But starting this week, the government mandated mask-wearing when out and about."

"Yeah, there are a lot of shady businesses peddling expired or even used masks to the public. But now, some production lines are back up and running, so the shortage should ease up gradually," Old Wu reassured Wei Xinguan.

"The real problem is, nobody knows when this damn epidemic will be over. And who's to say when it'll hit our neck of the woods? We've got to stock up for ourselves."

"Alright, let me shoot you the numbers of a few medical equipment shops. Give them a call and see what they've got."

Old Wu swiftly sent Wei Xinguan a handful of store contact numbers via WeChat.

Wei Xinguan wasted no time dialing the first one: "Hey there, do you guys have any masks in stock?"

"Sorry, we're completely sold out at the moment. Still waiting on a restock," came a sweet female voice on the other end.

He dialed the number of the second store.

"Hello, do you have any masks available?"

"Please hold on for a moment; let me check," a male voice responded.

Wei Xinguan's heart quickened, a glimmer of hope igniting within him.

"We do still have some, but they're just dust masks," the male voice conveyed regretfully after a couple of minutes, but he didn't disconnect the call.

Then, Wei Xinguan overheard a conversation between two individuals on the line before the male voice returned, saying, "Sorry, even those masks are completely sold out."

Thankfully, on his fourth attempt, Wei finally struck gold. There were still some available at the fourth store. But it was a race against time—first come, first served, no reservations.

"I promise I'll be there in fifteen minutes; please hold some for me!" Wei pleaded urgently over the phone.

Without wasting a moment, he snatched his coat from the sofa and dashed out, urgently telling his wife, "I've got to hurry, or they'll be gone!"

### III

Wei Xinguan rushed all the way, disregarding any rules, and reached the West Gate Mall as swiftly as possible. He leaped out of the car and strode inside with determination.

Pushing open the heavy glass door, he entered a bustling scene of shoppers, none of whom seemed to be wearing masks.

The pharmacy section already boasted a lengthy queue, predominantly filled with Asian faces. Standing ahead of Wei Xinguan were a mother and her daughter, who appeared to be around ten years old. When their turn came at the counter, the woman requested to purchase a thousand masks. However, the clerk responded, "I'm sorry, we're limiting purchases to a hundred per family to enable more people to buy."

The woman paused momentarily, then glanced at the girl and murmured, "Alright, make it two hundred. We're two separate families."

As she finished speaking, she gently tugged at the back of the girl's clothes with one hand.

The girl, appearing a bit disgruntled, glanced up with an odd expression before lowering her gaze and addressing the clerk: "She's my mom, and we're one family."

The clerk's face momentarily registered embarrassment but quickly became a friendly smile.

The mother's cheeks flushed crimson instantly as she hurriedly completed the transaction, avoiding eye contact. With her head bowed, she grasped her daughter's sleeve and hurried out of the store. Once outside, she pointedly jabbed her finger toward the girl's head, muttering as they walked, her tone laced with reprimand.

"Only 100 per family?" Wei Xinguan expressed his disappointment visibly.

He quickly calculated that the limit of a hundred masks wouldn't suffice for his sister-in-law's family of three. Since he needed to purchase some, he might as well procure them for his parents and siblings back home, too. It was the first time he actively considered buying items for his family back in China after years of living abroad. Moreover, considering the unpredictable nature of the virus, who knew if it might eventually reach Canada? For the time being, it hadn't appeared in the western prairie province where he resided. Yet, with a substantial Chinese immigrant population, he envisioned that the influx of people returning home for family reunions would spread the sickness like leaves scattered by the wind after Chinese New Year.

Back home, Wei Xinguan phoned his son, who was working in the United States, alerting him to the rapid spread of the epidemic and urging him to promptly purchase some masks for stockpiling.

However, his son responded sarcastically: "Dad, don't go looking for trouble where there isn't any, and don't diagnose illnesses that don't exist, all right?"

Wei Xinguan seethed angrily but refrained from arguing with his son. Instead, he inwardly scoffed, "Humph, what does a young man like you know? I bet you'll come running to me for help when the time comes!"

IV

Wei Xinguan sat on the sofa, his gaze fixed blankly on the two boxes of masks before him and his mind occupied by his son's dismissive words. He let out a heavy sigh.

Observing his despondent state, his wife joined him on the sofa, gently patting his leg as she inquired, "What's weighing on your mind? Wasn't it just that the store limited purchases to a hundred per family? Take me there, and I'll queue to buy another hundred."

Wei Xinguan's eyes widened slightly at his wife's offer, a glimmer of hope stirring within him. But then, the memory of the mother and daughter at the pharmacy dampened his spirits once more.

"Let's forget about it. We can't stoop to such deceitful tactics. We'll find another solution."

"Old Wu gave you a few more store numbers, didn't he? You still have two left to call. Keep trying!"

His wife's words spurred Wei Xinguan back into action, and he quickly retrieved the remaining phone numbers.

Well, luck finally smiled upon him this time. With just one call, he struck gold. They had masks in stock and urged him to hurry over.

Wei Xinguan swiftly snatched up his clothes once more and dashed out, prompting his wife to follow suit and quickly don her attire. This time, she insisted on accompanying him.

Upon reaching their destination, Wei Xinguan's wife remained in the car, instructing him, "Go in alone first. If they're still limiting purchases to 100 per family, I'll buy another 100 once you're out."

Wei Xinguan had no choice but to go by himself. Before long, he emerged carrying two boxes of masks.

Through the car window, Wei Xinguan's wife could tell from his sullen expression that something was amiss. Secretly pleased with her intuition, she hurried to open the door, preparing to get out of the car. But to her surprise, Wei Xinguan was livid: "Damn shameless! Canada is also profiting from our national crisis! This morning, a box was only twenty bucks, and now it's damn forty!"

Wei Xinguan's wife realized that either her husband had been deceived or she had misunderstood something.

She decided to inquire in person. Stepping into the large wholesale store for medical equipment, she spotted a blonde girl arranging shelves. Approaching her directly, she queried, "Excuse me, the masks we purchased from another store two hours ago were priced at only twenty dollars per box. Why have you suddenly doubled the price to forty dollars?"

The blonde girl appeared momentarily flustered before responding, "We just received a shipment from another store. They raised their prices, so we had to adjust ours accordingly. Did you know that prices in Vancouver have soared to fifty or even a hundred dollars?"

Shocked by this revelation, she felt an urgent need to purchase more masks.

However, upon reaching the counter, she witnessed a crowd inquiring about masks, only to be met with the disappointing response: "Sold out."

Wei Xinguan had to dial the last drugstore on the list. The response came swiftly: "Sorry, we're completely out of stock."

V

Wei Xinguan and his wife realized it wasn't enough, even with the two hundred masks they had managed to obtain. They allocated fifty masks for their son as a priority, another fifty for themselves as reserves, and the remaining hundred would be sent back to China to be distributed among several families. However, this allocation felt somewhat tight.

"How about this? Tomorrow, let's drive to nearby small towns and check if any masks are available. Those areas have fewer Chinese residents, so perhaps there won't be as much competition for masks," Wei Xinguan suggested, the idea suddenly sparking in his mind.

"That's a fantastic idea! Whether we find masks or not, let's treat it as a little outing," Wei Xinguan's wife responded, giving him a thumbs-up.

In the evening, Wei Xinguan scoured the internet for towns near their city and pinpointed two locations approximately one hundred kilometers away.

The following morning, Wei Xinguan and his wife embarked on their journey, driving towards the closest small town.

As they approached, the town revealed itself like a scene from a winter fairy tale. Wisps of smoke billowed from the chimney of every house while the roads remained eerily quiet, devoid of cars or pedestrians.

Wei Xinguan parked the car in front of a sizable supermarket and headed straight to the pharmacy inside. Unfortunately, the clerk delivered disappointing news: "We originally had two thousand masks in stock, but they were all purchased by a Chinese individual last week."

They exchanged glances before stepping out of the store. Wei Xinguan nodded thoughtfully, remarking, "See, someone beat us to it!"

As they arrived at the second town, Wei Xinguan noticed a gas station along the roadside and pulled in to refuel and use the restroom.

"Good morning!"

Wei Xinguan's wife opened the door to the gas station shop when she was greeted in Chinese.

"Hello, are you Chinese? Where are you from?" Wei Xinguan's wife couldn't contain her excitement. Her English wasn't proficient, so she suddenly became quite talkative.

"Sichuan. How about you?" the other person responded.

"Hey, fellow Sichuanese! We drove here from Edmonton and were hoping to find some masks for sale in your town," Wei Xinguan's wife exclaimed excitedly.

"Masks? Yes, we have them here. But I only sell to Chinese people. Please don't mention this to anyone else, okay?" the landlady whispered.

"Like finding a needle in a haystack! Today's trip wasn't in vain!" Wei

Xinguan's wife clapped her hands, nearly jumping with joy.

"Seventy dollars per box; how many do you want?" the shop owner inquired, getting straight to the point.

"Seventy?! We bought them for forty yesterday," Wei Xinguan's wife exclaimed, her eyes almost popping. She couldn't help but feel a pang of regret for not mentioning that they had purchased the first batch for twenty dollars a box.

"Yeah, now it's nearly impossible to find them for less than a hundred on the market. Some may accuse us of profiteering from a disaster. But let me ask: has the Canadian government declared a state of emergency? No, right? Have they mandated wearing masks? No, right? So, we're simply adjusting to market demand, not profiteering. Whether you choose to buy them is entirely up to you. I still need to set aside a few hundred for my friends," the landlady explained.

"I want them, I want them! Give me five hundred," Wei Xinguan's wife eagerly interjected. However, Wei Xinguan had finished refueling and entered the shop to join the conversation.

"I only accept cash," the landlady smiled at Wei Xinguan. Then, she turned around and called in English, "Kevin, drive back home and get five hundred masks. Our customers need them."

**VI**

Wei Xinguan and his wife wasted no time. They drove directly to the courier company, mailed a hundred masks to their son, foregoing any for themselves, and sent the rest back to China.

"Phew ...." Once back home, Wei Xinguan sank into the sofa, exhaling deeply as if he had just completed a monumental task and finally allowed himself to relax.

Turning to his wife, he said, "Let's not tell our son for now. He'll only complain. Let him receive them; he'll have to thank me when he needs them!"

That night, Wei Xinguan had his wife fashion a makeshift mask out of tissue paper, snapped a photo of himself wearing it, and sent it to his son, eager to boast about their accomplishment of obtaining masks over the past two days. However, he made no mention of mailing masks to him. Upon seeing the photo, his son left a message saying, "You guys are really something, huh? In North America, it's the sick people afraid of infecting others that wear masks!"

His son's words stoked Wei Xinguan's anger. A week later, they received a returned package slip from the U.S. postal service with "No one to receive" written on it. Three weeks later, they received a photo from their parents on WeChat depicting them wearing masks and giving the thumbs-up, accompanied by a message: "We have received the masks, but they arrived a bit late. Masks are readily available everywhere in China now."

# Jian Qian Wearing Red Dance Shoes

"Ring, ring, ring …."

"Hello, is this Sister Yan? I found a foreigner who is willing to marry me. We're going to register tomorrow, but I need a witness. After thinking about it, I believe you're the most suitable person. Can you help me?"

As soon as I had picked up the phone and said "Hello," I heard that familiar voice sounding urgent again.

It is often said that southern women are gentler in character, speak slowly and smoothly, and lack retroflex sounds in their Mandarin, which adds extra charm and occasionally reveals a bit of elegance or delicate beauty.

However, despite being from Suzhou, a picturesque water town south of the Yangtze River, Jian Qian was not such a woman. Ever since I first saw her at the airport, she struck me as a bird that had been mistreated. Finally, she was released from its cage, flying recklessly in the free sky with wide-open eyes.

When she saw her name on the sign I held at the airport exit, she reached out with both hands and flew straight at me, almost knocking me over, even though it was our first meeting. After that, she started talking non-stop, her excitement making it hard to believe she had been on a plane for almost fifteen hours.

"Wow, the sky here is so blue, and even the air feels sweet. When the plane announced we had entered Canadian airspace, I couldn't take my eyes off the window. The rivers below were dark, the forests were deep green, and the clouds floating past were white. I am so excited. I barely closed my eyes during the nearly fifteen-hour flight. My efforts finally paid off …." She spoke like reciting poetry, though the lines didn't rhyme.

"You need to rest. Let your mind quiet down for a while."

This was my first impression of my tenant, a woman who seemed a bit frivolous. Whether it was disdain for her excitement or genuine concern for her need to rest, I fell silent and stopped talking.

My husband, Xuan, worked in another small city more than five hundred kilometers away and came home for a week every three weeks.

We bought a big house not long ago and just moved in. The spaciousness of the house made me feel a bit uneasy, so we decided to rent out two rooms. First, it would provide me with some company, and second, the rent could help with the mortgage.

We posted the rental information on a local website, and Jian Qian was the first to contact me. She was a single girl and worked as a computer software designer in China. She had paid an agency to obtain a six-month work visa and was now working as a packer at a food processing plant in our city. My knowledge of her was limited to this. Although I couldn't understand why she would give up a superior job in China, I needed a tenant, so she became my first one.

Jian Qian was a petite woman with a somewhat pale complexion. She had a variety of hats, but her favorite was an octagonal one made of snowflake-patterned fabric. She wore her hair pulled back with strands falling on either side of her ears. She wore a light brown wool cardigan over a beige wide-necked T-shirt, revealing her collarbones. Her coat featured a pattern of brown rocks, the sea, and what seemed to be a ship. Her pants had brass zippers on both sides, and the legs were slightly long, so she liked to roll them up a bit, the cuffs covered her feet were clad in canvas shoes with red edges. At first glance, she appeared very avant-garde. But when you looked in her 28-year-old face, you saw the persistence and determination only in a man's eyes.

"My mom said that when I was five months in her belly, the doctor said I was a boy, but for some reason, by the seventh month, I had become a girl. I was supposed to be a boy," she often told me.

She came to Canada to find a foreigner and marry him.

There had been occasional inquiries about renting the room in the past few days. Seeing I still needed to rent another room, she widened her eyes and hinted, "Why not rent it to a foreigner? Foreign men are very gentle. Every time I walk to the store, they help me open the door, and I've heard ...."

"Why rent it to a foreigner?"

I knew what she meant, and before she could finish, I bluntly interrupted her, making her feel unhappy.

"I would never do such foolish things as soliciting customers at home," I said, slightly angry.

I despised her and didn't want to talk to her. Although we shared a kitchen, I always cooked when she wasn't around. But she had no friends here, so she seized every opportunity to chat with me in the kitchen when I was cooking. I couldn't resist her cooking skills, which were sometimes truly tempting to someone like me who could only make scrambled eggs with tomatoes.

"Wow, I went to see a movie last night, and they told me I needed to show my ID card because they thought I was under 18," she said, looking proud as she glanced at herself in the fridge mirror while putting a cup of milk in the microwave. It had only been half a month since she had received her first paycheck, and she had gone to see a movie with a foreign student she met online.

"Yeah, foreigners tend to see Chinese women as being five to ten years younger, while we see foreigners as being five to ten years older. It feels basically correct."

This had been one of my biggest observations since coming to Canada, often making me feel dizzy and think I was much younger.

"Wow, it feels great. I look so young in their eyes, which makes me much more confident," she said, shaking her head with pride.

After just a month, she became busier and busier, going out almost every night and coming back late. Sometimes, she even called to say she wouldn't be coming home. Although I didn't like her very much, I still worried about her.

"Have you found a boyfriend? Is he a foreigner?" I asked one day while we were both busy cooking dinner in the kitchen.

"Yes, did you guess?"

She seemed slightly surprised by my question and even a bit flattered. She quickly put down the knife she was using to chop vegetables and moved closer to me, nervously pinching the edges of her apron with both hands.

I figured she had wanted to tell me for a long time. It is a common ailment for women in love. Whether others are interested, they can't resist sharing their happiness.

"What does he do?" I asked, seeing she was eager to talk.

"Oh, he's a black man from another province in Canada. He's still in college and speaks a little Chinese. He lived in Taiwan Province for two years. He said he likes Chinese girls but only wants to live together, not get married. So I think I'll give up. I didn't come here to fool around. I want to stay by getting married, and I aim to marry a foreigner."

I had barely asked a question, and she was already chattering away like firecrackers. However, after hearing her words, I was left speechless.

My second tenant was finally found. He was a man named Hong who had just graduated from the University of Toronto and had come to work in our province. Hong was from Sichuan, and his cooking skills were even better than Jian Qian's. I had always heard that Sichuan men could throw anything into a pot and, with a couple of flips, turn it into a dish. Now, I finally saw it for myself. So, the three of us each cooked a dish and had a potluck together.

When two single tenants met, there were always endless topics to discuss. Hong seemed to have feelings for Jian Qian, and they often planned to go shopping together on weekends. Hong always carried a lot of stuff back home by himself. But Jian Qian only had eyes for foreigners; she didn't see Hong as a man.

"I'm moving out. My boyfriend Mike wants me to move in with him, and he's thinking about marrying me," Jian Qian announced one night as Hong and I watched TV in the living room.

"Move out? Now?"

Surprised and a little confused, I jumped up from the sofa.

"Where are you moving? It's late now," Hong said, standing up with a frown.

"My boyfriend's car is waiting outside. I'm moving to his place," Jian Qian said, suddenly grabbing my hand with a bit of embarrassment and swaying slightly.

I quickly went to open the door. Sure enough, outside in the pitch-black darkness, I could see a small truck with its engine still running and a man sitting in the driver's seat. I waved for him to come in.

I eyed the young man who entered with suspicion, making him too embarrassed to raise his head.

He was a slightly chubby, not very tall young white man with golden short hair standing upright on his head. The heels of his jeans were worn out by his black sports shoes, and the length of the pant legs made me worry that he might trip while walking.

They locked themselves in the room to pack while Hong and I stood stupidly in the living room. Although the TV was still on, neither of us was paying attention.

Wasn't this happening too fast? It felt like a car speeding towards the end of the road, suddenly making a ninety-degree turn, catching everyone off guard.

"You don't need to refund the rent. It's my breach of contract. Consider it a penalty."

She had only two suitcases and finished packing in less than half an hour. Jian Qian held some jingling small bags, and her boyfriend carried a suitcase in each hand. Hong and I stood there with empty hands hanging down, watching their car drive away.

"Yeah, I hope you find your paradise."

Looking at the now-empty room, my heart felt strangely empty, filled with a peculiar melancholy. I genuinely wished her well and hoped her dream would come true, but everything felt so unreal at the same time.

I lost contact with Jian Qian and could only reach her through email. However, I haven't sent her an email or received any messages from her. Shortly thereafter, Hong also returned to China.

Seeing the once-bustling room, my husband asked me, "Do you want to rent the house again?"

Perhaps due to Jian Qian, I didn't want to rent the house anymore. I yearned for a simpler life. Having a tenant had been just a chapter in my life, but these stories have brought me too much worry, making me feel burdened and suffocated.

Finally, I saw Jian Qian in a bustling Chinese supermarket. I grabbed her as if she would disappear if I let go.

"You! What's going on with you now? Why haven't I heard from you at all? Why didn't you call me?"

Jian Qian was chatting intimately with a scruffy white old man beside her.

My sudden grab and shout startled her, making her gasp, clutch her chest, and stomp her feet.

Seeing me grab Jian Qian and not understand what I was saying, the old man looked at me in confusion. Then he glanced at Jian Qian, and, seeing that she was starting to talk to me, he stepped aside with an understanding look.

"I changed boyfriends. It's him."

Jian Qian nervously pointed at the old man next to her. I had already guessed as much from the man's expression just now.

"I'll call you. Your phone number hasn't changed, right?" she said hastily before I could ask more questions, and she hurriedly walked away, pulling the man along.

I stood there foolishly, watching their backs until they disappeared. It seemed as if their steps slowed down more and more until finally, they were walking slowly, and I saw her sinking down. A voice in my heart cried: "There's a hole ahead!"

That night, I had a strange dream. I dreamed of the magical red dancing shoes in the movie Red Shoes on Jian Qian's feet. She wore these beautiful red dancing shoes, weaving through a crowd of foreigners.

Jian Qian had been in Canada for five months, and her work visa was about to expire. I still hadn't heard from her. I wrote her several emails, but she didn't reply to any of them. To be honest, from the beginning, I never understood why a girl who could be completely independent in China would go through so much trouble to work as a laborer abroad and insist on marrying a foreigner.

I sighed with mixed feelings when I heard the news of her marriage. It was both a premonition I had had and something unexpected. Despite my initial dislike for her, she considered me her only confidant, and I couldn't let her down.

The next morning, my husband and I went to the store, bought a large bouquet of roses, then found the address she had given us.

It was a big villa with pink stone walls, a tall, thick column on the high roof, a three-door garage, and a neatly trimmed green lawn that looked like freshly cut hair. Tulips were blooming around the lawn, and metal butterflies with spread wings adorned the flower beds, indicating it was a wealthy household.

I was pleasantly surprised.

"She finally got her wish!"

We rang the doorbell, and a middle-aged man in smart attire opened for us. As we walked into the living room, we saw Jian Qian. She was wearing a light pink dress, probably brought from China. Her made-up face looked a bit dry and showed some signs of fatigue. Still, this outfit accentuated her charm as a woman from a water town south of the Yangtze River.

"What a beautiful bride!" My heart was filled with immense joy. But then I noticed a man standing beside her, wearing a zippered shirt, jeans, and sneakers.

Approaching them, we handed the roses to her. She gave me a perfunctory hug, but it felt noticeably different from our first embrace at the airport.

She glanced somewhat reservedly at the man beside her, then took his arm, her face blushing slightly as she said, "This is my husband, Clayton. He is from Mexico and is a designer at a curtain factory. We're getting married right here today."

Upon hearing her words, my head buzzed with heat, and I grabbed my husband's arm, tuning out any further introductions.

The middle-aged man turned out to be their lawyer; this was his house. We were there to act as witnesses for their marriage.

As the lawyer asked questions and reviewed the legal procedures, I felt like I was listening to gibberish. Nothing seemed real except for the bundle of fresh red roses in Jian Qian's hands. The words "melancholy" and "wedding" couldn't connect. I simply couldn't believe such a wedding existed.

The question repeatedly echoed: "Did she really just marry herself off like this?"

"We don't have a house, just renting a room together, so we can't invite you to our home."

As we stepped out of the lawyer's house, Jian Qian's smile seemed awkward, and I could clearly sense a hint of bitterness in it.

Jian Qian's face looked much older than before. The dry Canadian climate had ruined her once delicate skin, even causing the makeup to start flaking off. In just a few months, she seemed like a completely different person.

"It's okay; today is your special day. We'll treat you to a big meal to celebrate," my husband said, assuming the role of a family member of the bride.

Our celebration took place at a Chinese restaurant in the downtown Chinatown. In recent years, immigrants from mainland China had filled the streets like the first snow of winter. We walked into a newly opened Anhui cuisine restaurant. The owner greeted us with a smile, and I asked him to bring out the best dishes because it was my friend's wedding day. The atmosphere at the table felt a bit heavy; everyone seemed hungry and focused on eating, with no extra words. As I looked at the spread of food on the table, I suddenly remembered the blessings, toasts, cheers, and laughter at my wedding banquet and even the raucous laughter during the bridal chamber teasing.

I couldn't help but softly ask Jian Qian in Chinese, "Do you feel happy?"

"Marrying him allows me to stay. I want this status, and I already have his child," she replied. She didn't directly answer my question, but her eyes flashed with an imperceptible sadness.

My heart ached a bit.

Another six months passed without any news from Jian Qian. Although my disdain for her had not completely dissipated, and I still couldn't understand her, I continued to feel sympathy and concern for her.

Whenever I went shopping, I looked around, hoping to encounter her again. I was anticipating, hoping for such a miracle to happen. I even went to the specific Chinese supermarket where I had unexpectedly met her last time, but the meeting didn't happen again.

Several months later, I finally received a package from her sent through the mail. Inside was a box containing a silver bracelet made from a silver spoon as a gift. A letter and a small photo of a baby were inside the envelope.

Her work visa had expired, and her husband couldn't stay with her in Canada. She had returned with him to his farm in Mexico.

The email read:

Dear Sister Yan, I know you don't like me, but you have always cared about me. When I married him, my difficult life began. He originally told me that marrying him would give me legal status to stay in Canada, but it was a lie. Now, I have returned to his farm in Mexico with him. My hands, once envied by many for typing on the keyboard, are now far away from the keyboard. I know you want to know why I had to marry a foreigner and stay abroad. At first, I thought the reason was simple. My first lover abandoned me to marry a Canadian immigrant, so I swore I would also go abroad and marry a foreigner. But now I realize that wasn't the real reason. Even I don't fully understand what the real reason is. Yet, once I had this idea, I couldn't stop focusing on foreigners, and I felt I had to fulfill this wish quickly. This is my choice and fate, so I can neither escape nor resist it...

# The Restroom Became Her Paradise

She mechanically entered the grimy restroom with leaden feet dragging and disheveled hair falling untended. She was too weary to lift a hand to brush her hair back. Without bothering to remove her pants, she slumped onto the toilet seat.

The stiff plastic cover seemed reluctant and protested with a snap.

The restroom floor, slick with grease, was strewn with discarded paper towels due to the overflowing trash can. A faucet, slightly leaking, dripped steadily. She found the sound irksome, reminiscent of something—like the lobby clock's ticking, pressing people to live busily.

Little did she anticipate that this restroom would become her paradise, the toilet becoming a heavenly, warm resting place amidst her weariness.

She was beyond exhaustion, too fatigued even to shed tears, simply sitting on the toilet seat blankly.

Back in her Chinese hometown, squatting toilets were the norm, both at home and in public facilities.

She reminisced about her initial encounter with a sitting toilet in Canada; after struggling for over an hour, she contemplated climbing atop the toilet to squat before eventually succeeding.

After finally finding this job, the Cantonese-speaking restaurant owner assigned her to work from 1:00 p.m. to 9:00 p.m., ensuring a constant stream of dishes to wash and vegetables to clean.

Her back throbbed as if on the verge of breaking, waves of heat swirling in her lower back, akin to a swarm of maggots gnawing at her.

Not a single chair was within reach. While aware of the chairs in the restaurant, they were off-limits for her.

Recollections flooded her mind of the comfortable moments in China when her family lounged on restaurant chairs, attended to by waiters...

Lost in thought, she absentmindedly dropped a chopstick on the ground and quickly squatted to pick it up. My goodness, what an unfamiliar sensation this was! It felt like a wonderful sensation she had never encountered in her memory; her sore waist and feet relaxed, and all the misaligned joints in her body realigned instantly. Since then, it seemed that whatever she held in her hands would inevitably slip and fall to the ground one way or another.

She sat numbly on the toilet seat, devoid of any call of nature, her head supported by her arms on her thighs. She wished fervently for time to halt, freezing everything at that moment and sitting comfortably on that toilet seat for eternity.

Before departing China, she had heard people say, "Endure three years of suffering at most for a lifetime of ease." Never having ventured abroad, she lacked a true understanding of the word "suffering" as described by others.

She had once curiously inquired of a colleague in the office who traveled abroad frequently, "What does suffering abroad entail? Must you stand under the sun all day?"

She thought the hardest suffering in China was endured by farmers exposed to the sun and rain daily. If suffering for three years abroad meant enduring similar conditions, maybe she could bear it.

"Are you going to be a traffic cop? Besides, Canadian cops don't typically stand at intersections directing traffic ...," that colleague, misinterpreting her question, responded in jest.

Today marked her third week since immigrating to Canada. Three years? One year had fifty-two weeks, totaling one hundred and fifty-six weeks over three years. Now, she finally understood the precise meaning of "endure." And what made her even more helpless was, even after enduring one hundred and fifty-six weeks, then what?

She recalled her arrival in Canada. Although dusk had not yet fallen, the sky was shrouded in darkness. An online friend picked them up and took them to the rented apartment, only saying, "A new life begins; take your time to adapt," before hastily leaving.

The apartment was empty, and the sky was pitch-black, with only faint streetlights casting a dim glow onto the ground where snowflakes fell like scattered cotton flakes. It was completely silent; even the cars parked by the roadside were all "dead" there, not moving.

She and her husband stood by the window, their two pairs of vacant, empty eyes hanging down, minds blank, without a word, resembling two statues standing in a lifeless world. Only their twelve-year-old son looked around curiously, continually asking questions, reminding her that there was still life.

They all said China was crowded and noisy, and immigrating to Canada promised a peaceful and quiet life. But on her first day in this "quiet" land, she had felt a tinge of fear.

Her husband had gotten up early the next day, attempting to find the library with broken English and stubbornly searching online for job opportunities back in their homeland. He resolutely returned to China a week later, leaving behind his wife and son.

With a bang, someone entered the restroom.

"Be careful, Helen!"

"Okay!" responded the crisp voice of a child to her mother.

"A girl sharing my name," she mused to herself.

Her mother had told her that when she was three months in the womb, her mother went to Hanshan Temple to pray and draw divination sticks for her. Holding the signed request, the abbot had foretold, "This child will reside in the Western world in the future. If a boy, call him David; if a girl, call her Helen, to avoid future changes ...."

"You have finally fulfilled your wish now," her husband said angrily as he left.

With a bang, the sound of the neighboring toilet flushing is akin to the relief of finally having your turn in a queue for the restroom: a moment of transition.

She rose helplessly, pulled out a piece of paper, rubbed her tearless eyes, and pushed open the door to walk toward the sink.

# A Homeward Journey

## I

In western Canada lies a small town called Okotoka. Rows of houses resembling matchboxes line the banks of the Lion River from a distance. Among its nearly thirty thousand residents, the majority are indigenous people. Having graduated from the Department of Psychology at the University of Calgary, Zu Hui worked as an assistant psychologist here. She had pursued her graduate studies in psychology alongside her work, aiming to obtain a certificate as a psychological counselor. Approaching thirty-five, she has never had the opportunity to meet a suitable partner, or perhaps she simply has no intention to do so. At first, her family, residing far away in Harbin, China, anxiously spread the word among relatives and friends, determined to find a suitable match for her. But as time went by, everyone stopped pushing, accepting her decision.

Following the conclusion of the COVID-19 epidemic, overseas Chinese were eagerly preparing to buy plane tickets to return home and visit relatives. For almost three years, aside from those who had urgent matters at home during the pandemic and had to buy expensive tickets to return to China, others were eagerly awaiting the end of the pandemic, the resumption of flights, and the decrease in ticket prices. Just as the air routes between China and Canada reopened, Zu Hui was eager to return home to celebrate her grandfather's eightieth birthday. Raised by her grandparents, her bond with them was even deeper than that with her parents. She checked flight tickets online daily, but they always seemed more expensive than anticipated. In the years before the pandemic, prices sometimes stood at only a few hundred Canadian dollars, similar to the prices from western to eastern Canada.

Zu Hui found online that there was only one direct flight per week, which was quite expensive, as were the flights with layovers. Finally, frustrated with searching, she asked a ticket agent for help. The agent displayed great enthusiasm and scoured options for her, eventually finding a ticket at a relatively reasonable price. Although the cost was double that before the pandemic, it involved an eight-hour layover in Osaka, Japan.

The extended layover gave Zu Hui pause as she pondered whether to accept the ticket due to her primary concern about the transfer in Japan. She couldn't tell her family about the layover there. Born in the 1980s, she grew up watching Japanese TV dramas like *Astro Boy, Attack No. 1,* and Blood Ties. Japan was familiar and unfamiliar to Zu Hui, devoid of direct personal experiences. As a result, she didn't hold the same hostility toward this country or its people as her elders did. After watching Japanese TV dramas, she even had some perplexing questions, wondering why humans clung to hatred instead of embracing forgiveness and reconciliation. Hitler initiated World War II, almost engulfing the entire world. Should people hate Germans now? Humans have engaged in numerous conflicts throughout history. If everyone held onto their grudges, wouldn't humanity be forever mired in animosity?

Canada is home to immigrants from all over the world, yet there are relatively few from Japan. During World War II, especially in 1942 when the Pacific War broke out and Japan attacked Pearl Harbor, the Canadian government responded to perceived security threats by enacting a series of measures, viewing Japanese immigrants as potential hostile forces, which led to the forced relocation of a group of Japanese individuals to the western region, including the town of Okotoka. After the war, the Canadian government apologized to the Japanese immigrants for its actions, and many Japanese immigrants returned to their homeland, while others resettled in Vancouver. Only a few Japanese descendants who have intermarried with the locals remain in the town.

Due to work, Zu Hui got to know a Japanese woman named Chiyoko who lived in the town. Chiyoko had a slender frame and spoke softly with a hint of proficiency in Chinese. She met her Canadian husband, Aidan, and married him in Japan. Aidan, of Japanese descent, had familial ties to the town—when his father was only 10 years old, his grandfather was exiled there. Aidan's father legally married an indigenous woman, and they had four children. With a deep-rooted appreciation for Asian culture, Aidan was a fervent advocate of multiculturalism, especially Eastern culture. After graduating from university, Aidan traveled alone to Japan. During an English-teaching stint at a local high school, he met Chiyoko, a teacher. Their union saw her English proficiency soar while his Japanese skills flourished. Several years later, they relocated from Japan to Shanghai, China, where Aidan taught English and Chiyoko taught Japanese.

The couple had had two children in Japan and a third in Shanghai. Aidan was diagnosed with liver cancer two years ago. Believing himself of indigenous descent with ancestors buried in the small town, he yearned to return there to join his family in the afterlife. As a result, the family had to return to Canada. As Aidan's health deteriorated, he became unable to care for himself. Chiyoko had to shoulder the responsibility of caring for her ailing husband and three children, so she couldn't work. Although government subsidies could cover their basic needs, the immense financial and emotional strain of caring for her family left Chiyoko on the verge of a breakdown, craving spiritual solace and support. Upon the recommendation of a specialist, she sought assistance at the psychological counseling center, where she met Zu Hui, whose work there and shared Chinese-Canadian cultural background facilitated their communication.

Hearing Chiyoko's story, witnessing her tearful despair, and understanding her past happy life, Zu Hui couldn't help but reflect on life's capriciousness. She realized that the vulnerability of humanity transcends national borders, with both the brilliance and darkness of human nature ingrained in the fabric of every society, which is not vast disparities between nations but individual nuances. However, she knew these sentiments must remain concealed within her heart, unspoken to her family. Although her father had not suffered under Japanese occupation, his father's vivid recollections seemed to impart a shared sense of anguish. During her schooling, visits to sites like the Japanese army's Unit 731 served as stark reminders of historical atrocities, reinforcing a collective memory of bloodshed.

Moreover, her great-grandfather had fallen victim to Japanese aggression.

"I don't want to see a Japanese again in my life! No Japanese products, ever!"

These were her grandfather's last words. Zu Hui could empathize with her grandfather's animosity because he had witnessed that massacre. Still, she couldn't understand the animosity harbored by her family and peers towards the Japanese from birth. If she were to transit through Japan herself, it would not only entail stepping foot in the "enemy's" territory, but it could also evoke fears of inviting misfortune upon her country and home in the eyes of her family.

"You don't have to disclose the flight details to your family. Just tell them it's a surprise!"

Zu Hui remained undecided, but the ticket agent's persistent call urged her not to procrastinate. With the deadline looming at four o'clock, she risked losing the reserved ticket, uncertain if she could secure the same fare again.

In the end, weighing the ticket price, Zu Hui resolved to proceed with the purchase, finally easing her mind.

## II

Zu Hui went to the manager's office to ask for leave. Regardless of the season, the tall and amiable manager always wore a black-gray tweed duckbill cap. Despite his French immigrant heritage, he embraced the DINK (Double Income, No Kids) lifestyle, resonating with Camus's philosophical inquiries into the meaning of life and human freedom and longed for travel and adventure.

"Spending eight hours at the airport is dreadfully dull. Why not seize this chance to explore Osaka? It's said to be a remarkably beautiful city. My wife and I are planning our next trip to various Asian countries," the manager said with envy and excitement in his eyes, momentarily removing his hat to give it a flick with his fingers before settling it back on his head.

Zu Hui was touched by the manager's suggestion. With the plane scheduled to land at Osaka Airport at nine-thirty in the morning and depart at six o'clock in the evening, she would have a good four hours of free time. Since she typically liked to plan ahead, this spontaneous decision was a departure from her usual approach. Perhaps this trait was inherited from her mother, who, having graduated from the Department of Chinese at a normal university in 1978, was deeply influenced by the teachings of *Mencius* and the *Doctrine of Golden Means*: "When affairs are going well, prepare for the possibility of failure." This proverb had been ingrained in Zu Hui's mind since childhood, a reminder from her mother during leisure times.

After dinner, Zu Hui took a box of blueberries from the fridge and soaked them in a bowl of lukewarm saltwater. Then, settling onto the soft fabric sofa, she cradled a cushion and began to envision her layover plans:

Location: Osaka Airport, Japan

1. Arrival

2. Confidently presenting her Canadian passport and exiting the customs and airport;

3. A long queue of waiting passengers for taxis outside the terminal;

4. Settling into the taxi, the driver greets her with a smile, "Where would you like to go?"

5. "With only a three-hour layover, please take me to the city's busiest and most vibrant spot. I'd love to experience Japanese cuisine."

6. "Then let's go to Dotonbori and Shinsekai."

7. "Sounds great!"

8. Before getting out of the taxi, she inquires, "Can you come back here to pick me up and return to the airport in three hours?"

9. "Certainly."

10. The driver arrives on time three hours later and successfully takes her back to Osaka Airport.

11. Departure.

The script was designed perfectly. Zu Hui rose from her seat and strolled into the kitchen, where she drained the blueberries soaked in mild salt water. Selecting one, she popped it into her mouth before heading to the living room mirror, positioned snugly against the wall. Tilting her head, she turned to face her reflection with confidence. This mirror, bought from IKEA, seemed almost enchanted, which had a knack for flattering one's appearance, casting a slender and statuesque silhouette. Standing before it, anyone would feel assured of their perfect figure. Zu Hui recalled a Brazilian classmate with a petite frame and ample curves who had visited once. Upon encountering the mirror's magic, she became so enamored that she never wanted to leave again. Finally, they struck a deal: whoever got married first would inherit the mirror as a gift.

Zu Hui pondered sharing her flawless plan with someone but hesitated to confide in her family. So, who could she turn to? In Canada, she had two close friends. Elder Sister Jiang was from southern China and had married a man from Fushun, once occupied by the Japanese in 1930s Liaoning Province, in northeastern China, before immigrating to Calgary. During Zu Hui's years at the University of Calgary, the couple had taken great care of her, inviting her over every time they made dumplings. They would freeze the dumplings for her to enjoy later, even on days when Zu Hui had classes. Occasionally, they took her to T&T Supermarket or Chinatown on weekends for grocery shopping. Zu Hui didn't expect Elder Sister Jiang's husband to share the same animosity toward the Japanese as her family members did. Three years ago, during a shopping trip, she excitedly introduced Japanese ramen to Elder Sister Jiang as Zu Hui reached for a pack of "Nissin Top Ramen (Chu Qian Yi Ding)," a delicious instant noodle from Japan. However, her enthusiasm was met with Elder Sister Jiang's husband's sarcastic remark, "Don't buy Japanese products while you're in my car."

"Don't mind him! He's stubborn!" Elder Sister Jiang interjected, firmly patting her husband's arm and shooting him a disapproving look.

Zu Hui brushed it off, assuming it was a jest. How could buying Japanese products be banned in his car? But to her astonishment, as she prepared to load the purchases into the car, Elder Sister Jiang's husband grabbed the steering wheel, fixed his gaze ahead, and adamantly refused to unlock the car door: "I told you, if you buy Japanese products, you should take the bus."

Zu Hui was shocked, her eyes widening in disbelief. It dawned on her that these fervent nationalists weren't confined to her family or to China but were worldwide. There was simply no room for Japanese products in their car. It was inconvenient to take the bus with so many things. Since then, she had refrained from buying Japanese goods in their car. If she disclosed her plan to transit through Japan, they might sever ties with her indefinitely.

Another friend crossed her mind, Yangzi, who lived in Ottawa. With a name that could pass for Japanese, she was unabashedly pro-Japanese. She liked to eat Japanese sushi, buy Japanese appliances, and even own a

Toyota car produced in Japan. Her mantra was simple: if it's good, it's good regardless of origin. The thought of Yangzi filled Zu Hui with a newfound vigor, akin to being injected with adrenaline.

However, when Zu Hui shared her transit plan with Yangzi over the phone, Yangzi's reaction was far from typical. She screamed almost hysterically, "Are you crazy? That's suicide! They just discharged nuclear wastewater!"

"So what? Didn't they get approval from the International Atomic Energy Agency?"

Zu Hui had already meticulously made her layover plan, so she didn't want to give it up. After all, the water she drank, the food she ate, and the air she breathed would be no different regardless of where she spent a few hours, right?

Unable to dissuade Zu Hui, Yangzi could only sigh and say that Osaka was an industrial hub and probably devoid of any noteworthy attractions.

Zu Hui shrugged indifferently, saying, "It doesn't matter. The world is so big. It's an opportunity to broaden my horizons. Anything beats idling away eight hours in one place."

Zu Hui felt a bit discouraged. It seemed that the whole world was against her layover in Japan. She needed a silver lining to lift her spirits. She remembered that she still had two hundred US dollars in cash. Two years ago, she had flown to San Francisco to meet her high school classmate, Zhengjie, who was on a business trip from China. He had handed her the remaining two hundred US dollars as he bade her farewell at the airport, deeming it useless upon his return to China. Since then, the bills had been untouched in her suitcase. With no immediate spending plans and no desire to exchange them for Japanese yen, little did she know they'd come in handy now as sufficient for layover expenses because Japan wouldn't accept Canadian dollars anyway.

Everything was ready except for one crucial thing. Zu Hui needed to undergo a virus test before boarding the plane. The ticket agent provided her with a link, indicating that only one clinic in Calgary conducted this test, and the cost was exorbitant. It was said that only the Chinese went there for testing. She needed to call it for reservation in advance, and the test result would be valid for twenty-four hours.

### III

Zu Hui arrived at Calgary International Airport early in the morning. After completing the check-in procedures and entering the departure lounge, there were still forty minutes before boarding. She bought a cup of Tim Hortons coffee and then aimlessly wandered among the few shops in the airport. She didn't need anything; she had already sent a box of health products home two weeks ago. Her parents often reassured her that China had abundant goods now, so there was no need to buy anything. However, browsing a small shop of Canadian specialties, she spotted a dark green neck pillow with a unique design and two layers of stepped increments. The fabric felt soft like velvet, offering high friction and firm support around the neck without losing shape. Though the price was steep, Zu Hui recognized her tendency to struggle with sleep during flights. If this pillow could help her rest well on the plane, she deemed it worthwhile. She didn't want to appear fatigued in front of her family, so she bought it.

Actually, Zu Hui had a fear of flying. Every time she bought a plane ticket, she would imagine terrifying scenes of air disasters she might encounter. Still, she couldn't succumb to these groundless fabrications and remain grounded. She endured constant apprehension, trembling with each minor turbulence throughout the flight, only finding relief as the plane regained stability. Interestingly, she would scrutinize her fellow passengers suspiciously amidst these fabricated scenes, seeking solace in the assumption that they all harbored good intentions and thus shouldn't meet a tragic fate.

"Hmm," she would reassure herself, "these people couldn't possibly be destined for ill fortune. This flight is not one bound for disaster! May God bless them all, and of course, bless me too."

In addition, Zu Hui also suffered from claustrophobia. A vivid memory from her college days haunted her. She had taken a road trip to the Rocky Mountains with two classmates on a hot summer day. Upon pulling into a rest area, her classmates headed for the restroom, leaving her in the car. The stifling heat intensified as the sun beat down on the vehicle, exacerbated by the dormant air conditioning. Sweat trickled down her body, and a sense of suffocation enveloped her, so she opened the car door in panic, desperate for air. Upon recounting her ordeal to her classmates, she realized she might suffer from claustrophobia. Since then, whenever she found herself in an enclosed space—on a plane or in an elevator—she made a concerted effort to divert her thoughts from the confines, steering her mind toward other distractions at the first inkling of claustrophobia.

As the plane reached Vancouver smoothly, Zu Hui met a young man at the airport, bidding farewell to his mother, who was returning to her home country. He had long hair and was dressed in a casual suit jacket, a pair of faded jeans, and canvas sneakers, exuding an air of arrogance and cynicism. Upon learning of Zu Hui's destination—Harbin--he entrusted her to take his mother to the transfer area in Osaka. Zu Hui readily accepted.

Zu Hui always preferred the window seat, flying or riding in a car or train. Gazing out at the world beyond was a source of solace for her during travel. Without the view outside, all she had were the screens of her phone or the backs of fellow passengers, which only heightened her sense of confinement.

After switching planes, she removed her neck pillow, settling comfortably against the window. It was half past ten in the morning, and Vancouver's sky stretched out in a flawless expanse of blue, unmarred by a single cloud. Staff were loading and unloading luggage while the occasional plane taxied across the tarmac, prompting a few drowsy passengers to stir and glance out the windows.

As the plane took off and soared over the lush and spacious grasslands, buildings dotted the distant hillsides. Yachts gently rocked on the sea below with their sails catching the breeze, while the occasional speedboat left a trail of white foam across the sparkling waters. When Zu Hui first arrived in Canada, she marveled at her seemingly improved eyesight, attributing it to her newfound ability to see distant places. However, she soon realized that it wasn't her eyesight that had changed but rather the clarity of the air that enhanced visibility.

Although it was a Canadian airline, most crew and passengers appeared

Chinese or Asian. There were likely some Japanese passengers, given that the final destination was Japan. For the first in-flight meal, passengers had two options: beef noodles or chicken rice, served with a small salad and a fruit pudding. Zu Hui chose the beef noodles. After the meal, the girl beside her pulled out her screen, put on her headphones, and started watching a movie. Zu Hui sneakily glanced at the screen: *Hero*, starring Zhang Ziyi, a famous Chinese movie star. Though she dared not assume, seeing Chinese subtitles confirmed that the girl was Chinese. Zu Hui had a preference for animated movies or movies about animals. She chose *Charlotte's Web*, a movie about a pig named Wilbur who grapples with fear and uncertainty about death. At the same time, seeing the natural order of life, a wise spider guides him to understanding. Witnessing Wilbur's journey, Zu Hui found solace in accepting life's cycle. If life and death were part of the rhythm of nature, there was no need to fear flying or worry about accidents.

Feeling tired after the movie, she stayed up late the previous night, organizing things, checking emails for urgent replies, and even setting up an automatic response. It was already one-thirty when she finished everything, took a hot shower, and got into bed.

Zu Hui drifted off to sleep with her neck pillow in place, entering a dream filled with peach-colored Japanese cherry blossoms and various sea creatures emerging from polluted waters. She witnessed fish and shrimp crawling ashore, tainted by nuclear pollution. In contrast, others remained in the water, lifeless and dense in their numbers. She was abruptly awakened halfway through her dream, only to find the girl behind her still engrossed in another movie, *Crouching Tiger, Hidden Dragon*, starring Zhang Ziyi. It seemed the girl was Zhang's dedicated fan. Zu Hui got up and went to the restroom. Upon returning, she succumbed to drowsiness again, drifting back to sleep without her neck pillow.

"Can I have a coffee, please?"

A male voice jolted Zu Hui awake, disoriented about how much time had passed. She frowned and mumbled, shifting her body to find a more comfortable position. But no matter how she adjusted, she felt uncomfortable since her head kept slipping down from the seatback. Absentmindedly reaching for her neck, she realized she wasn't wearing her neck pillow. Therefore, she turned her head and looked around, then rose to rummage through the heap of clothes and blankets beneath her. Despite her efforts, she still couldn't find it. A sense of unease crept over her—how could it vanish like that? Gradually, a realization dawned on her, followed by a surge of anger, ready to boil over.

When the plane began its descent from cruising altitude, the flight attendant happened to deliver a cup of coffee to the man behind her and was about to leave. Zu Hui seized the moment, sensing an urgency to find her missing neck pillow before landing.

She turned to the attendant and asked, "Excuse me, could you help me? I can't find my neck pillow."

The flight attendant frowned, indicating she didn't quite grasp the situation, prompting Zu Hui to elaborate. While not exactly a detective, Zu Hui enjoyed delving into criminal cases and occasionally discussed unsolved mysteries with fellow internet users. Although losing a neck pillow hardly constituted a major case, she was almost certain she could solve this mystery.

Growing impatient, she turned to the man behind her and inquired, "Excuse me, have you seen my neck pillow?"

He was a young white man in his twenties with a scruffy beard that appeared singed. Clad in a faded rust-colored T-shirt, he possessed average features yet emitted an air of slight disrepute. Balancing a coffee cup in one hand, he deftly unfolded the small table on the seatback with the other, conversing with the Asian woman beside him. He paused briefly when Zu Hui queried him about her missing neck pillow. Setting down his coffee, he flipped open the table and glanced around, both on the floor and in the vicinity. Then he looked up at Zu Hui, shrugging his shoulders for a negative answer. Zu Hui looked serious, didn't say a word, and stared at his movements intently. Meeting Zu Hui's serious gaze, he seemed to falter under her scrutiny. Reluctantly, he spread his previously crossed legs and leaned down to peer beneath the chair where, neatly nestled as if on a shelf, lay Zu Hui's neck pillow! His expression shifted to mild surprise as he retrieved it, extending it towards Zu Hui with a somewhat sheepish demeanor. Though grateful, Zu Hui's thanks were tinged with reluctance.

Zu Hui's frustration simmered as she retrieved her neck pillow, delaying her return to her seat.

Casting a pointed glance across the aisle, she couldn't help but express her disdain, muttering, "Behold, the white bastard you're dating."

The woman, seemingly unfazed, remained absorbed in her own world, negligent of Zu Hui's remark as she huddled onto the coffee table.

"It must have slipped beneath the seat," the flight attendant said with a smile, unaware of the tension, and then left.

Zu Hui pondered silently, her thoughts echoing skepticism.

"His legs were in the way? Could a snugly fitted fabric loop have rolled so neatly?"

Though silent outwardly, her inner voice was resolute, "Hmmph."

As Zu Hui disembarked the plane, her anger lingered. She stood up early, glancing back at the two individuals behind her. They kept their heads down, seemingly oblivious to her presence, waiting until the rest of the passengers had disembarked before stirring.

"Many people idolize white folks, extolling their supposed superiority. Who would have thought such cheap behavior existed!" Zu Hui seethed inwardly as she left her seat.

**VI**

Zu Hui hastily lifted the window shade as the plane descended over Osaka's Kansai Airport. The sky outside was shrouded in haze, resembling nothing but smog! In an instant, Zu Hui's excitement plummeted as if the plane had suddenly nosedived from high altitude. All the beauty she had anticipated and imagined faded, like a dream gone with the wind.

Upon disembarking, she almost forgot to accompany the elderly woman for her flight connection. In contrast, the elderly woman remembered, so she quickly approached Zu Hui and greeted her. She stayed close by her side with aimless words, as if afraid of being left behind.

As they walked, the elderly woman opened up about her life. Hailing from

Heilongjiang Province, she had been widowed at a young age, raising her son single-handedly, scrimping and saving to send him abroad for education. Though her son had succeeded as a manager at a logistics company in Vancouver, he remained unmarried at nearly forty.

"Why doesn't anyone notice my son?" she lamented, wishing she could showcase his talents to the world.

Learning that Zu Hui was also single, she eagerly suggested they could make a good match on WeChat, extolling her son's virtues, from his car and house to his accomplishments. Politely declining the offer, Zu Hui had no interest in such arrangements. When they reached the connecting gate, Zu Hui realized she had forgotten all about her sightseeing plans in Osaka. It was only after ensuring the elderly woman safely entered the transit passage that she remembered her predicament that she might not make it through customs in time.

Zu Hui felt a surge of panic, but she knew her priority was to swiftly assist the elderly woman before addressing her own predicament. Glancing behind her, she spotted a young, attractive mother with her son, who appeared to be around six or seven years old.

The boy gleefully rode on the top of his suitcase, using its wheels to coast along, exclaiming, "Mom, look at me!"

Zu Hui hurried over and realized that this mother and son were also heading home to visit relatives. She quickly entrusted the elderly woman to them. She rushed back to the escalator, only to find it ascended and didn't descend. Frustrated, she spotted a police officer passing by and eagerly approached him to ask for directions to an information desk. Despite her attempts to communicate through gestures, the officer couldn't understand her. With a resigned sigh, Zu Hui reluctantly gave up.

In her despair, she noticed a currency exchange booth near the elevator and quickly sought assistance on how to leave. Inside were two young staff members, a man and a woman. After Zu Hui explained her situation, the woman shook her head regretfully. She told her that leaving was no longer an option. Zu Hui felt as anxious as an ant on a hot pan, pacing back and forth in the corridor. Unwilling to give up so easily, she decided to make another attempt.

Returning to the currency exchange booth, she asked the man, "Excuse me, how can I go downstairs?"

"Sorry, there's an elevator ahead, but it's for staff only," the young man pointed to the corner elevator.

At this point, Zu Hui didn't care anymore. Her priority was to find the exit. Upon encountering the security personnel downstairs, she perhaps could explain her situation and gain permission to leave with some luck. After all, opportunity favored the proactive, not the passive. Armed with this mindset, she pressed the elevator button. To her pleasant surprise, the doors opened, and she descended swiftly. Stepping out onto the lower level, she approached the security checkpoint. The serene hall was devoid of passengers, with several idle security personnel engaged in casual conversation, one of whom even absentmindedly tapped a metal detector in his hand. As Zu Hui drew near, they all turned their heads alertly, fixing their gaze on her.

Sensing the tension, Zu Hui hesitated to approach too closely, shouting from a distance instead, "I need to leave! I possess a Canadian passport and wish to explore downtown Osaka during my layover."

Several people stared at Zu Hui with wide eyes, showing no response. It was evident they didn't understand.

After a moment, a stern-looking girl, proficient in English, waved her hand at Zu Hui and commanded, "Go back! Go back!"

Zu Hui had no choice but to retreat in disappointment. People were strange sometimes; the more unattainable something was, the stronger their desire for it. Her longing to visit Osaka downtown was stronger than ever before. She remained unwilling to give up easily, determined to stick to her plan.

So, returning to the currency exchange booth once more, she inquired, "Excuse me, where can I find an information desk?"

This was her last attempt.

The staff members were extremely patient, one telling Zu Hui with a smile, "There's a desk next door with a telephone on it."

Zu Hui hurried over, and indeed, there was a telephone on the table next door, with a sign standing next to it that read, "Information Inquiry Phone."

She dialed the number and explained her situation.

The person on the other end kindly told her, "I'm sorry, but it's impossible to clear customs."

Finally confirming that she couldn't clear customs, Zu Hui felt profoundly disappointed. By then, she was sweating profusely, her heart heavy with grievance, and a deep sense of loss enveloped her as if she had fallen into an abyss. With no other options left, she could only slink back to the departure hall again.

V

Zu Hui's mood had soured considerably. Her steps seemed particularly heavy like a lovelorn soul unable to meet her awaited lover. She settled into a chair by the window in the lobby aimlessly, her gaze vacant as she stared outside. The Osaka sky seemed to mirror her melancholy as it gradually began to drizzle.

Would these eight hours on like this? Surely, something must be new to see or learn to make this trip worthwhile, right?

Feeling disoriented, she pursed her lips and stepped into the restroom, only to find a luggage rack inside, which was low and perfect for larger items, so her carry-on luggage fit snugly on top. It was her first time encountering such a warm and considerate restroom design. But what embarrassed her was the bewildering array of functions on the flush toilet. She couldn't comprehend many features, from warm water flushing to heated seats and drying functions. As she prepared to leave, she instinctively glanced back at the toilet. She noticed that the water inside was yellowish-gray, somewhat murky. Immediately feeling embarrassed, she thought she had forgotten to flush. Pressing the flush valve, she attempted to clear the water, but the water remained the same color even after rinsing. Then, it dawned on her that untreated seawater was used for flushing to save on water and sewage treatment costs.

"Japanese are indeed clever!"

Since the airport toilets intrigued her with their novelty, she decided to explore more unseen things here. After all, different countries boast different cultures.

Feeling a bit hungry now, Zu Hui began to look for something to eat. Ahead, a woman caught her eye with her unusual sneakers, which separated the big toe from the other four toes, a design different from typical sneakers. While Zu Hui had seen socks with toe separators before, shoes like these were new to her. Intrigued, she approached the woman to strike up a conversation and ask if the shoes were comfortable. The woman was friendly but couldn't understand what Zu Hui was saying, so they awkwardly bid farewell.

Further ahead, a crowded bakery caught Zu Hui's attention. Someone at the entrance handed customers a red plastic basket to hold their desired items. Inside, a pretty girl offered samples of pastries to customers who swarmed around the shop. Zu Hui immediately spotted her favorite "Shiroi Koibito" sandwich cookies and couldn't resist picking up two boxes. Then she suddenly felt hesitant about buying so much—it might reveal her travel plans to her family.

As Zu Hui passed a cosmetic store, a woman in heavy makeup outside greeted her in Chinese, "Hello, may I help you? We have very good cosmetics."

Surprised, Zu Hui asked, "How did you know I'm Chinese?" because she didn't utter a word, and her face looked like other Japanese.

"I deduced it from observation," the woman replied with a shrewd smile. "Generally, locals wouldn't be so interested in wandering around the airport. Also, I heard you speaking Chinese to another lady on my way to work just now. You just didn't notice me."

Zu Hui thanked her and continued looking for food. What to eat? After scouring the area, she found herself at a loss. Sushi and noodles were ubiquitous in Canada, but she figured she might as well try something new since she was there. Looking around, she spotted a food cart with colorful items displayed along the wide street. She hadn't noticed it on her initial pass-by. Approaching closer, she found Japanese seafood snacks. Each item had a distinct price, and plastic replicas offered a tantalizing food preview. Zu Hui's eyes lit up at the sight of eel, sushi, lotus root, seaweed, and fried shrimp with rice—all resembling works of art with colors that made her drool. As the fried shrimp with rice was labeled the last one, she quickly grabbed it to purchase, momentarily forgetting Yangzi's advice about avoiding Japanese seafood.

With food in hand, she craved a drink. Not far away was a Starbucks coffee shop with a long line. Zu Hui wasn't typically a fan of Starbucks because she found their coffee too strong and sleep-disrupting. She preferred Tim Hortons coffee without caffeine, but it was a Canadian brand, not as widely available internationally as Starbucks. With limited options, Zu Hui joined the line. In front of her stood a man of ambiguous nationality, wearing a floral shirt and with dark skin resembling that of an Indian. When it was his turn to pay, he casually took a handful of coins from his pocket. Zu Hui's eyes widened because she loved collecting coins. After the man paid, she eagerly asked him in a low voice.

"Excuse me, could we exchange a few coins?" Zu Hui inquired politely.

"Sure, I also enjoy collecting coins from different countries," the man responded with a friendly smile.

He handed Zu Hui a Japanese coin with a square hole in the middle. Delighted, she glanced at the variety of coins in the man's hand and wished she had asked for more. Unfortunately, she only had one Canadian dollar in her wallet.

With a tinge of regret, she murmured, "I really wish I had another Chinese coin on me."

She wanted to exchange more.

"Which country are you from?" the man inquired, perhaps catching Zu Hui's murmur.

"Canada."

"Canada?! I've been there, and it's incredibly beautiful! People are very friendly there."

The man's eyes sparkled with admiration.

"Yes," Zu Hui responded proudly.

"I'm Filipino, and I love traveling." The man introduced himself before asking, "Where are you headed?"

"China."

"China? A fascinating and mysterious place. The Great Wall, the Forbidden City, and the pandas ... I hope to visit there someday."

At that moment, the man's wife joined him, and they exchanged a few words in a language Zu Hui couldn't understand. As they prepared to leave, the man reached into his pocket again, selecting two newer coins for Zu Hui.

"Goodbye, it was a pleasure exchanging with you," he said.

His wife cast a glance back at Zu Hui as they walked away.

"A sensitive woman," Zu Hui chuckled lightly to herself.

Balancing her coffee cup and food, Zu Hui made her way to a small table by the window in the café. She placed the items down, pulled out a chair, and carefully opened the food box.

"Wow, it looks exquisite. Where to begin?"

The beautiful food gave her pause. After a moment of contemplation, she had a sudden inspiration. Japanese cuisine with coffee—a novel combination! Would the flavors complement each other? Intrigued, she swirled the coffee in her cup, combining two seemingly disparate elements. She captured a photo from the optimal angle, creating a culinary "family portrait."

Kansai Airport, built in 1994, is situated on an artificial island in Osaka Bay, surrounded by the sea. Outside the window, the rain persisted, casting a thin veil over the glass, adding to the prevailing gloom of the already gray world. The sky, the ground, the buildings—all enveloped in a pallid shade of gray, seemed to echo the somber mood. It felt like a collective melancholy had descended upon the world, as if the entire sky, earth, and human race had succumbed to despondency. The vast airport stood sparsely populated with planes, while the control tower loomed like a solitary figure in the distant mist.

During this scene, two men conversing in northeastern Chinese accents caught Zu Hui's attention. She turned to find them going to the adjacent table. One tall, one short, both appeared to be in their sixties. The taller man carried a black violin case, while the shorter one's case was pink. They settled into their seats, placing their food bags on the table before leaning their violin cases against the window and setting down their backpacks.

Upon spotting the pink case, Zu Hui couldn't help but feel a sense of excitement.

"Perhaps it's for his granddaughter," she thought. "Maybe they brought their grandsons to Japan for some musical events."

After a brief wait without anyone else appearing, Zu Hui realized that the cases belonged to the men. The pink violin case by the window caught her attention, arousing her curiosity. She subtly adjusted her chair, feigning a change in posture but actually angling herself so that the tall man's back obscured her face, allowing her to observe more discreetly. The tall man wore a white baseball cap, a black leisure suit, and a pair of black sneakers. Leaning back in his chair, hands resting on the armrests, his posture showed confidence, even though his face remained unseen.

On the other hand, the short man wore a white sports suit with red accents and white and green high-top sneakers, topped off by a purple-red baseball cap. Their voices kept low as they conversed over their meal, preventing Zu Hui from catching their conversation. Nonetheless, she sensed an unusual intimacy between them. Suddenly, it dawned on Zu Hui that she might have stumbled upon a remarkable secret. When the short man rose to clear the table, Zu Hui noticed an earring on his ear—just on one ear.

Zu Hui instantly understood that they were gay.

"No wonder the shorter one's violin case is pink, and they exude a sense of mystery!"

Zu Hui felt a mix of amazement, admiration, and envy towards them. It reminded her of a college lecture where an elder had shared the persecution faced by homosexuals in Canada during the 1960s and his own experiences. He and his partner were dismissed from their jobs due to their relationship. They had to resort to clandestine meetings in shadowy corners after being reported multiple times with police investigations looming over them. The pace of societal change was staggering, but now, these two "uncles" from China could openly and unabashedly show their love.

## VI

Eight hours slipped by quickly, with the clock's hands seeming to sprout wings and each minute passing with a Zen-like tranquility for Zu Hui. Boarding the Air China flight brought forth a distinct sensation. The flight attendant's Mandarin was melodious, the cabin crew strikingly beautiful, and their smiles sweet.

Zu Hui instinctively raised the window shade as the plane smoothly ascended into the sky. The rain had stopped, and the sky was gradually darkening and clearing up. The sparkling lights of Osaka downtown resembled numerous colorful building blocks nestled in the expanse of the Pacific Ocean.

"Just over three hours until I'm home," Zu Hui exclaimed, too exhilarated to contemplate sleep.

"Ma'am, is this yours?"

A male voice interrupted her thoughts from behind, bearing an accent that piqued Zu Hui's curiosity.

Glancing back, Zu Hui saw a hand holding out a neck pillow that had rolled behind her seat. Touched by the gesture, she was instantly reminded of the contrasting behavior of the "white bastard" earlier in her journey and how disdainful it had seemed. Determined to express her genuine gratitude, she rose deliberately, preparing to thank the person behind her.

A man and a woman were seated behind her, smiling kindly as Zu Hui rose. The man, appearing in his fifties, wore a neatly draped black trench coat, exuding an air of gentlemanliness. The woman, in her twenties, wore a beige trench coat and light makeup; her eyes narrowed into gentle slits when she smiled, radiating an aura of gentleness and delicacy.

She sweetly addressed the man with a "Thank you!"

Zu Hui's gesture seemed slightly exaggerated, bordering on melodrama even to herself. Nonetheless, the pair behind her responded with warm smiles and nods, displaying genuine friendliness and courtesy.

The man's face flushed slightly with shyness as he introduced himself, " 甭 (béng) 客气 (Never mind). I'm Mishima ( 三岛 ), and I don't speak Chinese well."

Zu Hui was surprised. Despite his limited Chinese, he had actually used the word "béng," an authentic term from the Chinese northeastern dialect, which at least indicated that his Chinese shouldn't be too bad.

Finally, the plane landed at Harbin Airport. Zu Hui walked alongside the couple on their way to collect their luggage. Through a few conversations, she learned that they were from Osaka and were father and daughter.

"My sister was born in Harbin. Her mother is Chinese. She is my father's first child, and we are half-siblings. Despite our different backgrounds, we share a close bond. Before the pandemic, we used to meet every year. As soon as it ends, we are eager to visit her. She is a university professor and I study Chinese culture at a university in Japan. This is my daughter Qianxun. We're going to visit my elder sister together. Then I'll take her to her aunt's university to study Chinese culture," Mr. Mishima said.

Although his Chinese wasn't very fluent, and he even stumbled a bit, his words were clear, and his tone was friendly and humble.

The brief exchange brought Zu Hui closer to the father and daughter, giving her a warm feeling of belonging as if she were among her own people. It filled her with ease and contentment. She decided at that moment that upon returning home, she would have a heartfelt conversation with her parents about a topic that had been weighing on her for some time:

"War may be guilty, governments may be guilty, but the people are innocent! Love, hate, affection, and resentment can never sever the thousands of connections between the people of China and Japan."

# The Nameless Notes

## I

As Mana entered the Student Council Office, Troon handed her two notes and a letter, saying someone had left them for her.

The notes were densely filled with English words, and though she didn't read them carefully, she felt curious.

Frowning, she asked three times, somewhat incredulously, "Are these for me? Are they really for me? Are you sure?"

Mana didn't expect anyone to leave her a long piece of writing, especially in handwritten English. Since immigrating to Canada, most of her friends were Chinese. Moreover, nowadays, even roommates a wall apart would text rather than bother with pen and paper.

Troon explained, "The notes and letter are from the Summer All-Canada Student Representatives Conference you attended. Remember the survey before the conference concluded, where delegates were asked to write about someone who had made the strongest impression during the event and explain why ...."

Mana's memory was jogged. Spotting her name, she confirmed that the notes were indeed for her and read them eagerly.

"Mana, it was a pleasure to see you again. From subtle details, I noticed your dedication to social activities. I see you as someone vibrant and full of life, which truly touched me. You serve as an inspiration for many!"

The note was unsigned, leaving Mana puzzled. Having interacted with many people at several provincial student representative conferences, she knew this person must have seen her and been deeply impressed.

As a middle-aged woman, formerly a doctor in her home country and now an immigrant in Canada, Mana had to set aside her education and work experience and start from scratch like those twenty-something youngsters, training as a nurse and getting elected as a student representative. Such circumstances might surprise people, but regardless of nationality, it was the reality of immigration.

Mana was touched. Who could be the author of these notes? Unable to guess, she shrugged it off, dismissing the writer as another admirer. She pocketed the note and briskly headed to the coffee shop, bought a cup, and, finding a secluded corner to savor it, opened the second note to read it carefully:

"Mana, I admire your determination to return to school and enhance yourself on your life's journey. The story about your daughter wanting to assert herself by saying 'No' to you at twelve deeply resonated with me. I often say 'Yes' to my mother and family, neglecting my feelings. Your narrative holds significance for me and is a great inspiration for self-care. I will learn to assert myself when necessary and say 'No.' Thank you for sharing your story!"

Mana recalled that this message must be from Violet, the English girl with long golden hair, a slightly upturned nose, and a sprinkling of charming freckles across her face.

II

In the summer, the Rocky Mountains, the emerald Lake Louise, and the towering Stone Mountain are shrouded in clouds. The rolling forests attracted tourists worldwide, setting the stage for the All-Canada Student Council Annual Conference.

Mana had met Violet in the hotel corridor on the first morning of the conference.

Violet had strode ahead with her long, curly hair fashioned into twin braids. Clad in a white T-shirt tucked into faded denim shorts and sporting light blue sneakers, she had exuded a vibrant energy as she traversed the carpeted floor.

Mana, with an innate appreciation for beauty, had admired the girl's fantastic figure as she followed behind.

"Such a slim waist and long legs," she had marveled silently.

Noticing a delicate rose tattoo encircling the ankle bone of Violet's left foot, Mana hadn't been able to help but think, "How unique!"

She had estimated the girl, radiating youthful vigor, to be no more than twenty years old.

Violet's uniqueness had immediately caught Mana's attention, which was gifted by God to appreciate beauty, especially since she had a daughter of Violet's age.

Entering the conference room, Mana sat beside Violet without hesitation.

The first thing on the agenda was introductions and sharing stories between neighbors.

"Your family must be proud of you for returning to school, right?"

Violet's eyes sparkled with a gleam that made even her eyes smile.

"Yes, my mother was an English teacher in China. Whenever I speak with her over the phone, she sometimes asks me to help correct her English pronunciation. And especially my daughter, she has even become my teacher."

Whenever Mana talked about her daughter, a proud smile lit up her face. She eagerly shared stories about her daughter.

Mana remembered one weekend when her daughter was twelve. She had invited her mother to her room. As Mana pushed the door open, she saw her daughter sitting at the table in tears, feeling a bit anxious without knowing what had happened.

Her daughter had cried out with her back to Mana, saying, "Mom, no matter what you asked me to do or say before, I always said 'Yes'! But now that I'm twelve, can I start saying 'No' to you?"

Mana had been taken aback by her daughter's words, realizing at that moment that her daughter was growing up, needing to think for herself, seeking independence, and requiring breathing space of her own.

As Mana told this story, Violet nodded in silence throughout, deep in contemplation.

Violet had only been married six months. Her husband's family were friends of her parents, both from England. They had known each other since childhood and entered university together. Last year, her husband hadn't graduated when he joined the recruiting team to enlist in the Navy. He said he would return to school after completing his service and take Violet to live in that seaside city after graduating. Violet's face blushed, her eyes filled with happy expectations.

Violet willingly showed Mana the small rose tattoo encircling her ankle bone to prove her happiness, saying it was traditional English culture. People believed her love would last forever if a girl's ankle bone bore a ring of roses.

### III

Mana sat alone outside the school's café, two notes resting quietly on the small table. With one hand holding a coffee cup and the other supporting her chin, her eyes stared absentmindedly at the distant street scene, a faint smile playing at the corners of her mouth. Outside the window, the poplar leaves began to turn yellow slightly, and a wild rabbit bravely scampered across the road in front of the door, disappearing in the blink of an eye.

Mana hadn't expected a brief exchange to make her the most memorable person for two classmates at that conference. Now she understood why Violet's eyes had filled with tears while listening to her daughter's story. It turned out that she shared similar struggles with her daughter of the same age.

Mana solemnly folded the notes, put them in her bag, and slowly opened the envelope. Inside was an email printed by the organizing committee, addressed to the recipients of the notes:

Dear conference delegates, as summer vacation ends and everyone returns to bustling school life, here are some personal notes written for you. We hope these notes will foster friendship and respect among you. We encourage students to communicate with each other, learn from each other, and have the opportunity to truly represent your school's students. We wish you all academic success!

Even before finishing the letter, Mana's eyes welled up with tears, memories of unforgettable moments rushing back to her.

# Fenfang in the Eastern Town of Toronto

## I

Fenfang had never expected that she, a woman in her fifties who had once lived on the fringes of society in China, would achieve fame in a foreign land, Canada. Her name graced the pages of the Fresh News of Grey County: "The Chinese Lady Is a Hero." Since then, the residents of Blue Mountains Town have started calling her the Chinese Lady.

When Fenfang was young, she was a tall, fair-skinned, and exceptionally kind-hearted girl from Hunan. After graduating from high school in 1983 without gaining college admission, she had joined a shoe factory where her father worked as a needlework operator. In the late 1990s, the factory management had collectively decided to sell the factory to a Taiwanese businessman. The technical workers who chose to stay had had their seniority recalculated. At the same time, the rest were offered a buyout of their seniority at 400 RMB per year. Fenfang sold her over ten years of seniority for 7,000 RMB.

Fenfang's husband, who was the warehouse keeper of the shoe factory, had been involved in a theft incident where he was struck on the head with a brick by the thief, leaving him in a vegetative state. Before the factory sale, he had received timely wages and medical reimbursement because of his work-related injury. However, after the sale, all medical benefits were lost. The couple had received less than 20,000 RMB for selling their seniority. Fenfang was thirty-six that year, and their son Xiaogang was only seven.

Better jobs in the city typically demanded applicants to be under thirty-five. Unable to secure a decent job, Fenfang had rented a stall at the farm products fair and started selling dumplings. Her dumplings had been delicious and authentic, and initially, business was fairly good. However, business had become increasingly challenging with an influx of laid-off workers entering the fair to sell dumplings, wontons, and even resell vegetables and fruits.

Four years later, Fenfang's husband, still in a vegetative state, passed away.

Kind-hearted people had started introducing potential partners to Fenfang. Two of them had outright rejected her upon learning she had a ten-year-old son, and there were even those who openly expressed unwillingness to assist in raising someone else's child. Finally, one day, a man who was 16 years her senior met with her, and the two chatted well, but the situation quickly shifted. As per the matchmaker, the man chose a younger woman instead.

After encountering several men who had either dismissed her due to her age or her having a son, Fenfang had realized that as time passed, finding a suitable partner in her thirties was already difficult, let alone in her forties. Men in their sixties even deemed her too old.

Fenfang understood that seeking a spouse as a woman paralleled searching for a job; both necessitated youth. Eventually, she had lost confidence in remarriage and pinned her only hope on raising her son to adulthood.

One of her neighbors, who had returned from Beijing to visit her hometown, advised Fenfang not to pin her hopes on finding a man. Given the difficulty of securing employment in a small town, she had suggested Fenfang become a live-in maid in affluent households in Beijing. This way, she could have food and shelter and earn money to support her son. Filled with resolve, Fenfang had left her son with her parents and went to Beijing alone, working as a domestic helper in the home of a real estate tycoon.

Her employer had treated Fenfang well, paying her promptly each month and granting her weekends off. She had sent most of her earnings to her parents, asking them to buy more books for Xiaogang and urging him to study hard with aspirations for a prestigious university. Fenfang learned that those among her high school classmates who had pursued higher education had become government officials or successful entrepreneurs.

II

One day, the nanny from the opposite building, Zhang Xiaoyu, saw Fenfang and mysteriously mentioned having seen an advertisement on the street offering 30,000 RMB for marrying a foreigner and moving to Canada.

A sudden spark lit up in Fenfang's mind: "Is such a thing possible?!"

On her way to the market to buy groceries, Fenfang had deliberately taken a detour, full of curiosity, and gone to the place Xiaoyu mentioned. Sure enough, there was an advertisement that read:

For 30,000 RMB, you can marry into paradise—Canada! Canada! No English is required. We can guide you to heaven. Payment in three installments: 10,000 RMB for finding a match, 10,000 RMB for translating letters and arranging meetings, and the final 10,000 RMB upon meeting. No refunds!

A wave of excitement surged through Fenfang. In her forties, still vibrant, she yearned for companionship, especially yearning for a home and hoping for someone to share an umbrella with the rain. Besides, her son Xiaogang needed a father.

Over the years, Fenfang's romantic aspirations had dimmed with each unsuccessful date.

Most single men in their seventies or eighties sought younger women. As many people joked, "Men's preferences for women never change. No matter their age, they always desire an eighteen-year-old."

This international marriage advertisement flickered like a fragile oil lamp for Fenfang, reigniting a nearly extinguished flame. Touched by the prospect, her criteria were simple: "A husband to provide for me." Finding a man who could provide security and treat her and Xiaogang well would suffice.

She began to weigh her options. With nearly 10,000 RMB in her bank account, borrowing 20,000 RMB from her sister could make up the required 30,000 RMB. But what if she lost this sum? Repaying her sister would take at least five years with her current income. Nevertheless, considering she might live another thirty years, if she were fortunate enough to find a supportive partner and a stable family, wouldn't the 30,000 RMB investment be worthwhile?

Fenfang subconsciously looked for Canada on the map in her employer's study from that day on. To her, this country was just a point of knowledge from her middle school geography book. She knew Canada's vastness and chilliness, recognizing names like Vancouver and Toronto, yet their true essence remained mysterious. Canada now held a profound significance for her. Whenever it was mentioned on TV or in the news, Fenfang tuned in with heightened attention.

One day, she deliberately visited the Tianyi Global Marriage Agency and Immigration Company. It seemed decent, with luxurious decoration and all the necessary certificates hung on the wall. It didn't strike her as a bogus company.

"Nothing ventured, nothing gained!"

After significant contemplation, Fenfang eventually spurred herself on. She was on the brink of wagering 30,000 RMB on her future, contemplating marriage to a foreigner and relocating to Canada. At worst, she thought she would end up spending her days as a live-in maid. Fenfang had resolved to take the plunge.

**III**

September marked the end of summer, yet weekends in Beijing still retained a lingering humidity. Along the North Street of Donghuangchenggen (Eastern Section of the Imperial City), the leaves of the sycamore trees were starting to yellow, rustling in the autumn wind. Pedicabs, bicycles, and a steady stream of vans and cars moved in an orderly fashion.

At the entrance of the Elementary School of Heizhima Hutong (Black Sesame Alley), an old man squatted on the ground, repairing a bicycle. One hand gripped the frame while the other turned the pedals. Leaning against the wall was a makeshift sign crafted from sturdy cardboard, crookedly displaying "Tire Inflation and Tyre Repair."

Across the street, a clothing store boasted a significant sale, with Wang Jie's (aka, Dave Wang or Wang Chieh's) song, "Do I Truly Have Nothing?" playing on the two-tone speaker recorder:

Whose heart flies in the sky above?

Whose fate drifts on the sea?

A wounded heart reluctant to speak.

The past and the future seem like a dream,

Leave the pain and beauty to my solitary self.

The unfamiliar melody echoes once more,

Do I truly have nothing?

Nearby, a public telephone booth resembling a large barrel with green sheet metal was covered with small ads for furniture making, painting, and sewer-dredging services.

Fenfang lingered in the vicinity for a while, observing the ebb and flow of people around the phone booth. Yet, she couldn't muster the courage to enter. A slight fear—she might be selling herself—nagged at her.

Finally, with the booth vacant, Fenfang gathered her courage and stepped inside. Taking a deep breath, she presented a crumpled notebook with phone numbers, cradling the receiver between her ear and shoulder as she dialed the number with her free hand.

"Hello, is this Fenxiang? It's me, Sister Fangfang. Do you have some spare money? Can you lend me twenty thousand yuan?"

Anxious to avoid hesitation, she rushed through her words as soon as the call connected.

"Twenty thousand yuan? For what? That's a substantial amount!"

Such a sum held weight in the 1990s, prompting surprise from Fenxiang at the other end of the line.

"I want to take a gamble on my luck!"

Fenfang explained her intentions to her younger sister.

"This is a bit risky. Make sure you fully understand and consider it carefully. Don't tell Mom and Dad yet. Let me discuss this with my husband and see if we can gather the funds."

Fenxiang, five years junior to her elder sister, had always got the delicious food saved by Fenfang. She would shift the blame to her elder sister whenever she erred, who endured the scolding without protest. As a primary school teacher alongside her husband, Fenxiang couldn't offer much assistance to her widowed sister. Yet now, faced with her sister's desire to alter her destiny, she had to find a way to lend her the money.

**IV**

Today, Fenfang was heading to Tianyi Global Marriage Agency and Immigration Company to sign the contract. She dressed in her favorite brown windbreaker and a pink scarf. Walking down the street, a breeze blew, causing the scarf to flutter in front of her chest, as did her heart. She carried ten thousand yuan in a red synthetic leather purse, hanging in front of her chest and covered by the windbreaker, nervously wary of potential thieves.

The marriage agency was located at the intersection near the Drum Tower. Its two glass doors were adorned with paper-cut dragon and phoenix motifs, exuding a festive atmosphere. The perceptive receptionist, Miss Zhou, immediately recognized the slightly timid woman in front of her as a returning visitor. With a warm smile, she handed Fenfang a glass of water, conducted a brief inquiry, and then ushered her into the office.

An hour of persuasion and promises later, the assistant, Little Deng, skillfully filled out the necessary forms for Fenfang. After photo-taking, payment, and receipt-receiving, it was time to return and wait for the news.

Exiting the marriage agency, Fenfang felt light-hearted, walking with a rhythm. Anticipation for the future filled her, transforming her mood into one of increased happiness and vigor, and she even found herself humming snippets of popular tunes.

As per the agreement, Fenfang had to visit the marriage agency weekly to check for mail. However, one week passed with no news, then two months, and eventually two months without any news.

Regrets started to creep in for Fenfang, questioning her impulsive decision and the expenditure of the ten thousand yuan.

In an attempt to console her, Miss Zhou remarked, "Fate plays a role in these matters; patience is key. We've facilitated numerous successful matches. Look, we have received many thank-you notes."

She took out a folder from the cabinet filled with expressions of gratitude from happily married couples.

Fenfang fell silent, harboring deep skepticism and suspicion that these "thank you notes" could be forged.

"Look, there's this."

Miss Zhou noticed that Fenfang was still shaking her head in silence, so she took out a bottle of Canadian specialty ice wine and a box of maple syrup from the cabinet, saying, "This is a gift from a woman who successfully married and immigrated to Canada, and she returned to visit her family not long ago."

"Be confident and patient!"

With these words, Miss Zhou slowed down her tone and reached out to gently hold Fenfang's shoulder.

Miss Zhou's words began to thaw Fenfang's heart and reignite her hope.

Two weeks later, a Canadian veteran named Douglas liked Fenfang and expressed his desire to contact her.

Little Deng had already translated the letter's contents into Chinese and provided Fenfang with a printed photo of Douglas to consider how to respond. After Fenfang wrote her reply in Chinese, she would bring it back. Then Little Deng translated it into English and sent it to Douglas. Before leaving, Little Deng reminded her that the second payment would be due at the next visit.

That night, Fenfang told the homeowners she had a headache and locked herself in her room early. Her heart raced with a mixture of joy and worry. Taking out the letter from her bag felt clandestine, causing her hands to tremble.

The man in the photo was nearly 1.80 meters tall, with a clean-shaven face marred by deep wrinkles. Clad in jeans, he stood by a lake, smiling at her as if asking, "What do you think of me?"

"Why would this well-built, healthy man of only fifty-one years old not choose a woman in her twenties or thirties? Why not someone without children? Could he be a scammer? But what could he possibly scam from me?"

Fenfang's heart raced, filled with uncertainties and suspicions. Her past rejections by men she had dated prevented her from easily believing in her stroke of luck. She carefully unfolded the letter translated by Little Deng and began to read:

"Dear Ms. Fenfang,

Hello! I am Douglas, a fifty-one-year-old resident of a quaint town called Blue Mountain, not far from downtown Toronto. As a retired soldier, I previously served as a mechanical engineer in the Army. Now, I run a small company specializing in mechanical and electrical repairs. I've experienced two failed marriages and have a daughter who has married and settled in the United States. A devoted Christian, I deeply appreciate Chinese cuisine, especially spicy dishes. After learning about your background, I am struck by your strong will and resilience. Your dedication to working as a family nanny in Beijing to support your child is admirable. I sympathize with your situation and want to get to know you."

The brief letter resonated with Fenfang, who read it repeatedly. Tears welled in her eyes as she reached the end, cascading down her cheeks with a salty taste. Unlike the usual expressions of sympathy and concern she had encountered in the past, Douglas's words of admiration touched her deeply.

At that moment, she seemed to rediscover herself: "It turns out that everyone lives with their own value."

V

A newfound sensation stirred Fenfang while the enchantment of a fresh world held her spellbound. She resolved to persist in taking the risk.

If Fenfang had initially been somewhat cautious when completing her personal resume, she now laid bare all her true circumstances in this letter. She believed that if Douglas turned out to be a fraudster, he would simply abandon her—a woman with no money.

Three months passed, during which Fenfang and Douglas exchanged over a dozen emails through Little Deng's translation. Douglas never showed disdain for her; he kept praising and encouraging her, even suggesting she dedicated time to learning English.

Douglas's letters served as a beacon of hope for Fenfang.

Once, Douglas excitedly asked Fenfang to buy a cellphone in a letter, expressing his desire to speak with her and hear her voice. He had found someone in his small town who could speak Chinese to help with translation.

Fenfang stared at the long string of numbers on the screen the first time the phone rang, her heart pounding. Overwhelmed with nerves, she answered with a trembling voice, " 喂，您好！ (Hello! How are you?)."

"Hello! Mr. Douglas wants to speak with you," a woman's voice, tinged with a Cantonese accent in Mandarin, came from the other end of the line. Goodness, in her extreme nervousness, Fenfang had momentarily forgotten that direct communication with Douglas was not possible.

Fenfang later learned that the woman on the line was the proprietress of the town's sole Chinese restaurant. Douglas, a fan of Chinese cuisine, frequented her establishment and had formed a connection with the family. This led to him enlisting the help of the proprietress for translation purposes.

Six months later, Douglas willingly settled the remaining ten thousand yuan and made an appointment with the marriage agency to rendezvous with Fenfang in Beijing. Upon hearing this, Fenfang experienced an overwhelming mix of anxiety and apprehension. Yet, a glimmer of joy lay buried deep within her.

Miss Zhou became even more attentive with a beaming smile, letting Fenfang offer them candies to celebrate it and saying that when she married Douglas, she mustn't forget to write a thank-you note to the company for their records.

### VI

The marriage agency arranged all the schedules. Little Deng accompanied Fenfang to hail a taxi, buying her a rose to meet Douglas at the airport.

The vast Beijing airport dazzled Fenfang, disorienting her as she struggled to navigate the complex network of overpasses and expressways, her mind clouded with an inexplicable mix of emotions. When Little Deng took them to the hotel, handing over the room keys to leave, Fenfang entertained the thought of fleeing with Little Deng.

Ultimately, Fenfang didn't flee. After Little Deng left, she and Douglas exchanged awkward glances, at a loss for words. Douglas maintained a smile, prompting Fenfang to reciprocate. However, she was too nervous to meet his gaze, shuffling awkwardly into the elevator.

The elevator boasted solid wood walls, exuding an antique and luxurious charm under the dim lighting. It was a far cry from the elevators Fenfang was accustomed to, typically plastered with phone numbers and advertisements.

Douglas opened the door and let Fenfang enter first. As soon as they stepped into the room, he tenderly kissed her hair. Nervous tremors ran through her, followed by a long-lost sweetness.

Seating herself on the sofa, Fenfang anxiously rubbed her hands together. Her facial muscles tensed, giving her the appearance of forcing a smile, unsure of what else to do.

Perching on the edge of the bed, Douglas nodded and smiled, the air around them seemingly frozen at that moment.

"Well ...," Douglas tried to break the silence, only to realize they couldn't communicate.

Standing up, he skillfully found the wardrobe and opened the suitcase to hang up his clothes.

Upon seeing this, Fenfang's nervousness dissipated as she hurried over to snatch his clothes.

This move by Fenfang was entirely natural, but it startled Douglas. It was the first time in his life that someone had taken something from him without asking. Yet, as he watched her skillfully arrange the clothes in the wardrobe, he relaxed, offering a nod and a smile.

Fenfang's second surprise for Douglas came while he slept; she quietly took his pants and shirt, washing them by hand in the bathroom basin. Despite being aware of the hotel's laundry service, she deemed it too costly and believed she could achieve a cleaner wash by hand.

Upon waking to find his clothes missing, Douglas heard movement from the bathroom. Startled, he leaped out of bed and rushed to investigate. Discovering his wallet and some loose change on the counter, he observed Fenfang washing his clothes in the tub. Breathing a sigh of relief, he shook his head before returning to bed.

This was how Douglas experienced the virtue of Chinese women. He had fallen deeply for this Chinese woman, who epitomized the ideal wife in his heart: honest, kind, and strong. Moreover, Fenfang could cook the Chinese food he liked, which felt like the icing on the cake.

A few months later, the wedding was held in Fenfang's hometown. Douglas settled the debt Fenfang owed her sister, provided living expenses for Fenfang and her son Xiaogang, and then returned to Canada to process the family reunion immigration for Fenfang.

Fenfang didn't harbor intense emotions for the man she had married. Language barriers hindered their verbal communication, leading them to rely on gestures and drawings to convey their thoughts. Her predominant sentiment was one of gratitude. She was thankful that this man had married her, grateful for his genuine care towards Xiaogang, and appreciative of his potential to shape her future, even though it remained uncertain. She sensed his deep respect for her, yet a tinge of inadequacy lingered within her. She felt she had little to offer Douglas except to cherish him, fulfill her duties as a woman, show him consideration, take care of him, and give him the warmth of home.

### VII

Fenfang's family reunion immigration procedures took only three months, with Douglas even booking her plane ticket, urging her to reunite with him in Canada as soon as possible.

Arriving at the Blue Mountain town from Toronto International Airport, it was almost midnight, enveloped in darkness. Fenfang could hardly make out her surroundings, the prevailing sensation being one of overwhelming silence.

When Fenfang woke up the next morning, Douglas had already gone out. It was silent everywhere, with only the occasional sound of a car passing by the door.

Sitting up, Fenfang leaned against the pillow, widened her eyes to look around, and then blinked hard, still unable to believe what she saw.

The room was neat and clean, with red sheets and quilts—the dowry her parents had gifted her upon marriage. The big wooden bed, brand new, emitted a faint woody scent; even the carpet had just been cleaned, exuding the fragrance of detergent. The air seemed to have been washed; everything felt so fresh, so unfamiliar.

Making her way to the kitchen, Fenfang noticed a note on the table with a drawing of a person exiting through a door, indicating that he had left. Drawings on the refrigerator depicted a cow (signifying milk in the fridge), bread, and eggs.

Despite not feeling hungry, Fenfang's mind buzzed with curiosity. Opening the door and stepping outside through a small balcony to the backyard, she beheld a meticulously maintained lawn resembling freshly cut hair, adorned with a tree bearing red berries and yellowing leaves scattered on the green grass like a picturesque painting. The sun beamed overhead, white clouds drifting in the azure sky while a flock of geese flew south for migration. Fenfang had never seen such a large villa; even in the real estate tycoon's house in Beijing, they just lived in high-rise apartments with no backyard.

She sighed, whispering, "I finally have a home!"

Fenfang surveyed the surroundings, then suddenly covered her mouth in shock, almost screaming, before quickly running back and tightly locking the door, her heart pounding heavily. It turned out that their backyard was connected to a small hill, which housed a large cemetery.

Douglas was willing to discuss anything, but when Fenfang broached the topic of moving, there was no room for negotiation. He didn't understand her fear of the deceased. Death was a natural part of life; the ancestors of the town were buried here, his parents were laid to rest here, and he, too, would find his final resting place here. This was the closest place to heaven.

Fenfang thought she had no grounds to argue on this matter. Since the house belonged to him, she had to go along. As the saying goes, "Marrying a chicken means following the chicken; marrying a dog means following the dog." But Douglas's words often reminded her of the slogan of Tianyi Global Marriage Agency and Immigration Company: "Thirty thousand yuan takes you to heaven!" Since then, Fenfang often teased herself, "I may not have reached heaven, but I'm certainly close; it's just next door."

## VIII

The townspeople were very friendly. Many knew Fenfang as Douglas's Chinese wife, and they all greeted her warmly. She gradually grew accustomed to the new environment, enjoying it very much.

Every Sunday, Fenfang accompanied Douglas to church. She couldn't fully grasp the pastor's sermons. Still, she cherished the peaceful and serene atmosphere, particularly the hymns sung by the congregation. Mrs. Mira, an 85-year-old lady, took it upon herself to teach Fenfang English and regaled her with stories from Douglas's youth when he had quarreled with her son.

One day, Douglas wanted to enroll Fenfang in driving lessons.

Still, she staunchly objected: "In such a small place, where you can walk everywhere within minutes, why bother driving? It's simply a waste of money!"

Douglas hated hearing Fenfang say one phrase the most: "Waste of money!" Whether he took her swimming, skiing, or staying in luxury hotels on weekend trips, she dismissed it all as wasteful.

Douglas was angry this time: "Not being able to drive is like not having legs; people will laugh at you. Everyone must learn to drive in Canada, just like everyone needs air!" After a brief pause, he continued solemnly, "What if one day I can't drive? What will you do?"

Seeing Douglas's face turning red as a tomato, Fenfang knew her husband was very angry and quickly apologized, "I'm sorry; I'll learn if you want me to."

Although Fenfang voiced her compliance, she obstinately thought, "It's not my money anyway, so do as you please with it."

A month later, Fenfang obtained her driver's license.

Douglas also found a weekend Chinese school in Toronto, where he dedicated two hours every Friday evening to studying Chinese. Fenfang accompanied him without complaint, driving more than a hundred kilometers to attend classes regardless of the weather, which persisted for two years.

Fenfang's son, Xiaogang, excelled academically in high school. With Douglas's support, he gained admission to the University of Toronto.

These days, he was touring Tiananmen Square and the Great Wall with his grandparents in Beijing, preparing to come to Toronto in a month.

Filled with joy, Douglas took Fenfang for a drive to Toronto to arrange Xiaogang's accommodation. During a pit stop for refueling on their return journey, Douglas encountered a customer who had previously sought his help with appliance repairs. Standing tall with hands on his hips, Douglas proudly told the customer, "My son has been accepted to the University of Toronto, and we just sorted out his accommodation."

"Your younger brother Xiaogang has been admitted to the University of Toronto. I'm so proud, haha. He is smarter than you. Invite your whole family to come back for Christmas ...." After hearing Douglas say these words to his daughter in the United States over the phone, Fenfang locked herself in the room and cried bitterly. She later regarded the tears as a poignant farewell ceremony, marking the end of her sorrow. She vowed never to shed tears so easily again.

Fenfang cherished her life even more, finding joy in planning to cook Chinese dishes that Douglas enjoyed each night. She felt content, imagining that without Douglas, she might still be working as a nanny in the home of a real estate businessman in Beijing, away from her son, watching the owner's children grow up day by day.

Their life was peaceful and comfortable, and Fenfang and Douglas were very satisfied with this lifestyle.

**IX**

Blue Mountain Town was a tourist destination in eastern Canada. In the summer, tourists come to the Blue Mountain Resort to golf, hike, and enjoy the Scandinavian Spa. In the winter, it became a hub for skiing.

In the whole town, Douglas was the only comprehensive mechanic and appliance repairman, renowned for his family business by all. Douglas built a small wooden house next to the garage just for storing tools, housing hundreds of various tools, some of which were passed down from his ancestors.

Fenfang was never a restless person, and after coming to Canada, the leisurely pace made her quite uncomfortable. In her free time, she liked to enter the small wooden house where Douglas stored his tools. Many of the tools were unfamiliar, and she was clueless about their usage. She only knew that they were her husband's beloved "children." She carefully cleaned them with a towel and neatly put them back in place.

Douglas greatly appreciated Fenfang's virtues and was very proud of her, "Many people in town praise my good fortune and commend you as a wonderful wife. Thank you, honey; I'm happy every day now; I'm truly blessed."

When Douglas spoke, he would often hold Fenfang's hands, using them to cover his face, and tenderly kiss them on both sides.

Observing Douglas's contentment, Fenfang felt immense joy. "Our town is a tourist town with only around a hundred local households. Mrs. Mira teaches me English every week, Wendy occasionally brings me flowers from her garden, Stephanie introduces me to her friends, and Mrs. Huang from the Chinese restaurant instructs me in cooking Cantonese dishes. The people here are so friendly to me, like a big family, and I want to contribute somehow, but I am unsure how."

"My honey, I adore you deeply. As long as you're happy, I'll support whatever you wish to pursue," Douglas seemed to miss Fenfang's point.

"Oh, I remember you mentioning that your tools are the most extensive in town, right? How about we open them up for free use to everyone in town? That way, they won't need to buy them, saving them from the hassle of sometimes having to go to Toronto to rent tools," Fenfang suddenly said excitedly, grabbing Douglas's hands.

"You? ... You're a genius! But is this feasible? It's an unprecedented innovation," Douglas was stunned momentarily, then hugged Fenfang tightly.

The news of the tool shed being open for free use quickly spread, and Douglas's face bloomed with smiles, telling everyone that it was his Chinese wife's idea.

Fenfang hung a notebook on the wall of the tool shed, requiring those who borrowed tools to leave their names. To Fenfang's surprise, people not only left their names but also often left flowers, vegetables, and occasionally,

Tom's handmade soap.

**X**

Fenfang and Douglas no longer needed to attend weekend Chinese school to communicate. She was becoming increasingly adapted to and fond of this place, growing to love the life here.

One evening, as she rolled dough for dumplings, Fenfang told Douglas, "I want to open a small shoe repair shop in town."

"Repair shoes? What do you mean?"

Douglas, watching TV, stood up and approached Fenfang, looking puzzled.

"I've been observing for a while and noticed that this place attracts tourists all year round. In summer, people come for mountain climbing and golfing; in winter, many come for skiing and hot springs. Once, I saw a tourist carrying expensive shoes, lamenting the loss and unable to find a repair place. Having worked in a shoe factory in China, I am familiar with shoe repair techniques. I could offer this service and earn some extra pocket money," Fenfang said, pausing her rolling pin and turning to Douglas.

Unbeknownst to Douglas, Fenfang harbored a small ambition in her heart: "If I earn money myself, I could support my parents during the New Year and festivals. I could also bring my younger sister's daughter to college by saving up."

"Honey, I don't need you to earn money. You've toiled hard before. I want you to live an easy and happy life. Your happiness is my happiness. It's as simple as that."

Douglas embraced her from behind, kissing her hair. Fenfang remembered their first meeting when he kissed her hair like this. Somehow, tears welled up in her eyes.

"Stop! Stop! If you really want to do it, then go ahead. I don't want to see you sad in tears." Seeing Fenfang tearing up, Douglas thought she was upset and raised his hands in surrender.

"No, no, it's tears of joy," Fenfang said, smiling awkwardly as she spoke.

## XI

Fenfang's Shoe Repair Shop opened near the gas station in Blue Mountain town. This business had never existed there before. Fenfang charged reasonably, attracting the locals and the ski resort, which regularly sent rental shoes for repair. Fenfang's reputation spread, drawing visitors from towns dozens of kilometers away who brought their shoes and leather goods for repair.

On a snowy evening, Douglas was repairing a neighbor's microwave oven.

"I'm going to the shoe store. The ski resort is picking up shoes tomorrow morning. I want to check and buy a bucket of milk from the grocery store at the gas station," Fenfang said as she stood up, putting down the carpet she was knitting with knitting needles.

"I'll go with you," Douglas said, putting down his tools.

"No need. The neighbor still needs the microwave oven tomorrow morning. I'll be back soon."

"Drive safely. Oh, take my phone with you."

Douglas took his phone from his pocket, reminding Fenfang as if she were a child.

"Is the pepper spray in your bag?"

Concerned for Fenfang working alone at the shoe repair shop, Douglas had bought her this pepper spray for safety.

"I know ... Mr. Old." Whenever Douglas repeated his reminders, Fenfang teased him with that nickname.

The town was small, with a total length of less than one kilometer from all directions. The snowfall tonight was a bit heavy, and the cars made a loud "coo" as they compressed the snow on the road.

Fenfang cleaned the shoes the ski resort would pick up the next day, locked the door, and walked into the adjacent grocery store.

No other customers were in the grocery store; only Annabel was working.

Seeing Fenfang enter, Annabel greeted her warmly, "Hello, Fen, what do you need today?"

After buying the milk, Fenfang headed towards the door of the shop. As she reached out to push the door, unexpectedly, someone outside pulled the door outward. Normally, people outside would let those inside leave first, but this time was different. Two men wearing winter hats that covered their faces stood outside. Instead of letting Fenfang leave first, they pushed their way in, with the second man using his back to shut the door firmly, swiftly locking it.

The first man held a black garbage bag and quickly rushed to the cash register, using a gun to coerce Annabel into giving him money.

Meanwhile, the second man extended his hand to Fenfang, demanding, "Money, give me money!"

Fenfang couldn't see the man's face, only his eyes darting around. His hand, clad in a thick, black glove, was like a claw about to crush Fenfang.

A moment of dizziness washed over Fenfang as she realized she was being robbed. Her legs weakened, stepping back, a chill running down her spine. Her head shaking, her eyes staring at the man with only a pair of eyes exposed, full of horror. She instinctively reached into her bag for her wallet, her hand brushing against the pepper spray Douglas had bought her. She shook slightly, feeling a bit more calm.

Annabel, visibly terrified, her hands trembling, pleaded with the man not to harm her, the keys in her hand failing to find the lock of the drawer.

In that critical moment, Fenfang had made up her mind. She reached into her bag, took out her wallet, and handed it to the man asking for money. As the man bent down to take the wallet, his guard lowered. Seizing the opportunity, Fenfang quickly took out the pepper spray and sprayed it into his face. The man clutched his face with both hands, shouting in pain. The other man turned his head to this side, not reacting yet, and Fenfang took a step forward, using all her strength, pressing the pepper spray against his face and spraying hard.

A bullet whizzed past Fenfang's ear and hit the wall.

Reacting promptly, Annabel pressed the button next to the cash box, triggering an alarm system.

A minute later, the sirens of police cars were blaring outside the store...

"According to police, these two young men came from the western province, planning to rob some money and return along the way. Their previous attempt went smoothly. Unexpectedly, they stumbled upon a Chinese woman this time," *Fresh News* reported.

# The Woman Who Won the Lottery

## I

"Why don't you write my story? I won Lotto 6/49!"

A stranger asked for my WeChat number.

"How did you know about me? And why do you want me to do that?"

Out of curiosity, my first question was direct after accepting her request.

"I read your series 'Chinese Women in a Foreign Land' from a friend, and I felt not every Chinese woman who marries a foreigner has a tough time. I'm one of the lucky ones."

She left this message, followed by a big mischievous and smiling face emoji.

"Congratulations! Not only did you find your happiness, but you also won Lotto 6/49. That's double joy!"

I genuinely felt happy for her.

"Ha, ha! A satisfying marriage is like winning Lotto 6/49, isn't it?"

Her face was full of delight.

Only then did I realize that her "Lotto 6/49" was her current husband, a Westerner nine years younger than her, who had never been married.

## II

Her name was Juan, a woman in her forties who had immigrated to Canada almost eight years ago. We agreed to have a chat at her house this weekend.

It was early September in the western Canadian metropolis, and the autumn chill was setting in. Standing at the highest point in the city, except for the cluster of high-rise buildings in the downtown area, other areas were dotted with patches of golden leaves, as if Monet himself were freely wielding his brush over the city's sky.

During the last long summer weekend, people took the opportunity to drive to the nearby Rocky Mountains for vacation. The neighborhood was deserted, with no one in sight. Not far away, a cat meowed.

Juan's house stood on a slope by the road in the neighborhood. Just as I approached the fence, I heard a woman's voice inside laughing heartily: "I got it! I got it!" in English with a typical northeastern Chinese accent.

I saw a tall, muscular man gently holding a woman's waist with both hands through the white wire fence. She was seated atop his shoulders, reaching out to pick an apple from a tree. The tree was laden with ripe red apples, and fallen ones lay across the ground.

I remained silent, not wanting to disturb their moment, just standing quietly outside the house. It was a quaint brick house surrounded by a freshly manicured lawn emitting the scent of newly cut grass. In the center of the lawn stood a majestic pine tree adorned with wooden chickens and ducks underneath and a red birdhouse swaying gently from its branches in the wind.

The garage door was open, revealing two parked cars inside, and the walls were adorned with various tools. Adjacent to the door stood a portable basketball hoop.

At the entrance, a set of small steps led to the solid wood door, its glossy white planks complemented by a hanging pot of pink trumpet flowers overflowing with vibrant vines. Affixed to the glass door frame was a large inverted Chinese character " 福 " (happiness), a symbol of fortune and blessings.

"Do you usually pick apples in this way?" I quipped as I rang the doorbell, skipping introductions momentarily.

"No, not at all. Henry mentioned the fresh apples on the tree when you arrived. He filled a basket when he suddenly spotted a big one high up. Next thing I knew, he was hoisting me onto his shoulders."

Juan spoke quickly, stifling laughter as her eyes narrowed into joyous slits.

Observing Juan, cradled by her husband like a princess, her petite frame standing at less than five and a half feet tall, her ordinary face unadorned with makeup, her short black hair tied neatly at the back of her neck, wearing a floral dress and a pair of delicate slippers with ten toes painted bright pink— she exuded an air of capability and neatness, radiating a sunny disposition.

"Henry, our guest has arrived!" she called out to the kitchen, leading me into the living room.

"Hi, I'm Henry. Welcome to our home," greeted the man before me, his slightly curly hair and white teeth contrasting his towering height of nearly six and a half feet. Yet, his bashfulness makes him seem like a shy young boy.

"This guy, he's not shy at all on stage in front of thousands of people, but he blushes when he talks off stage. Alright, alright, go and wash the apples," Juan intervened with a smile, nudging Henry toward the kitchen.

Henry trotted back to the kitchen gently, running water echoing from within.

The house was impeccably tidy, with a dulcimer in the corner, a colorful and vibrant abstract line drawing on the living room wall, and a large glass fish tank by the door, home to several small tropical fish leisurely swimming within.

"I'm Chinese, but I've never believed in feng shui. I think it's superstition. Hey, but my Henry is a believer. Being a designer, he studied some Chinese feng shui in school."

"Tell me, how did you win this '6/49'?" I pressed eagerly, a hint of impatience in my tone.

"Ha, ha, if you want to know, I feel embarrassed," Juan replied, settling beside me, hands clasped together with a shy smile.

"You know, nowadays, everyone finds partners through marriage websites. Some sites are free, but most are unreliable, except for the paid ones. That's how I got the '6/49.'"

"Please have some fruit."

Henry came out with a plate of fruit. The apples were scrubbed clean, and even the stems of the strawberries were meticulously cleaned and arranged within.

"Xiaowei's taekwondo class is about to end. You guys chat; I'll go to the gym to pick him up."

Henry held the car keys, ready to go out.

I rose from my seat and inquired with a friendly smile, "Juan said she won the '6/49.' What's your opinion?"

"No! No! No! She's wrong. I won the 6/49!" Henry retorted playfully.

It seemed this was a well-rehearsed joke between them.

Henry shook his head with mock seriousness as he approached Juan, his hand gently caressing her arm, his gaze fixed on her, before leaning affectionately to rest his face against Juan's head.

**III**

Juan appeared to be an unassuming Chinese woman. This kind blends into the crowd without drawing attention, seemingly ordinary like a daisy swaying on the prairie, unnoticed by passersby. But she was a "hidden gem," growing more appealing with closer scrutiny. In college, she had pursued a degree in dulcimer performance. Upon graduation, she had married a classmate who had attended her commencement recital with her elder brother. Within a year of their marriage, she had become pregnant. However, her towering, six-foot-tall husband always disdained her petite stature, plain appearance, lack of domestic skills, and incessant criticism marred their relationship.

After three years of marriage, the couple had immigrated to Canada under the sponsorship of Juan's elder brother. Juan had established a dulcimer teaching studio to recruit students while her husband struggled to secure steady employment. Frustrated by meager earnings from casino work, he had nearly succumbed to a gambling addiction. Finally, he had resorted to returning to university for further education, where he had become entangled with a wealthy foreign student. When the student became pregnant, he had abruptly demanded a divorce from Juan, leaving behind their five-and-a-half-year-old son in her care.

"I'm a divorced woman with a child, and Henry is unmarried, nine years younger than me. I never thought he would choose me," Juan said with a hint of pride.

"Have you ever asked him what he likes about you?"

I confessed that I had a preconceived notion of marriage being about "a talented man and a beautiful woman." At least, I thought they didn't seem very compatible in appearance.

"Oh, I was surprised myself. I'm simply a perfect person in his eyes. He says he loves me whenever I ask him because I'm kind-hearted, independent, and raising a child independently.”

“What do you like about him?”

“He’s kind, practical, spoils, sincerely lives with me, and gives me all the money he earns for me to manage. He’s also very pleasant and humorous; his hobby is acting in plays with a group of people. Being with him seems like nothing can bother me. No matter what happens, he can always make me laugh.”

She paused for a moment, smiling as if savoring something.

“He also says I’m very beautiful.” She covered her mouth with both hands a little shyly, her eyes narrowing into slits with laughter. “But, in my ex-husband’s eyes, I seemed to be a woman without merits—short, unattractive, careless, heartless, and can’t cook. I’m still myself, except I’ve improved my cooking a bit. Nothing else has changed, but the shortcomings in my ex-husband’s eyes are not present in Henry’s eyes. For example, I’m short, but he thinks a kind heart is more important than appearance. When I play the dulcimer, my ex-husband thought it was noisy, but Henry says I’m most beautiful when I play it. Anyway, he finds me pleasing wherever he looks.”

Juan talked about her Henry as if the whole room was full of sunshine.

“Love is blind. I sincerely praise you.”

<h3 style="text-align:center">IV</h3>

Bang! Bang! Bang! The sound of a basketball hitting the hoop came from outside.

Juan stood up, walked to the window, pointed at Henry shooting hoops outside, and said through the gauze window, “He treats Xiaowei as if he were his own son. Look, they’re playing basketball together, getting along so well. Sometimes, I chat with him and say, ‘You don’t have a child, and maybe we can still try for one with medical advancements nowadays.’ He unhappily asks me, ‘Didn’t we have a son?’ It makes me feel embarrassed.”

“What does he do for a living?”

"He's a civil engineer. He goes to work at seven in the morning to avoid traffic jams and has to get up at half past five. So, I get up at five every day to prepare breakfast and lunch for him and my son, the same as clockwork, never missing a day for five years. I bought these lunch boxes with red, yellow, blue, green, and white lids. I always try making different breakfasts and lunches for them from Monday to Friday."

Juan opened the cupboard, which was full of lunch boxes: large ones for the main meal, small ones for fruit, and some for snacks, all neatly stacked in different colors.

"Sorry, Xiaowei fell down, and his foot is bleeding. I'll get the band-aid for him."

The door suddenly opened, pushed by Henry who didn't even take off his shoes, and rushed into the house with a look of apology and anxiety on his face.

Juan and I ran out and saw Xiaowei sitting on the ground, his big toe bleeding.

Henry took the band-aid and cotton swab and knelt down, taking hold of Xiaowei's foot in his hands and pressing the bleeding wound with the cotton swab, his movements as skillful as those of a surgeon. Gradually, the bleeding stopped, and he wrapped the wound in the band-aid.

"What a perfect father-son moment!"

The scene before my eyes suddenly made me understand why they both felt like they won the "6/49" in this seemingly ordinary marriage. They appreciate each other in their marriage and even regard cultural conflicts as an opportunity to learn from each other. It's also because they embrace the trivial details of life and take on different roles due to their different perspectives, just like the neatly organized lunchboxes Juan has arranged.

# A Woman from China

My name is Christi, and I'm eleven years old. During the Chinese Film Festival in Kathmandu, Nepal, our school organized a screening of the Chinese film *Waiting for the Wind*. It showcased Pokhara, one of the world's top three safest paragliding spots, and our revered "Living Goddess." I've heard that another Chinese film, *The Great Escape in Nepal*, is also being filmed in our country. I also watched an American disaster movie, *2012*, with my classmates. Nepal is a stunning country at the foot of the Himalayas, often described as the closest place to heaven. The movie portrays it as the location where Noah's Ark, the savior of all mankind, was constructed. However, in my heart, the true Noah's Ark lies across the Himalayas in our neighbor, China.

## I

Today, Friday, my sister, who teaches English at our school, called my mom early in the morning, saying, "Mum, tell Christi that the school is closed today, and there will be no classes."

Lying in bed, I listened intently as my mother asked anxiously, "Why no classes? Is it just the sixth grade not having classes, or is the whole school closed?"

"Strike? Hmph, another strike!" my mom exclaimed unhappily, then hung up the phone.

Secretly, I rejoiced in my heart! In Nepal, we have school on Saturdays and only Sundays off. Heh, heh, I won't have classes for two days this week. How awesome!

Just yesterday, I received my midterm exam results, all A+. In celebration, Mom rewarded me with chewing gum. I felt deserving of some rest!

However, I pretended to be asleep and didn't respond because I knew if I showed the slightest reluctance to go to school, she would immediately stand with her hands on her hips, glaring at me with her big eyes. Often, her forehead bore a red tikka (a red vermilion mark symbolizing auspiciousness and good fortune), with two deep black lines drawn at the corners of her eyes, making them appear even bigger, rounder, and scarier.

She married my father when she was only fourteen, and my sister was born when she was fifteen. She said, "I became a mother to care for the little birds before my wings were not yet fully grown."

When I was five years old, I stayed with my mother in the village of Damak to take care of my grandparents. In contrast, my father took my eleven-year-old sister to work in a gold shop in Kathmandu, crafting jewelry for the customers.

In Nepal, every household treasures gold. Both men and women adore wearing gold and silver jewelry. When my sister and I turned one year old, my father gifted us a pair of exquisitely crafted gold earrings.

My grandpa inherited his skill and was renowned in our village of dozens of households. Even women from neighboring villages sought him out for jewelry making. That's how my mother met my father.

Whenever he got drunk and merry, he would proclaim, "I may not possess gold, but my craft is worth its weight in gold. I won't starve in this lifetime, nor will I allow my family to suffer."

However, just a year ago, he returned to the village with a young, fashionable woman, whom my mother revealed was the daughter of a gold shop owner. She proposed that if my mother agreed to divorce, she would provide a substantial sum of money.

My mother held me tight and wept bitterly. The only condition she laid out was for my father to fund our relocation to Kathmandu and ensure my enrollment in this private school. She believed my sister had received a fine education and was now teaching at this school. And she couldn't bear to disappoint me. She firmly believed girls could only secure a bright future through quality education.

Our principal, a university graduate in the United States, returned to Nepal with a vision to establish a school. Despite the higher fees compared to public schools, we pride ourselves on being a bilingual institution that prepares students for future studies abroad. With over five hundred students enrolled, our school regularly hosts volunteers from around the globe, sharing insights about their countries and teaching us various games. Many alumni from our school have pursued higher education at universities worldwide.

My mother's aspiration is to send me to study in New York, as she has an American friend named Pete residing there.

**II**

She didn't wake me up as usual today, so I drifted back to sleep and immersed myself in a dream. In it, I stood amidst the bustling streets of New York City, gazing up at unfamiliar traffic lights and towering skyscrapers, feeling utterly lost and unable to find my way home.

Suddenly, I was jolted awake by the sound of my younger aunt, who resides downstairs, entering our home. Their voices echoed loudly as they conversed:

"Why isn't Christi at school today? Upendra mentions that a Chinese woman will move in next door to you," my aunt exclaimed.

"A Chinese woman? I have no idea! When does this happen?" Mother's voice rang out with surprise.

"Upendra cleared out the living room across from your house yesterday, and it's now ready for her to move in!"

My aunt's voice carried a hint of pride, as she always seemed one step ahead of her older sister regarding neighborhood gossip. Just like last night, there was a commotion in the courtyard across the street, and a police car arrived. A crowd gathered to witness the spectacle, but my aunt swiftly pieced together the entire scenario in just two minutes. Returning to inform us, she revealed that Oso's two wives had been in a heated altercation. Oso intended to take his younger wife to work in Dubai. Still, the older wife had intervened, sparking the conflict because the younger wife had allegedly conspired with Oso to abandon her in Kathmandu to care for their parents-in-law. Oso's younger brother and sister-in-law had also become embroiled, blaming Oso for favoring the younger wife. It was quite a lively affair for a family residing in the same building!

"A Chinese woman!" I exclaimed excitedly, leaping out of bed and startling my mother and aunt seated beside me.

I've never been to China, but I know our two countries share a border. My textbook introduces iconic landmarks, such as the Great Wall of China and the Potala Palace in Tibet. Many classmates fantasize about visiting China one day to scale the Great Wall. I vividly recall last semester when we hosted Chinese volunteers at school. They were all college students, and one of the sisters stood out with her striking beauty, sporting a gentle face framed by glasses. Her flowing long hair, jeans, and sneakers gave off such a cool vibe! She taught us Chinese and encouraged us to consider studying in China in the future. Sadly, I can only now remember " 你好 " (*nihao*, Hello in English).

"If only I could speak Chinese! I wonder what the Chinese woman moving in will be like. Will she communicate with me in English? Will she be friendly?" I pondered silently.

I dislike it when people display arrogance, like Qianda in our class. She flaunts her metal brace as if to emphasize her family's wealth. Whenever she speaks, she deliberately touches her braces with her hand. I've heard her father doesn't earn much money working in Korea.

### III

The Chinese woman has finally moved in!

I heard a stir outside and quickly opened a corner of the cloth curtain, wrapping it around my neck as I stuck my head out, curious to see what was happening.

Wow, I've never seen such a colossal suitcase before! Upendra and her Nepali friend were struggling to move it.

The Chinese woman wore sunglasses and carried another small suitcase in one hand, with a double-shoulder backpack on her back.

She sported a wheat-colored hat and a light green floral skirt and tied two braids like mine, though hers were coiled at the back of her head and lacked the blue ribbon we typically use at school. Her feet were adorned with white plastic sandals, topped with a plastic flower of the same color. I bet I've never laid eyes on such exquisite shoes before.

Why are Chinese women so beautiful?! She offered me a sweet smile, appearing older than my mother but without the same round belly. Seeing her was as invigorating as sipping a chilled Nepali Bhadgaon yogurt on a sweltering day.

My aunt, carrying my two-year-old cousin Mina, hurriedly ascended the stairs to join the gathering, and Mina still suckled on her mother's nipple.

Rima from the third floor, holding a handful of pumpkin leaves (a staple vegetable in Nepal), leaned against the staircase railing, her gaze curious as she looked downstairs.

As our eyes met the Chinese woman's, she gently set down her suitcase and clasped her hands together in greeting: "*Namaste!*" (Hello)

"*Namaste!*" I quickly released the curtain and politely folded my hands across my chest.

Auntie and Rima echoed, "*Namaste!*"

Then, I observed that she extended her hand and lifted the curtain, which was so tarnished that its original hue had faded into obscurity.

She turned to Upendra and requested, "Could you please remove this? I don't need it."

Our building has three floors, each with a bathroom and kitchen for the tenants. There are five households in total, and each household has a cloth curtain at the entrance to block the view inside because we're not used to always closing the door, as it feels like rejecting interaction with our neighbors.

Upendra was a young man in his twenties who had studied Japanese for nearly two years, like many people in Nepal who plan to work in Japan after graduation. I heard that Upendra's uncle and aunt had opened a Nepalese restaurant in Canada, saved some money from selling our traditional food, and used it to come back and renovate this building. Upendra lives on the second floor and manages the building for his uncle. However, Upendra's management is really poor! He never waters the flowers, leaving them to flourish or wilt. To retain moisture at the roots, all the flowers have become particularly tenacious, with their leaves shrinking smaller and smaller, clearly lacking water. He also often forgets to fill the water tank on the roof, causing us to stop having water twice a week. I heard other landlords clean the water tank every six months, but we have never seen him clean it. Oh, don't even mention the water in our house; it's as yellow as urine most of the time! It forces us to drink bottled water.

But my mother says, "It's normal for young people to be lazy. He's not managing it well, so we can rent a cheap house. But now that this Chinese tenant has arrived, I hope Upendra's management will improve!"

<h2 style="text-align:center">IV</h2>

When my mother called me to wake up this morning, I immediately sprang out of bed. I was still excited about our new neighbor who moved in next door yesterday—a foreigner, a Chinese woman.

My aunt once mentioned that in Nepal, it's a longstanding tradition for people to seek job opportunities abroad to earn a living. Almost every household has a member working overseas. My uncle, for instance, is currently employed by a shipping company in Malaysia. She also mentioned that it's highly esteemed in Nepal to forge friendships with foreigners, as young Nepalese individuals constantly seek opportunities to work abroad. My mother is discussing with her friend on the phone, mentioning that over fourteen thousand young people in Kathmandu took the "Qualification Examination for Korean Language Unified Employment Abroad" last week.

I eagerly longed to meet our new neighbor right away. I yearned to befriend a foreigner, especially someone from China. I envisioned sharing my report card with her, expressing my desire to visit China, see the Great Wall, learn Chinese, and study there.

However, after lifting our door curtain several times and finding the brown wooden door opposite still closed, I couldn't help but feel disappointed.

My mother noticed my preoccupation and gently braided my hair as she spoke reassuringly: "She only arrived yesterday. Perhaps she's adjusting to the time difference (Nepal is two hours ahead of China). I'm sure she needs some rest today. You'll likely meet her when you return from school in the evening."

## V

At school, time seemed to drag on unusually slowly. During lunchtime, I sat with my close friend Ashiya. I excitedly shared the news about our new Chinese neighbor next door, filling her with envy.

I've had the pleasure of meeting Ashiya's father before; he's a Nepali truck driver who always sings China's praises. Ashiya shared that he hasn't forgotten the hardships caused by India's blockade against Nepal in 2015, and he remains grateful for the assistance provided by the Chinese government during that critical time. His fervent wish is for Ashiya to learn Chinese, study in China, and forge friendships with Chinese people in the future.

As school ended at six o'clock, my mother awaited me at the gate.

When I spotted her, I couldn't contain my excitement and questioned her, "Mom, did you meet the Chinese lady? Did you talk to her? How is she?"

Standing behind me, Mother adjusted my backpack with both hands and shared, "Yes, we had a chat. She even gave each neighbor a little gift—a red 'Chinese knot.' She explained that it's a traditional Chinese gift believed to bring luck. My English is limited, but I can understand that much."

"I'm familiar with 'Chinese knots.' Last term, a student volunteer from China gifted our school a large one. They even taught us how to make them."

"Shiristi, let's be respectful. Instead of referring to her as the 'Chinese lady,' remember, she has a name. Her name is Surya."

My mother draped her arm around my shoulder and lowered her head to speak to me.

"Surya?! What a beautiful name! In Nepali, it means 'sun.'" I playfully flicked my right index finger near my ear a few times, gently tugging Mother's arm back and hopping backward as I teased her.

"Yes, her Chinese name is hard for us to remember. She mentioned that even her Nepali friends struggled to recall it, so she adopted a Nepali name, Surya. It instantly stuck with us. Heh, heh, it's quite a special name." Mother giggled, covering her mouth with one hand, a habit of hers while speaking.

My footsteps quickened, almost like I was eager to sprint back home immediately.

## VI

In Nepal, dinner typically takes place around eight, sometimes even later. It's customary for us to switch off the lights after dinner and retire to bed early to conserve electricity. However, many individuals rise around five in the morning, as adults believe the air is freshest before the sun ascends.

As we neared home, my mother went to the nearby store to buy vegetables while I eagerly made my way toward the large iron gate of our yard. Just as I rounded the corner of the alley, I encountered a young woman who appeared to be a student. She carried a bag with toothpaste in one hand and a box of tea leaves in the other, imploring passing pedestrians, "Please help me! I'm a business student, and this semester is my internship. I need to sell some items to customers to pass and graduate."

Observing people sidestep her without making purchases stirred a sense of sympathy. Suddenly, my thoughts turned to Surya: "She just arrived yesterday; she must need something!"

I waved to the intern, suggesting that someone might be interested in her items, and eagerly guided her to push open the gate of our yard. We swiftly ascended the stairs to our upstairs.

However, Surya's door remained shut.

Undeterred, I felt confident that Surya would appreciate me. Approaching her door, I raised my hand and lightly knocked a few times, calling out excitedly, "Excuse me!"

The door swung open, revealing Surya dressed in a light yellow T-shirt paired with jeans. Across her chest, the T-shirt bore a line of black English words: "Just do it." Her hair cascaded freely over her shoulders, lending her a youthful appearance. At that moment, I estimated her age to be around thirty, possibly younger than my mother. With one hand holding the door ajar, she held a pen in the other as though she had been writing something.

As Surya caught sight of me and the intern, she appeared slightly bewildered, unsure of what was happening.

Without waiting for Surya's response, I eagerly pointed to the intern and exclaimed, "Hello! She's a business trainee. The items she's selling might be just what you need. If you purchase from her, she can graduate!"

Driven by my enthusiasm, I pulled the intern into Surya's room without her consent.

Setting the bag down, the intern began to unpack, revealing toothbrushes, hand soap, wet wipes, mosquito repellent, tea leaves, and even diapers.

Upon hearing the intern's introduction, Surya shook her head and smiled, "Thank you, but I already have these items. And I certainly don't need diapers!"

I stood by, feeling a bit anxious for the intern.

"Please consider buying something. If you make a purchase, she can graduate! Without your support, she might not be able to pass!"

"Don't Chinese people have money? Surya is Chinese; she must have money. But why won't she help?"

I couldn't help but feel disappointed upon seeing Surya decline to buy anything.

"Shiristi!" my mother's voice rang out, elongating the last letter of my name.

Startled by the call, the intern seemed flustered and hastily packed her belongings into her bag before departing.

"You can't simply bring strangers into our yard! Surya is new to Nepal; she doesn't know anyone, and it's inappropriate to bring strangers into her room!" my mother scolded me sternly as she called me into the house.

I didn't argue back as usual; instead, I sulked on the ground, completing my homework silently and joylessly. A hint of resentment began to brew within me towards Surya. I felt she wasn't very friendly because she was unwilling to help others. Once finishing my assignments, I sought solace in playing with Mina at my aunt's house on the first floor, feeling bored and disheartened. Eventually, I trudged back up to the second floor, my steps heavy and disappointed. The clicking sound of my mother's thick, hard plastic slippers echoed on the staircase as I ascended.

"Shiristi, I have a gift for you!"

Surya's voice reached my ears as she appeared at her door.

"A gift!"

Upon hearing these words, I immediately perked up.

"It's an automatic pencil. I know you're a kind-hearted child, and I appreciate your concern today," Surya explained as she handed me the pencil. "However, I don't require the items the student is selling. Moreover, as a business student, she needs to develop her sales skills independently rather than relying solely on others' assistance and sympathy."

"Wow, what a beautiful pencil! A small pink plastic doll holds a rubber ball on top, and the pen shaft is covered with cartoon patterns. This is the most beautiful pen I've ever seen!"

My mouth was wide open, completely ignoring what she was saying.

"Made in China! Hmph, Qianda will never make me jealous of the pencils her dad bought from Korea again!"

I turned over the gift repeatedly, even carefully reading the English on it. My mind was filled with joy and pride, completely forgetting that I had once said I didn't like Surya.

## VII

School ended a bit early today. As soon as I reached the corner, I saw a square machine making a hissing sound hanging on the balcony of Surya's room.

"Wow, the Chinese are really rich! It seems like no one in our area has air conditioning yet. After following my sister to the KL Tower shopping mall, I only learned what air conditioning was. It was so cool and comfortable inside!"

I widened my eyes with amazement.

Just as I pushed open the iron gate of the yard, I saw Surya gesturing with little Doha's mother on the first floor. They couldn't understand each other's language and were smiling awkwardly.

They seemed to have found a savior when they saw me enter and immediately started talking to me. Surya spoke in English, and little Doha's mother spoke in Nepali, hoping I would translate for them.

Doha's mother pointed to a pink plastic pipe at the corner of the wall outside her room. She asked me to ask Surya if the water from the pipe could be drunk because it was icy cold. Her son Doha had secretly drunk from the pipe several times when she wasn't looking.

I took two steps back and looked up along the pipe, seeing it connected to the air conditioner upstairs, with clear water flowing out of it.

Doha, who is five years old and a mischievous little boy, stood at his doorstep, holding his head and grinning proudly at us.

I translated Doha's mother's words to Surya, and she quickly shook her head, saying, "No, no! The water from the pipe cannot be drunk!"

"She said it can't be drunk," I turned to tell Doha's mother.

"Then why did she shake her head but say it can't be drunk?" Doha's mother asked me, frowning in confusion.

This question stumped me for a moment. I blinked and thought for a while, then realized that shaking my head means yes in Nepal, and nodding means no!

"But your aunt said it can be drunk! She said the air conditioner installer told her. She also said this water is cleaner than the water in our tank," Doha's mother said, still puzzled after hearing my explanation.

When I asked Surya again, this question also seemed to stump her. Indeed, the water stored in the tank in our yard looked much dirtier than this water.

She frowned, thought for a while, and then said uncertainly, "I really don't know! But I think it's best not to drink it. The water looks clear but comes from a machine, so it's not sanitary."

After speaking, Surya rolled up the pipe and hung it high. Now, little Doha couldn't reach it anymore.

"Oh, my, what's happening! The air conditioner at home is leaking water!"

Shortly after, we heard Surya open the door and run downstairs, shouting.

Mom and I didn't know what was happening, so we rushed out of the house and followed her downstairs.

It turned out that after she rolled up the drainage pipe, the water from the air conditioner flowed back and was now gushing out from the wall of her room.

*Meri abassai* (Oh my God)! It was hilarious!

## VIII

"Shiristi, see if Surya has hung a curtain on her door. She won't close the door anymore."

A few days later, Mom quietly told me after waking me up in the morning.

I jumped out of bed and ran to lift the curtain at our door, seeing a cloth curtain hanging on the opposite door. The floral cloth was beautiful, with yellow sunflowers on a light green background.

A week passed, and I became friends with Surya. She showed me the children's storybooks she had brought, told me about China, and wrote my name in Chinese on paper for me to keep. Oh, I liked her so much.

One day, I discovered she had a hobby: she liked eating chicken feet. On the weekend, I took her to the meat shop to buy some, but they said they would give them to her for free because Nepali people don't eat them. She was so happy and let me try some after cooking them. Afraid Mom would be unhappy if she found out, I secretly tasted a bit in her room. Wow, it was so delicious.

This time, I couldn't help but tell her, "I like you so much!"

"Then can you tell me what you like about me?" she asked with a smile.

"Well, you are very friendly, you are very beautiful, you know many things I don't know, and your room has cool air conditioning. My mom likes listening to you talk; she thinks your voice is pleasant. She wants to chat with you but regrets needing me to translate because her English is limited."

Oh, I couldn't seem to say much. In the end, we made a deal not to litter anymore.

That day, Upendra notified us tenants that we had to move out within a month because Surya would rent the entire house to turn it into a family inn. We were all very sad and didn't want to leave, but we had no choice.

I told Mom, "Surya will need workers for her family inn. Ask her to hire you so I can see her every day."

"You're so smart. I've already asked. She said it's still in the planning stage and won't hire anyone yet, but maybe in the future," Mom said, tapping my forehead with her henna-stained finger.

Hearing Mom's words, I was so disappointed that I almost cried.

My aunt's daughter Mina's birthday was this weekend, and Mom and Aunt were discussing how to celebrate.

"We must invite Surya!" I shouted from the side.

Mom and Aunt both laughed, "We will definitely invite her. We all like her. Since we're moving next week, we'll invite her to enjoy Nepali cuisine."

Alas! If only we could continue living here, even if it was nearby. But Mom asked many people, and they all said there were no vacant rooms for rent, so we had to move to the far west. But I will remember and miss her, Surya, a Chinese woman who brought beautiful memories to me.

# Shoemaker Old Zeng

## I

It was a Sunday in Nanchong, northeast of Sichuan Province, China. The lingering summer heat made it a bit sultry, but a gentle breeze and a few fan swipes made people under the shade of a tree feel pleasantly cool.

It was just past six o'clock in the morning, and the cicadas in the trees had already begun their rhythmic chirping. Some villagers, heading to the early market, had made their way into the urban area, shouldering baskets and carrying goods on shoulder poles. An old farmer with a chicken tied to his shoulder pole was among them. Suddenly, the chicken broke free with a swift whoosh, startling the old farmer, who dropped his basket and chased after it. The chicken hopped and squawked, landing right before the shoemaker, Old Zeng.

"For country fellows, it is not easy to raise chickens and ducks! They keep you on your toes. Morning, bro!"

Old Zeng swiftly approached, deftly catching the chicken by its wings and setting it into his basket, where it settled without protest.

"Nice and cool this morning, isn't it? Morning! Thanks a lot!"

The old farmer, dressed in a simple white coat and shorts, with grass shoes on his feet and a weathered straw hat atop his head, bade farewell before shouldering his pole and disappearing into the distance.

Old Zeng lived in Duweiba Township on the far side of the Xiqiaohe River, where he had learned his trade from his father in his youth. As his father aged and could no longer work, Old Zeng would trek to Nanchong city, carrying his shoulder pole basket. He had set up his shoe repair stall near the People's Club by Wuxing Garden, a routine he had maintained for over a decade. During this time, he witnessed many events and encountered diverse people. Once, he even received a pair of high heels for repair, though he was at a loss as to how to mend them. Taking them home, he handed them over to his wife to try, nearly causing her to sprain her foot in the process. After that mishap, his wife often boasted in the township about her experience, claiming she had once worn high heels despite foot-binding traditions. Later, the

People's Club transformed into a People's Cinema, leading Old Zeng and his fellow shoemaker, Wuwa, to be relocated to a corner near the cinema stairs.

Old Zeng wore a weathered, long band across his chest, his hands bearing calluses, with fingertips marked by blackened wrinkles and nails, some areas adorned with adhesive plasters. There was a copper pin on his right ring finger, and he wore a pair of straw sandals made from woven grass. Perched on a foldable canvas stool, he leaned against a tall eucalyptus tree, a shiny bamboo shoulder pole propped beside him. Neatly arranged in front of him on a wooden box were various repaired shoes, some paired, some solitary. To his right sat a hefty iron shoe stirrup last for hammering nails, while to his left rested a bamboo basket brimming with shoes for repair and materials for mending.

The movie today was The Story of Liubao Village, its poster showcasing a truly stunning actress.

Gradually, ice cream and cold water vendors, sugarcane sellers, bicycle repairmen, and people intending to see the Zoetrope (a device for watching animations through narrow slits) gathered around.

Old Zeng's first customer was a young boy who brought in a pair of shoes, explaining that the sole was coming off and needed to be glued. He planned to pick them up after the movie ended.

As the sun climbed higher, the sky turned piercingly blue, devoid of clouds. Summer had entered its second phase. Only a few people rode bicycles along the road, mostly some pulling rickshaws. Dust occasionally swirled up from the gravel road. Pedestrians mostly strolled along the stone-paved paths on either side, each person fanning themselves against the heat. Elderly individuals wielded palm-leaf fans, while younger ones chose reed fans, giving them a slightly exotic air.

"I saw a crazy woman singing at the chicken market yesterday. Surprisingly, she has quite a voice," remarked two young women as they walked by.

"Oh, the woman you mean? I saw her near the Siji Mall last time, singing to her children. She had her face painted, looking rather pitiful."

As they chatted, they indulged in refreshing white sugar ice creams.

Old Zeng overheard their conversation and quietly pondered, "How come I've never witnessed such a lively scene in front of the cinema before?"

## II

"Up early on Sunday, Old Zeng?"

"Old Zeng, I need a rubber sole for my newly made shoes."

"Off to the movie again? The Story of Liubao Village—good flick, great tunes."

Though Old Zeng hadn't seen it, he had heard the chatter after the screenings.

"Youth in the Flames of War is tops. Cross-dressing and battles—more thrilling."

A young man dropped his Jiefang shoes off and dashed to the cinema.

"Still holding onto those shoes, Old Zeng? I offered to buy them, but you won't budget."

A woman gestured to a pair of shoes leaning against the tree.

"Sister Zhang, my father always said I must have a conscience, even in shoe repair. What if the owner comes for them?"

"It's been six months already. If they were coming back, they would have by now. My daughter's feet have outgrown them, and I no longer need them. I won't bother you further. I have to catch the bus to Dujingba Township for work."

With that, she hurried off towards Mofanjie Street.

Sister Zhang was referring to a pair of dark red leather sandals for children, punched with petal-shaped holes, which looked like high-quality shoes at first glance. Most children from ordinary families wore homemade cloth shoes, so having rubber soles added was considered a luxury. They were certainly not the shoes a child from an ordinary family would wear. Old Zeng vividly remembered that they belonged to a young woman—tall, with two braids tied up into a big bun at the back of her head, wearing a corduroy coat, and speaking in a foreign dialect. Old Zeng had even examined the shoes then and estimated they were for a seven- or eight-year-old girl based on the size. The leather was of good quality, but the heels were badly worn, and the buckle on the side was loose, needing a piece of similar leather and a few stitches to fix.

The repair had long been done, but the woman had never returned to collect them. With so many people coming and going daily, Old Zeng never saw her again.

### III

After finishing the cold noodles his wife made for him and gulping down the porridge from his lunchbox, Old Zeng started feeling drowsy. He lifted his head, leaned his whole body against the tree trunk behind him, and drifted into a half-asleep state. A cool breeze blew by, and he faintly heard some pleasant singing from a distance:

"The moon wanders through clouds like white lotus flowers, and the evening breeze brings bursts of joyful singing. We sit beside the tall stacks of grain, listening to our mother recounting the past events. We sit beside the tall stacks of grain, listening to our mother recounting the past stories."

"Hey, don't underestimate her. She sings better than Guo Lanying (the song's original singer)."

"Where did this crazy woman come from? So eerie!"

"You don't know, huh? She's been around for a long time. She runs around singing this song every day."

"Thank you. Don't say anymore! Let's listen to her sing!"

The song was accompanied by some noisy chatter.

Old Zeng, in his drowsy state, felt like he was dreaming. The clamor sounded like the lively scene under the stage in their village, where they used to listen to Sichuan Opera. The actors would start banging drums and gongs before they even appeared on stage, and when they finally did, they would strike a pose and start singing.

But this girl's singing was really nice. Old Zeng listened agape, drooling a little from the corner of his mouth.

Suddenly, the singing stopped, and he heard someone shouting, "Don't touch them!"

This shout jolted Old Zeng awake from his dreamlike state. He opened his eyes abruptly and saw a dirty woman standing before him with disheveled hair, staring fixedly at that pair of leather sandals.

This woman was tall, with a thin face and unkempt hair. She wore an unidentifiable open-front shirt and dark blue pants, and her feet were in wooden sandals. She quietly knelt on the ground, holding one of the shoes in one hand and gently caressing it with the other as if she were caressing her own child.

"It's the crazy woman again; why does she like those shoes? She can't fit into those shoes either," the old lady selling cold water said loudly, laughing as she spoke.

"Old Zeng, this lady fell in love with you!" Wuwa yelled at him with a tilted head.

"Crazy woman, sing another one," a passerby teased her.

No matter how people teased or provoked her, her hands repeatedly caressed the shoes, and a faint smile appeared.

Old Zeng was stunned by the scene before him. Through the messy hair of the crazy woman, he vaguely saw something familiar.

"It's her, the owner of the shoes I've been waiting for for six months!" Old Zeng suddenly realized.

"These shoes belong to your daughter. You brought them to me for repair half a year ago. Look, they're fixed now," Old Zeng eagerly explained as he picked up the shoes and handed them to the woman.

The woman snatched the shoes from his hand, hugged them to her chest, and stared blankly at him for a couple of seconds before swiftly standing up and staggering away.

This sudden action caught Old Zeng and the onlookers by surprise. For a moment, everyone was speechless, staring in astonishment as they watched her leave.

After that, Old Zeng never saw the woman again.

Later, he learned from another woman who came to have her shoes repaired that the crazy woman had a tragic story. Her husband, originally an accountant from Guangdong Province who had been assigned to their countryside, couldn't endure the loneliness and hardships of rural life. He sneaked into Hong Kong alone, sending money twice and some clothes, including the children's leather shoes, but vanished without a trace. Less than two years later, her only daughter died of pneumonia due to a severe fever. Unable to bear the double blow, the woman lost her sanity. However, it was rumored that her condition gradually improved after she received her daughter's shoes, and at least she stopped wandering aimlessly.

The story of the crazy woman spread widely in Nanchong, with several versions circulating. Sister Zhang seemed to have heard about it, too.

One day, she passed by Old Zeng's shoe stall and remarked, "You repaired her shoes and kept them for six months but didn't get a penny. It's not worth it."

Old Zeng remained focused on repairing the shoes in his hands, not bothering to lift his head.

"Sister Zhang, don't speak nonsense. Let me tell you, it's a blessing that I kept them for her. Haven't you heard? She got better when she saw the shoes, as if she had seen her child again. Saving a life outweighs building a seven-storied pagoda! As my father always said, one must have a conscience!"

# Walking Over the Bridge

In our city of Nanchong, Sichuan Province, China, there's a prevailing custom among older women to adopt their husband's surname. Auntie Tang, whose actual surname is Du, is universally known as Auntie Tang due to her husband's surname being Tang.

Auntie Tang's husband is a skilled clock repairer. He is not particularly advanced in age, probably in his thirties. He's tall and thin, not much of a talker, always adorned with thick glasses, and has a polite and cultured demeanor that gives him a somewhat elderly appearance. When my mother was putting me to sleep, the melodic strains of Mr. Tang playing the erhu next door often drifted in. The rhythm of my mother's hand clapping me to sleep was like a beat to his melody. His deep, mellow playing often served as a soothing lullaby for me. Growing up, my mother mentioned that Mr. Tang's family was well-off in his youth. Their clock shop was a family heirloom, and he learned the craft from his father, intending to inherit the business from him. However, with reforms, the shop transitioned into state ownership, and he became a salaried clerk.

I don't remember if I started calling him "Uncle Tang" or if my mother did, but that's what we both called him.

I vividly recall the most magnificent clock shop on Renmin Middle Road in Nanchong. Auntie Tang would often take me there in the afternoons. On our return journey, we'd buy fresh spring onions, garlic shoots, and other vegetables from the market.

My favorite part of visiting Uncle Tang's clock shop was standing beneath the large clock in the entrance hall, gazing up at the owl with its big eyes rotating left and right. My eyes would track its movements, eagerly waiting for it to chime "ding-dong" every half hour and "ding-dong-ding-dong" every hour. As a child not yet four years old, I couldn't understand how its eyes moved or how it knew when to chime. I was convinced that there must be a tiny person inside it.

Upon entering, you would find Uncle Tang's repair counter behind a tall wooden cabinet to the right. Each time I saw him, he wore a magnifying glass over his right eye, framed by numerous copper rings. The glasses had no hooks, making it a marvel how they stayed on. I would always insist on trying them, too. When I called out, Auntie Tang would lift me up from the ground, and Uncle Tang would remove the magical contraption. With a "hey," it would miraculously fit between his upper and lower eyelids. I would grin happily, and Auntie Tang would beam proudly.

Sometimes, when there were no customers in the shop, Auntie Tang would point to the watches in the glass case one by one, saying, "This is a Swiss watch; this is a Roman watch; this is a Tianjin watch; and there's the Seagull watch and the Shanghai watch." Whenever she said "watch," she elongated the word like an expert. I didn't understand much, but I knew the ones with the golden hands must be expensive because my mother had a ring of that color.

Auntie Tang was short, with short hair clipped with two steel hairpins above her ears. She was said to be a distant relative of Uncle Tang from the rural town of Banqiao Town, Xichong County. She didn't have a job or children. Besides housework, one thing she did every day was to wash Uncle Tang's white satin shirt.

Sometimes, she would mutter, "Your Uncle Tang is so particular; his clothes mustn't have any wrinkles." Ordinary households didn't have electric irons, so she washed the shirt and stashed it with rice water. She would then hang one end of a shiny bamboo stick on a branch in front of the door, slip one sleeve of the starched shirt over it, then the other, and use both hands to gently pull and smooth out the wrinkles. Finally, she would use a clothespin to lift the other end of the bamboo stick and hang it on another branch. With the shirt fluttering in the breeze, it looked like a kite dancing in the wind.

My father served in the border troops in distant Tibet and could only come home once a year. My mother was a caregiver in the Nanchong Military Sub-Region Headquarters and usually had no free time. Seeing me, my mother fretted. She wrote to my father suggesting that they give some money to Auntie Tang and ask her to take care of me at home. Auntie Tang agreed but refused to take any money, and she even often gave me some extra change to buy snacks. These included sesame candies, orange slices, dried persimmon slices, a piece of sugarcane, or my favorites, *guokui* with *liangfen* (crispy pancakes with bean jelly ) and fried peas.

When my mother found out, she felt guilty, but Auntie Tang said, "It's okay; the money I saved buying cheap vegetables is enough."

It was July 1, 1975. Auntie Tang was very busy those days, taking me to the "New Market," "First Market," or "Wuli Shop" every day to buy fresh chili peppers to make chili sauce. That day, she bought two baskets of fresh red peppers, cut off each stem with scissors, and then fetched two buckets of water from the well near the yard. After washing and drying them, she poured them into a large wooden basin usually used for bathing, placed the cutting board in the middle, picked up her knife, and began chopping.

She chopped while chatting with me: "The child who spat into the well got caught again today. His father doesn't care, so I'll help them punish him!"

"The chili sauce made at home is tastier and fresher; it can last a whole year."

Then she said, "Today is July 1, the birthday of the Communist Party of China. We'll see the bridge opening after I mince the chili peppers."

"My mom told me yesterday that today's bridge opening will be lively."

I loved lively events, especially when Auntie Tang took me because there would always be delicious food.

I obediently stood aside, picked up a fire hook, and drew on the ground before the door.

"A nail doesn't stick out, hang two small leather balls in the house, don't eat for three days and nights, and spin with hunger."

This was how Auntie Tang taught me to draw a human face.

Perhaps Auntie Tang was too focused; she didn't notice as I approached the large wooden basin. Suddenly, a grain of chili pepper jumped into my eye. I threw the fire hook and burst into tears, rubbing my eyes vigorously with both hands.

Trouble—both eyes were burning.

"Oh my god, what should we do!"

Auntie Tang stood alarmed and disregarded everything to pry my hands away.

I cried and screamed loudly, "My eyes hurt so much!!"

Auntie Tang panicked, picking me up and comforting me, promising to buy me candies. I didn't listen or want anything. I kicked my feet frantically, only aware of the pain.

Perhaps tears washed away the chili, and gradually, my eyes didn't hurt as much, but they still stung and wouldn't open properly.

Auntie Tang held me with one hand and pointed to the flowers by the roadside with the other, saying, "Look, look at these beautiful flowers. It's the oleander flowers you like the most."

I still didn't want to open my eyes.

She picked one and handed it to me, saying, "Look, don't you always ask me to pick them for you?"

I stopped crying and reluctantly opened my eyelids slightly, vaguely seeing a pinkish-red color. I petulantly knocked the flower out of her hand and continued to cry.

Maybe from crying too much, my voice wasn't as loud, and I heard a voice floating by, "What's wrong with this child, crying so loudly? Are you abducting the child?"

"Damn it, you're the one who stole the child!" I heard Auntie Tang retort angrily.

Then, I heard cries of "Sesame candy! Knock sesame candy!"

"Tossed Clear Noodles in Chili Sauce!"

*"Guokui with liangfen!"*

A string of melodious shouts drifted away from me. I leaned against Auntie Tang's shoulder, my sobbing gradually weakening, and I could hear her breathing clearly.

Auntie Tang carried me from Heping West Road to the Red Guards' Garden, passing by the Municipal Committee Building and the Geological Bureau and then walking along the riverside to the intersection of Mofan Street. Gradually, I heard the deafening sound of gongs and drums, "clang-clang-dong-dong," followed by the crackling of firecrackers.

I stopped sobbing, thinking people were celebrating the Chinese Lunar New Year, and my eyes didn't hurt as much. Auntie Tang saw my eyes were open, and her worried expression softened.

"I told you, today we have something lively to see. Look, the Jialing River Bridge is opening."

"What's going on? My sugar cane and sesame rods have been removed from their pan!" I heard an old man shout. Several women were busy around him, paying him no attention.

Auntie Tang put me down and helped the old man pick up the fallen pan full of sugar cane and sesame rods. Then she took out a coin, saying she would buy them for me to eat.

The old man quickly pulled a piece of paper from his waist pocket, picked up two pieces, and said, "No need for money; I won't sell them either. Take them back for the child to eat. I've never walked over the bridge; today's a good day."

Auntie Tang took the sugar cane from the paper, blew off the dust symbolically, broke it into small pieces and put one in my mouth.

"Quickly, let's go walk over the bridge!"

It was like a bustling rural market, with people coming and going. People from dozens of miles away had come, and it was as lively as New Year's Day, with firecrackers going off and the big gongs on Liberation brand trucks being banged by four people. Some were dancing, some were playing waist drums, the ferry boats on the river honked, and there were hundreds of cars.

I had seen people dancing and playing waist drums before but had never seen so many cars together. At that moment, my eyes widened like saucers.

After stowing away his scales and poles, a straw hat man grabbed the unsold small cabbage and joined the crowd.

Someone asked if he could buy them, and the old man said, "Come with me; you can't sell on the bridge; follow me, I'll sell them to you at a lower price when we get there."

Oh, that bridge felt so long, like I could never reach the end. Gradually, I lost interest in crossing it, and my eyes started hurting again. I began to sob, saying my eyes hurt and I couldn't walk anymore, asking Auntie Tang to carry me.

Auntie Tang had no choice but to squat down, bend over, and let me place my hands on her shoulders. She picked me up and continued walking.

I don't remember how long we walked, only hearing many people on the bridge talking:

"This is my second round trip already."

"This bridge is great; we have no need to take the ferry anymore!"

"The ferry costs two cents each way and four cents for a round trip to sell vegetables. You can't even earn a few cents daily if you don't make money."

"It's convenient to go to Longmen market now, huh?"

"It's even more convenient for us in Gaopingba, huh?"

"Did you know this bridge is over 780 meters long? It's quite a walk."

I vaguely remember Auntie Tang's back being soft, like a broad and sturdy bed. With every step she took and every sway of her body, I felt like I was sleeping in a mother's cradle.

"What's so good about this bridge? It hurts to walk; it's better to take the boat!"

I murmured, nested on Auntie Tang's back, and gradually fell asleep.

....

The next time, and the last time I saw Auntie Tang, was almost 40 years later. Uncle Tang had been gone for many years, and Auntie Tang's back was too old to carry me anymore. When she saw me, her face lit up like a beautiful flower, while I hugged her with tears streaming down my face.

When she heard that I had returned from abroad and came to visit her that day, she slapped her thigh and said, "I knew this girl was special. See, was I right or what?!"

I quickly said, "Auntie Tang, I came today to bring you a gift."

She waved her hand dismissively, "No need, no need. I lack nothing. Look, the house I live in was given to me by the government as affordable housing. Life is getting better and better!"

I said, "Auntie Tang, I know you lack nothing. My gift for you today is to take us on a walk across all four bridges in Nanchong."

"Lass, things have changed a lot. I've heard that there are already four bridges over the Jialing River in Nanchong, but I haven't been there. I can't walk anymore. Unlike the old days, I could carry you, a big lump, and run so fast."

Holding her, I said, "Auntie Tang, we won't walk today. We'll take a car and follow the route we used to take to walk the bridges, and then we'll walk each of the four bridges."

"You've really thought this through, girl. Auntie Tang has been lucky in this life."

At that moment, I saw tears shimmering in Auntie Tang's eyes.

# San Er Passed Away

## I

Jia Wen rose from the bed as he typically did early Saturday. Glancing at the clock on the opposite wall, he noted it was only half past five.

He slipped into a vest and socks, his steps soft on the plush carpet as he tiptoed to the door of the adjacent room. Peering through the crack, he observed the night light still softly illuminating the foot of the bed, and his wife, still asleep, emitted a gentle snore. Suppressing a smile, he returned to his room, gently closing the door behind him.

As he turned to open the blinds, the dazzling sunlight instantly blinded him. Outside the window, snowflakes like goose feathers drifted slowly downward.

"Alas! What a snow in April!" he sighed, resigned to the unpredictable weather.

Winter seemed particularly prolonged in Alberta, western Canada, this year. Yet, for him, the temperature mattered less than the presence of sunshine. He loathed this sunless weather, which left him inexplicably melancholic.

"Let's catch up on the news," he muttered, settling at his desk with a hint of despondency and powering up the computer with his thumb. The bulky desktop made a familiar "click" as it whirred to life, reminiscent of an old car revving its engine.

The headline on the BBC was a "Titanic Tragedy Special Memorial Event". Today was April 15, 2012—the 100th anniversary of its sinking.

Bad weather and headlines of a significant tragedy—his heart sank again as he sighed deeply. With little inclination to read the news, he reached for a weathered candy box produced in Hong Kong labeled *fada* (Prosperous) on the bookshelf. Inside lay a *New Testament* with yellowed pages and a black sheepskin cover. His mother, who had lived to be 102 years old, had passed away just a few months ago. Her final wish to her son, uttered before her passing, had been unexpectedly about his embracing the church and becoming a child of the Almighty God in his lifetime.

This request wasn't burdensome, but it felt somewhat contrived to him as a materialistic thinker. Although he had not formally attended the church, his mother's wish weighed heavily on his mind. Recently, he had found himself compelled to delve into his mother's thoughts. The paper of this Bible was as thin as silk, bearing the inscription "Presented to Lianfen, from Yucheng in 1947" on the title page. Handwritten annotations adorned the blank spaces of the scripture pages, some faded, serving as a testament to his mother's cherished possession. His mother wouldn't have preserved and studied this book for decades without her reverence. The act of devotion deeply impressed him. This book, preserved and cherished by his mother for so long, offered a glimpse into her unwavering faith, and the person who gifted it to her must have held a special place in her heart.

The snow outside became more fierce, and the sky turned foggy. He stared blankly out of the window. A gust of wind was blowing snow from the opposite roof, and his mood changed from melancholy to anxiety and to fear.

Alas! He was an old man now. His physical ailments increased, and his artistic sensibilities became more volatile. Once, upon hearing an old song from a popular TV series during his university days, he found his eyes welled up with tears.

His wife had teased him, saying, "How did you become as sentimental as a woman?"

He remained silent, not refuting her words, understanding that it was entirely due to his advancing age and growing experiences. He had begun to reminisce more often, and the softness in his nature had gradually emerged, making him more sentimental. Wasn't this exactly what his mother used to talk to him about?

As the snowfall gradually lessened and the sky began to clear, the neighbor next door started shoveling snow, the iron shovel making a rustling sound as it penetrated the snow layer.

He put on a thick coat, a hat, a scarf, and gloves and opened the garage door. Carefully, he used the shovel to pile the snow on both sides of the driveway and sidewalk, then used the snow blower to clear the snow connecting to the neighbor's path. By the time everything was tidy, his wife had already prepared breakfast.

**II**

Jia Wen planned to go to the bank to deposit a check today and then head to the post office to send a meticulously crafted painting to his classmate Guangwei, who resided in Hong Kong. Guangwei was the eldest among their four roommates during his time at the National Taiwan University of Arts, affectionately referred to as "Big Wei" ( 伟 大 , Greatest) in jest, following their age order. With Big Wei's youngest son set to marry this summer, he had requested a gift from his friend, an already renowned painter, a meticulously crafted painting as the most appropriate wedding present.

Starting with the post office, Jia Wen mailed the carefully packaged painting before proceeding to a nearby bank.

Upon entering the bank on Saturday morning, the lobby was relatively quiet.

Just as he reached the waiting sign, a lady with a bright smile appeared behind the counter, introducing herself with, "Good morning, sir! My name is Nancy. How can I help you?"

Presenting his wallet, Jia Wen retrieved a cheque and handed it to Nancy with both hands.

"Hello! I'd like to deposit this cheque, please."

Nancy's fingers moved swiftly, making rhythmic "clack" sounds as they tapped on the keyboard, almost as if engaged in a joyful dance.

Later, she inquired quietly, "Would you like a printed statement of your account balance?"

"Yes, please. Thank you!"

"Your account balance is, um ...." Nancy's voice trailed off as she reached for the slip emerging from the printer. Suddenly, her smiling face froze.

Her eyes locked onto the slip of paper with a peculiar expression akin to someone who had seen a ghost or hit the jackpot. She was so engrossed that she nearly forgot to hand the paper to the waiting customer.

Jia Wen stood patiently in front of the counter, squinting slightly as he waited for clarification, his brow furrowed in curiosity.

Upon regaining her composure, Nancy handed him the note, her eyes widening incredulity.

"Oh my God! I've never seen anything like this before."

Jia Wen quickly took the slip and examined it. The account balance displayed $33333.33. His heart skipped a beat, taken aback by the striking figure!

He pocketed the slip without much thought, exiting the bank and going home.

**III**

When Jia Wen returned home, he found his wife had already gone. A note on the table indicated that she had left lunch prepared, and it read, "Our daughter called that our grandson had a slight cough, so I've gone to offer some steamed sugar water. Lunch is ready; help yourself."

He placed the bank-printed slip in a large envelope filled with various receipts, intending to sort through them later. Just as he was about to sit down for lunch, the phone rang, interrupting him with its persistent chime.

Answering with a simple "Hello," he was met with an urgent voice on the other end.

"Is this Jia Er speaking?"

"Yes, Big Wei," he responded, recognizing the caller's nickname.

"I just sent the meticulous painting this morning. Hey, don't worry. It's already framed and ready to be hung in your son's new house."

The mention of "Jia Er" instantly identified the caller.

"Jia Er, I'm not calling about that. Have you heard San Er, our roommate, has passed away? He is gone! He just died yesterday. He was on a business trip to Australia for a conference, but he drowned while swimming alone in the sea. His wife and children all rushed to Australia today."

Big Wei's words poured out in a rush; his voice increasingly choked, devoid of any jest.

"Ah! How could this happen …."

Jia Wen sank onto the sofa, his mind reeling.

San Er, whose real name was Cheng Wanshan, was the third oldest among the four roommates. With the name Shan sounding San in some Chinese dialects, they affectionately called him "San Er." He had grown up near the sea from a family of fishermen, often claiming that seawater was as essential to him as air. He was always drawn to the water and would dive in whenever he saw the sea. Who would have thought he had drowned himself?

Jia Wen sat on the sofa, reminiscing about the times he and San Er had spent sketching on the streets and in parks, visiting the library, dining out, and sharing late-night snacks during their university days. Waves of sorrow washed over him, tears welling up in his eyes.

Suddenly, the numbers printed on the bank slip flashed in his mind. Rushing to the drawer, he retrieved the slip of paper with trembling hands. Tears streaming down his face as he stared at the figures. He was convinced that 33333.33 was a message from heaven, a sign of his sincere roommate and friend, San Er, being in trouble—perhaps even deceased!

The heavens seemed to have spoken, and his late mother's words echoed in his mind. With tomorrow being Sunday, he made a firm decision to attend church.

*Manna Liu*（嘉妮）

# Naturalization

The citizenship oath ceremony for Chen Guangze was scheduled for ten o'clock the next morning. He had meticulously double-checked his essentials the night before, anxious not to forget anything. He even rehearsed the Canadian national anthem, "O, Canada!" several times to ensure he remembered the lyrics for the ceremony. Setting his alarm for eight in the morning, he allotted ample time for a refreshing shower.

Given the inconvenience of parking in the city center, he had taken some change from his elephant-shaped piggy bank to purchase bus tickets the previous night. He vividly recalled acquiring this piggy bank from an antique shop shortly after he arrived in Canada. His ex-wife, Amy, keen to conceal her age, humorously claimed she was born in the Year of the Elephant. They stumbled upon the piggy bank during their first month of immigration, and she eagerly spent two dollars on it.

From childhood, Chen harbored a superstitious belief in the adage that good things come after hardship. Recognizing the solemnity of the naturalization oath, he planned to depart early. However, an unsettling premonition lingered before he left.

Despite reserving ample time to catch the bus, he arrived at the station ahead of schedule, only to realize he had missed the previous bus after a fifteen-minute wait.

This setback reinforced his conviction in the proverbial notion that "good things come after hardship," intensifying his anxiety and panic about potential subway delays or entry issues at the venue.

Fortunately, he finally boarded the subway. He had taken the subway many times before, always wondering why there were no ticket inspections. But today marked an encounter with ticket inspections conducted by several police officers at the front of the car.

He felt a bit like a fortune teller today, his intuition sharper than that of a blind seer. When passing the bridge, the subway unexpectedly paused for five minutes, prompting Chen's musings on the concept of "good things come after hardship" and a sense of inexplicable indignation.

As the subway carriages grew increasingly crowded, an elderly lady boarded just before the midway station. Her trembling demeanor and gasping plea for a seat without lifting her head, "May I have a seat? I'm old ...." prompted a young man, resembling a Chinese overseas student, to offer his seat promptly.

Seated diagonally across from Chen, the elderly lady piqued his interest as he observed her peculiar appearance and actions. He had never observed a woman so quietly and attentively before. She looked at least sixty years old, adorned with a few ostentatious shiny rings on her fingers, one gleaming on her thumb. She wore a black jacket, a pair of light green pants, and a pair of ill-fitting sneakers. Her gray hair was haphazardly tied at the back of her head. Her face bore wrinkles like scars from burns. Clutching a dirty pillow in her left hand and several plastic bags in the other, she sat down, inadvertently dropping one of the bags to the ground. Despite her aged countenance and disheveled attire, she nonchalantly engaged with her phone, oblivious to her surroundings.

To Chen's surprise, she embarked on a loud, impassioned phone conversation, seemingly oblivious to the public and holding the phone to her mouth like a microphone. My God!

She called her boyfriend: "If you invite that woman out on a date again, I won't go anymore!"

Maybe the person on the other end of the line was trying to explain, but it made her even angrier, so her voice increased: "You did make coffee for her yesterday! Do you know? You are in trouble now!"

The old lady's voice grew hoarser and more frightening. She verged on hysteria as she uttered the last two sentences. Her face, already etched with wrinkles, contorted even more grotesquely, bordering on ferocity.

Her hoarse, frantic voice reverberated through the carriage, drawing amused glances and stifled laughter from fellow passengers. Most of the passengers were young people heading to college classes.

Amidst the quiet carriage, Chen refrained from laughter, reflecting on Shakespeare's adage that "love knows no age." He pondered the irony of societal expectations regarding age and love, feeling embarrassed at the spectacle unfolding before him. He took out his phone, put on his headphones, and started to review the national anthem he had to sing today. However, that hysterical voice kept echoing in his mind.

"Good things come after hardship."

As the scheduled time for the oath-taking approached, Chen's anxiety mounted, exacerbated by confusion over the multiple exits at the subway station. Fortunately, a group of police officers stationed at the exit facilitated his timely arrival at the oath-taking venue in City Hall.

By this time, a lengthy queue had formed in the hall. Just as he rushed to the queue, he was unexpectedly accosted by a girl midway through the line. Turning his head, he recognized her as Joy, the acquaintance from the naturalization exam just two weeks ago.

"I'm leaving for China in two days. If I don't get my passport on time after naturalization, I won't be able to return to Canada. What should I do?"

Joy grasped Chen Guangze, the only familiar face in the crowd, and asked anxiously.

"It's best to ask the staff. I'm not sure either," he replied, shaking his head and attempting to retreat to the end of the line.

Joy seized him once more, saying, "You're really straightforward. Stand here with me, and don't go to the end."

He shook his head again and proceeded towards the end of the line.

Everyone had to undergo immigration paper checks and surrender their maple leaf cards before registration. The staff explained that they would ask three serious questions before the oath-taking first, whether he had a criminal record. Second, whether he was loyal to Queen Elizabeth, he didn't comprehend the third question but attempted to answer "Yes" and surprisingly passed.

The heavy doors of the hall were shut after the naturalization participants and their families entered the venue. The judge, clad in a red robe, began narrating her story (it is said that she recounted the same story every time). It was a tale from long ago when many believed Canada was brimming with gold, prompting her parents to immigrate. Upon seeing snow for the first time, her father famously dubbed it "white gold."

A grand screen displayed Canada's history and culture, accompanied by the national anthem.

The judge continued fervently: "Canada is a big family. One hundred and ten individuals from forty-seven countries speaking diverse languages have gathered to join this warm, free, democratic family. Let's build it together!"

Applause resounded, and Chen was truly moved at that moment, his eyes welling up with tears. It was a big family, and he had now become a part of it.

The men on stage taking the oath were dressed in suits and ties, while the women wore elegant skirts. Chen pondered that despite obtaining a Canadian passport and citizenship, he had still felt deeply connected to his Chinese roots while deciding what to wear the previous night. Hence, he chose to wear a dark blue Zhongshan suit from China.

As Chen raised his hand to take the oath, a complex mix of emotions washed over him, signifying the culmination of his journey toward citizenship.

Chen felt very tired that night. He lay down early but couldn't sleep. After much tossing and turning, he finally got up and wrote a long letter to his wife, who was doing business in China. They had been married for four years without children, living separately without caring about each other. Plagued by thoughts of the elderly lady on the subway, Chen resolved to address the stagnant state of his marriage.

A month later, Chen went to the court to submit divorce papers. When he returned home, he received a notification in the mailbox to collect his Canadian passport, marking a new chapter in his life.

# A Single Mom

## I

The delineation of her identity left me somewhat perplexed. I found myself grappling with whether to classify her as Chinese or Vietnamese. Her parents were Chinese immigrants who settled in Vietnam, yet she had never acquired Chinese citizenship. She was born near the Nanhe River in Vientiane, the capital of Laos, and her parents christened her Nan'an. From a tender age, her parents enrolled her in a bilingual school, ensuring her proficiency in both Vietnamese and Mandarin.

As Nan'an embarked on her second year of university in 1977, Vietnam initiated a sweeping anti-Chinese campaign. Consequently, her parents' tea shop in Vientiane was forced to close, compelling them to liquidate all their possessions for gold to flee back to China. Escape was perilous; each refugee had to pay 10 taels of gold to the "snakeheads," individuals aiding others in clandestine entry into China, for passage on the boat. Even the gold carried by refugees wasn't immune to danger; if they encountered marine police and refused to hand it over, they would be pushed into the sea and drowned. Many were promptly stripped of all their possessions. Over time, refugees devised strategies to safeguard their gold, such as stashing it in small pouches, hanging it on ropes affixed to the side of the boat, and submerging it in the sea. Thus, some managed to evade plundering.

After enduring the perilous voyage alongside Nan'an and her family, they eventually reached Guangxi Province. Facilitated by the snakeheads within the refugee camp, they boarded a smuggling vessel bound for Hong Kong. However, while evading pursuit by maritime authorities, tragedy struck as their boat capsized, claiming the lives of Nan'an's parents and younger sister, leaving her as the sole survivor rescued by Hong Kong police. Ultimately, she found sanctuary in a Canadian refugee camp in Hong Kong and was eventually resettled in Canada.

## II

On Saturday morning, Vancouver's bustling Chinatown welcomed visitors with its vibrant energy. Nearby, nestled within a Mandarin-speaking church, was the "Future Children's Chinese Class," where Nan'an brought her child to register.

"Good morning, teacher! My name is Tianxing," greeted Nan'an's child, a captivating figure with undeniable beauty. Rosy cheeks adorned his fair complexion, while deep-set eyes shimmered with stunning blue irises. A pair of oversized glasses perched upon his prominent nose, occasionally prompting him to adjust them with a gentle push. Curly golden locks were adorned with vivid blue hair clips, and when he smiled, dimples graced each side of his mouth, lending him the charm of a lively doll.

"Your daughter is absolutely charming! And her grasp of Chinese is commendable," I remarked, pleasantly surprised by the doll-like child's efforts despite the occasional imperfection in pronunciation.

"Ha, ha, my apologies! He's a boy. He's six years old this year, gifted in languages, and he has a keen interest in China," Nan'an clarified with a smile. "I've been teaching him Chinese at home, but I'm not a professional teacher. I hope he can learn here and make some friends who speak Chinese. I dream he'll have the opportunity to travel to China one day."

As soon as Nan'an spotted me, she struck up a candid conversation.

She had a typical Asian visage, with brown skin dotted with freckles adorning her flat face. Her eyes were wide-set, with a large, round nose and slightly upturning nostrils. Her dry hair, tinged with yellow, was casually tied back. She stood at an average height, with a relatively slender upper body but a prominent posterior.

My initial thought was, "This child must be adopted!"

The disparity between mother and son was striking, leaving little room to discern any shared DNA.

"No problem at all. He can join our beginner class on Sunday afternoons. All the kids in the class are his age. And we'll be organizing summer camps in China in the future."

I instantly fell in love with this child.

"Sure, but I'll need to make some time arrangements. I work on Sundays," Nan'an said, with her head down, a slight furrow in her brow, appearing somewhat uncertain.

"It's okay; his dad can also pick him up if he's available," I said, worried about losing this student after hearing her words.

"He doesn't have a father; I'm a single mom," Nan'an replied straightforwardly, causing embarrassment and regret to wash over me for my careless assumption.

"We've got Mommy's love, right Tianxing?" she spoke, pulling her son close to her side with one hand.

Blushing slightly, Tianxing looked up at his mom and nodded shyly.

### III

Nan'an eventually enrolled Tianxing in our Chinese school. He proved to be a bright, spirited child with a vivid imagination. In word games, his talent for mimicry outshone that of his peers, gradually elevating him to the leader among the children in the class.

Halfway through the semester, a captivating incident unfolded in the classroom. One day, a Chinese parent expressed her desire to withdraw her daughter from school, citing Tianxing's behavior as the cause: "Tianxing is nothing but a little troublemaker. He brazenly told Anna that he intends to marry her someday! How can I allow my daughter to be influenced like this?"

With a fierce glare directed at Tianxing, the mother's impassioned words left a non-Chinese-speaking foreigner nearby bewildered, casting a puzzled glance in my direction.

"Tianxing, why did you tell Anna you want to marry her when you grow up?" I asked gently, waiting for Nan'an and Tianxing in the classroom after class. Squatting down to meet Tianxing at eye level, I held his hand, awaiting his response.

"My shoelace came undone, and she helped me tie it. She also said I'm very handsome. So, I decided to marry her when I grow up," Tianxing explained, his face uplifted with his eyes blinking innocently, displaying no trace of adult bashfulness.

As I gazed upon the endearing face before me, I found myself reluctant to impose adult perspectives or traditional norms onto him. It dawned on me that many times, the world as perceived and envisioned by adults was far more tainted than that of children's innocent purity.

Nan'an arrived to collect Tianxing, her countenance aglow with delight as she insisted on presenting me with a sizable papaya.

"This week, the boss finally raised our wages. Many of us would have been compelled to seek alternative employment without it. Thank you for teaching Tianxing; he adores attending your classes."

"Congratulations!" I exclaimed, cognizant of single mothers' challenges, genuinely sharing her joy.

"Thank you! I've been employed at a clothing factory for over fifteen years. Starting at seven yuan per hour, with a meager raise of point two five yuan annually, I've reached thirteen yuan. Despite being deemed a skilled laborer, the increments were infrequent, with some of my colleagues not seeing a raise for several years," Nan'an revealed, a flicker of pride gracing her features.

"Why not seek out a new opportunity swiftly? The minimum wage in BC province is nearly the same, right?" I inquired upon hearing Nan'an's explanation.

"Well, I've grown accustomed to it. Pursuing a new job without proficient language skills would likely result in minimum wage, regardless of where I go. Here, at least, I possess some experience and acquaintances. It's preferable to avoid being exploited," Nan'an explained, a tinge of resignation shadowing her expression.

Nan'an's words were a stark reminder that unseen struggles persisted even in this seemingly idyllic setting.

"Tianxing, look what Mom bought for you—Batman," Nan'an exclaimed, presenting a splendid toy box brimming with various-sized Batman figurines.

"He's been asking for it for nearly a year. I promised to get it for him once I received a raise," Nan'an chuckled, her entire face illuminated with laughter as she spoke.

"Oh, look, he inherited his father's French romanticism—tongue kissing."

Tianxing jumped up and kissed his mom on the mouth.

"He's too cute; how could his father bear to abandon him?"

I was moved and began to blurt out nonsense again.

"He doesn't have a father; I conceived him with purchased sperm."

This statement shocked me; I didn't expect such a seemingly ordinary woman to have such progressive thoughts.

**IV**

"Why not seek a partner to marry and raise children? It would provide the child with a father figure," I suggested to Nan'an, knowing her to be a forthright woman and feeling comfortable broaching personal topics as our acquaintance deepened.

"I did try to find someone, but I didn't meet anyone I truly liked," Nan'an replied, her expression akin to a princess resigned to her fate.

"You should never marry someone you don't genuinely care for, especially just to have children," I concurred, agreeing with her sentiment.

"But I adore children and long to have one to share my life. Pouring my love into raising a child is fulfillment enough for me," she explained.

And so, Nan'an proceeded to recount her journey to motherhood.

Ten years ago, Nan'an made the firm decision to forgo marriage. Determined to have a child, she navigated the labyrinthine process of acquiring sperm at the hospital. This endeavor proved arduous and time-consuming, with endless queues, appointments, and medical evaluations spanning nearly three years. Yet, what lingered most vividly in her memory was the painstaking process of selecting a sperm donor.

Within the hospital, she was presented with photo albums showcasing potential sperm donors, meticulously categorized by age, nationality, skin color, educational background, and more. Before making her choice, Nan'an was required to sign an agreement stipulating that any contact or inquiries regarding the child's father would be strictly prohibited post-birth.

Having grown up in Vietnam, a nation once colonized by France, Nan'an harbored a profound affinity for the French. During her college years, she had even admired a French classmate. However, following the tumultuous events surrounding the anti-Chinese campaign, her aspirations and connections to the past faded into distant dreams.

She chose sperm from a young French man, a university student exuding charm and charisma, with golden curly locks reminiscent of the individual she once admired.

"You know, he embodies the essence of being French, born with a penchant for affection. When he was born and laid eyes on me, he leaned in and planted a kiss on my cheek," Nan'an recounted with a proud grin.

Tianxing's cheeks flushed slightly as he looked up at his mom, pushing his glasses up with his hand.

"Mom, I really do love you!" he declared earnestly.

Nan'an gently removed the hairpins from Tianxing's head and announced, "Let's go; I will take you to get a haircut and give you a Robin haircut inspired by Batman."

"Goodbye, teacher!" Tianxing waved gleefully at me before turning around, clutching his mom's hand, and bouncing away into the distance, their figures gradually fading from view.

# The Melancholy of Returning Home

At dusk, Su Shanshan's international flight took off from Vancouver and, after more than ten hours of flying, finally landed safely at Chengdu Shuangliu International Airport. Before the plane even came to a complete stop, the cabin was already bustling. People impatiently unbuckled their seatbelts and stood up to retrieve their luggage, turning the aisle into a chaotic scene. The captain's warning came over the intercom, but it seemed to fall on deaf ears as everyone continued with their own actions.

Shanshan sat in her seat, her face showing fatigue and bewilderment. She watched as the people in front of her pushed backward and those behind her surged forward, feeling a tinge of envy. These people's journeys were filled with joy and anticipation, while she felt as if she were nailed to her seat, unable to move.

The sound of unbuckling seatbelts echoed in the cabin. Shanshan thought, "Oh, how eager and excited they are. Family, friends and a warm home must await them at the airport exit!" She clasped her hands and placed them on her lap, staring blankly at every corner of the cabin as if in a vast theater, the only audience member in the entire venue.

Outside, the sky was beginning to darken. The setting sun cast a faint red glow on the edge of the gray sky, resembling a bleeding wound slashed by a sharp blade across the vast horizon. A plane stood quietly on the ground, and two workers in orange vests were unloading luggage onto a cart. Seeing this scene, Su Shanshan found it somewhat amusing and couldn't help but laugh. She then adjusted her posture to make herself more comfortable, resting her face on her hand, her elbow on the oval window frame, and fell into deep thought.

Twenty years ago, at the end of that summer, the Sichuan Basin was like a giant steamer, making everyone sweat profusely. At this airport, the nearly forty-year-old Shanshan, her husband, their eight-year-old son, and six large suitcases emigrated to Canada. Fearing their workplace wouldn't approve, they dared not tell their friends openly. Her brother and sister-in-law were firmly opposed, saying they were too selfish to leave their aging mother for others to care for.

                                          *Manna Liu*（嘉妮）

On the day of departure, no relatives or friends came to see them off. In the early 1990s, western cities were not yet developed, and compared to bigger eastern cities, it was rare to see people going abroad. Upon learning that they had bought international flight tickets, the check-in staff led them to a specific waiting area away from the bustling terminal. Her husband took out immigration papers and passports for a final check. At the same time, their clueless son sat on a chair, licking a "Yili Brand Ice Cream" and swinging his feet that couldn't reach the ground. The large waiting hall was empty except for their family of three. Shanshan sat beside her husband, watching him flip through the documents, thinking, "Is this the immigration paper that took three years to get?!" Her heart was filled with a complex mix of anxiety and a tinge of regret. She and her husband hadn't thoroughly considered why they wanted to emigrate, what the foreign country would be like, whether they could find jobs there, and if the decision was too hasty. Yet, simultaneously, she felt excitement and anticipation for the new life ahead. Her husband's college classmates had emigrated in the 1980s, and every time they called for advice, they heard encouraging words. Upon learning that they had received their immigration papers, the classmates enthusiastically helped arrange airport pickups and housing.

"Although the house isn't ours, at least we'll have a place to stay as soon as we get there, like having a home."

They had already been dismissed from their workplace and had no way back. The die was cast, and she could only comfort herself.

"Ma'am, it's time to disembark."

Shanshan was lost in thought and interrupted by a smiling flight attendant standing in the aisle. She returned to reality and realized the once noisy cabin was empty. The cabin, devoid of its bustling passengers, felt like a fish that had suddenly been gutted, lifeless.

"Oh."

She bent down to pick up her backpack below her seat and walked towards the cabin door. The handsome captain and two flight attendants stood at the door, smiling as they saw her off. To them, this marked the end of a pleasant or arduous journey, and now they eagerly anticipated going home. Despite the woman's apparent reluctance to leave, they still smiled.

Shanshan walked out of the airplane aisle with her backpack and carry-on luggage. Over the years, the country had changed so much that even the airport had become dazzling and luxurious. The long walkways were now equipped with moving walkways that transported people. The walkways were flanked by huge glass frames, and various advertisements flickered vividly under the colorful neon lights. The unfamiliarity made her feel timid like she had come from an undeveloped village to a developed city. She recalled a novel she had read, *Chen Huansheng Goes to the City*, an award-winning short story by Gao Xiaosheng in the early 1980s.

"Since no one is here to pick me up, why rush?"

With no destination for the night, Shanshan didn't know where to go after collecting her luggage.

The other passengers had already arrived at the luggage carousel, eagerly awaiting their luggage. They craned their necks, staring at each piece of luggage that emerged from the black hole, afraid of missing theirs. By the time Shanshan arrived, only her suitcase was left on the long luggage carousel, circling round and round alone on the black conveyor belt.

Although Shanshan had only returned to visit her family a few times, she called her mother once a week. Her mother often nagged, "Shan'er, come back and visit whenever you can. I'm getting older every year. As long as I'm here, there's a home. But when I'm gone, the home will be gone too."

At the time, she couldn't understand how true and cruel her mother's words were. Hearing them repeatedly annoyed her; she even resented her mother's nagging. It seemed like her mother was trying to force her to return. In reality, it wasn't that she didn't want to go back; in the early years after emigrating, she and her husband were struggling in the mire of life, unable to extricate themselves. Life after immigration was far from easy, as her husband dejectedly described it: "Falling from heaven into the dirt!"

Their first trip back to visit family was six years after immigrating. Looking at the pile of nutritional supplements they brought back, her in-laws pursed their lips. They said that so-and-so had sent money from abroad to buy a house for their family, and so-and-so had sent money for their siblings' weddings. The implication was clear: why hadn't they seen them return in glory? But they had no idea how hard it was to earn that money. After the subsequent two visits, her husband simply refused to go back. In recent years, as Shanshan's job stabilized and they bought a house and a car, she became even more reluctant to return, fearing the embarrassment of divorcing her husband. Once a family of three, now she was alone. Although her son had graduated with a Ph.D. and worked in the United States, which sounded like a proud achievement, would it be considered coming back in glory?

Shanshan grew up in a small county town, often called a tomboy, climbing trees and houses like the boys, sometimes even fighting with them. However, when she was in the third grade, her parents divorced. Her father remarried and moved to another city with her brother, later having a daughter, Xiaoqian. He passed away before sixty due to illness. Once, a female classmate argued with her and insulted her, saying, "Your mom's divorced!" At the time, she didn't feel anything, thinking, "What does my mom's divorce have to do with me?" But later, she vaguely sensed that the girls started avoiding her and didn't like playing with her. No matter, she played with the boys instead. She developed later than other girls, and her period didn't come until she was almost fifteen. Around the age of thirteen, she began to understand things, sensing the shame brought by her parents' divorce. She suddenly realized that divorce could be used to insult people. Gradually, her "wildness" began to subside, and she preferred reading at home instead of going out. As an adult, she vowed that once she got married and had children, she would never divorce and never let her children suffer the same humiliation she did due to her parent's divorce.

But in the end, she had to accept the reality of divorce!

Upon arriving in Canada, they had to find a school for their son. The school assigned an ESL teacher for him and arranged for a bilingual child to be his deskmate and help him. Desperate to validate their decision to immigrate, Shanshan eagerly asked her son about the Canadian school just two months after arriving. She sought comfort and recognition from his satisfaction to confirm the correctness of their decision. Her son said, "The school here is good; there's no homework every day, but if only my school in

China could be moved here, it would be even better." Over time, her son grew to love everything about Canada, lost contact with his classmates in China, consistently ranked at the top of his class, and developed a passion for various sports.

After Susan and her husband went to a language center for a test, they waited for the government to arrange their English learning. During this period, her husband, who studied Chinese, diligently sent out resumes everywhere but received no interview invitations. With the help of friends, he finally found a job at a bar. A week later, when he received his first paycheck, he bowed his head and wept. A graduate of Beijing Normal University who had risen to the position of section chief in the education bureau, he was now cleaning toilets and serving drinks in a bar in Canada. The psychological barrier was insurmountable. Gradually, he didn't earn much money and became a regular at the bar, spending almost all his earnings there. Leveraging her English major from back home, Shanshan quickly found a job as an office assistant at a Chinese law firm. Later, she worked part-time while studying to obtain a secretarial certificate from a university, eventually landing a job at a Western law firm. Her husband's decline made Shanshan feel as if the sky was falling. Over time, she began to handle various issues independently and tried hard to help her husband quit drinking. But her husband was a difficult person to change. Although he eventually overcame his alcohol addiction, he still couldn't find a satisfactory professional job due to his language barrier and ended up delivering takeout. Seeing his wife secure a stable job, he felt ashamed and unable to face the challenges of life, ultimately falling back into alcohol.

Witnessing their daily arguments, their fifteen-year-old son calmly said, "Dad, Mom, if you can't get along, you should get a divorce. It would be better for everyone!"

In most families, children fear their parents' divorce. Faced with parental arguments, children often cry and beg for them to stay together. In China, many parents wait until their children have taken the college entrance exam before divorcing, creating a trend known as "college entrance exam divorces." However, a child actively advising their parents to divorce was a first for them.

"It seems that parents' so-called consideration for their children is entirely unnecessary," the couple thought, shocked and helpless at their son's advice.

They calmly went through the divorce process. After the divorce, her husband moved to another city.

Shanshan felt guilty for not being able to bring her mother to Canada. Occasionally, her mother would mention on the phone, "Someone said your daughter and son-in-law are in Canada. Once they settle down, they'll bring you over to enjoy life ...," implying that she should have the opportunity to bring her elderly mother over for a visit. Shanshan never responded to this. After estimating her daughter's situation, her mother never raised it again.

"Xiaobin, I must return to China. I want to visit my mother's grave; I miss her very much. She passed away suddenly. At that time, I had a spinal fracture and was undergoing surgery, so I couldn't return. Additionally, I want to handle my retirement procedures in China," she told her brother over the phone.

She had only one brother in China, so she had to notify him about her return.

Her brother's response was brief: "Oh, got it. I'm on a business trip. If you need anything, talk to Xingxing." And that was the end of it.

Xingxing was her brother's wife, who managed all family affairs. Before her departure, Shanshan couldn't determine whether her sister-in-law was willing to host her. So she mustered the courage to call her brother's home.

Her sister-in-law's voice was a bit cold: "Oh, you're coming back? ... You know after Mom passed away, we sold the old house. Sorry, our second child is preparing for next year's college entrance exam. We recently adopted two cats, and the spare room is for them."

Feeling anxious, she recalled her mother's frequent words. Her mother's passing toppled the family tree and took away the home in her heart. Now, returning meant seeing only a grave. This thought pained her deeply. She arrived in her hometown, facing the brightly lit city without knowing where to go.

She once discussed this topic with her Indian friend, Kiran: "Our cultures are quite similar. In Indian culture, parents are considered the core and spiritual pillar of the family. We also have a saying: 'As long as parents are there, the home is there (Mata-Pita ho toh ghar ho).'"

Kiran shared a story with her.

In a small Indian village where Kiran once lived, there was an elderly couple, Ram and Subhrol. They had two sons, Rajeev and Shankar, and a daughter, Anita. Shankar grew up and moved to a big city, becoming an architect. Still, he returned to the village every year to visit his parents. Over time, his parents passed away.

One day, Shankar decided to visit his hometown. He first went to his elder brother's house, a hardworking farmer with his own family and land. At the door, his sister-in-law greeted him, but her expression showed displeasure.

His brother came out, and Shankar tentatively asked, "Brother, I have nowhere to go right now. Can I stay at your place for a few days?"

His brother looked troubled, saying, "Shankar, I understand your situation, but you see, my house is small, and the children are all crammed into one room. Why don't you try your sister's place?"

His sister had married into another village and was doing well.

Full of hope, Shankar explained his situation to her, but she sighed, "Brother, it's not that I don't want to help you. You know the rules of my in-laws' house. Bringing you here suddenly would cause a lot of trouble. I'm really sorry."

Feeling disheartened, Shankar had to stay at the village's only small inn. The death of his parents not only took away his loved ones but also the home in his heart. He became a rootless wanderer without a spiritual home. From then on, he never wanted to return to his hometown.

Outside the airport was a long line of taxis. Shanshan approached one and got in, immediately looking for the seatbelt.

"Back from abroad, huh?" the driver suddenly remarked.

This comment acted like an activation code, instantly opening her mouth that had been shut for almost twenty hours.

"How did you know?" she asked, clearly curious.

"People returning from abroad have all become foreigners. Their first action after getting in the car is to look for the seatbelt," the taxi driver replied with a smile.

"Oh, I've been abroad for twenty years. To this country and this city, I've become an out-of-place stranger. But am I considered Canadian?"

A tinge of sadness welled up in Shanshan's heart.

Technically, she should be considered a foreigner. Five years after immigrating to Canada, she had applied for citizenship. The reason wasn't that she disliked her Chinese identity but because her son's school was planning a summer trip to Egypt. A Chinese passport required a visa, which was quite troublesome. Her son was only thirteen and couldn't apply for citizenship independently; he needed a guardian with a Canadian passport to take him. All his friends were going, and she didn't want to disappoint him. In truth, she often struggled with identity and cultural recognition, a feeling that only emerged after she moved to Canada.

"Where would you like to go?" the taxi driver asked, turning his head.

"Please find me a hotel."

"Oh, you don't have a home here? I can tell from your accent that you're from Chengdu," the driver continued, trying to engage her in conversation, but she had lost interest.

In winter, Chengdu was foggy, with neon lights in the city casting a cold glow through the mist. Shanshan couldn't feel even a hint of the joy of being welcomed home from those flashing lights.

"So, where is my home?"

The driver's question made her break out in a cold sweat. She felt embarrassed to say she was a local. If she was, why would she be staying in a hotel?

The taxi's radio was playing a heart-wrenching song by Li Lele:

In a strange city with strange people,
Dragging my weary body, where should I go?
Leaving you, leaving you, just trying to escape,
Hiding in a corner, crying my heart out.
In a strange city with strange people,
Tearing my heart apart, I've been hurt completely,

Lonely, I wander in the deep night,

My desolate figure, accompanied by sighs.

Finally, Shanshan checked into a hotel that catered to foreigners. With the approach of the Spring Festival, there were few business travelers and tourists, making the hotel seem deserted. The room had no heating, with a large bed covered in white sheets placed coldly in the center and a pile of white pillows staring at her indifferently.

Feeling utterly disheartened, she dropped her backpack on the floor and slumped into the chair in front of the bed, staring numbly at the cold room as tears streamed down her face.

Later, she decided to fill a basin with hot water, letting the warmth embrace her cold body. At that moment, she felt an immense need for a listener, preferably with a warm hug. She needed to vent and be heard. But that listener couldn't be her son, who worked as a lawyer in the United States. This resulted from her efforts, the first time since emigrating that she felt a sense of pride upon returning. Perhaps this was one of the reasons motivating her to come back.

Who knows?

Unable to sleep at night, Susan lay on the spacious bed, took out her phone, and casually scrolled through WeChat messages from friends. One was from her good friend Yumin, asking if she had arrived safely.

It was daytime in Canada. After hesitating for a moment, Susan dialed a WeChat call. As soon as the call connected, she cried, "Sister Yu, I had no choice but to return. Both of my parents have passed away, and I wanted to come back to visit their graves. I also need to handle my retirement procedures here. My brother is doing quite well financially, living in a big house and running a small factory. But right now, I'm staying in a hotel. I think this will be my last visit to China; I don't want to come back again. I have no home here."

"I understand, I totally understand! Don't be too sad; try to think positively. This is reality, this is life. When my parents were alive, they told me similar things, but I didn't feel it then. It wasn't until last year, when I returned to move their graves, that I deeply realized their words were true."

As Yumin said this, tears streamed down her cheeks and into her mouth. The same situation deeply pained her heart.

Ring, ring, ring...

Suddenly, Susan's phone rang. It was an unfamiliar number.

"Hello, is this Susan? This is Aunt Wen. Xiaobin told me you came back to China."

Aunt Wen was Shanshan's father's second wife and Xiaobin's step-grandmother. Due to her mother's obstruction, Shanshan had only met her twice.

"Oh, Aunt Wen, yes. Uh, I ... I returned to visit my parents' graves and see if I can handle the retirement procedures here."

Aunt Wen's call took Susan by surprise, making her somewhat incoherent.

"Oh, welcome home, welcome home. Coming all the way back, how can you stay in a hotel? I'll have Xiaoqian drive to pick you up and bring you home!"

Aunt Wen's words were warm and firm.

"Home? Stay at home ...?"

The call had ended, but Shanshan remained in a daze, still immersed in what felt like an unreal dream.

# The Scent of Blood and Flowers

## I

Xia Yue hurriedly exited the coffee shop, clutching a cup of coffee. Today was New Year's Eve in Canada and New Year's Day in China, and she needed to rush to work for half a day.

Xia Yue worked at an insurance company with over a dozen branches spread across different cities in Canada. The company employed more than twenty Chinese immigrants. Still, it did not grant them a holiday for the Chinese New Year, stating that no such regulation existed in Canada. However, her department manager was relatively understanding, allowing her to come in the morning to organize a contract and call a client, after which she could go home early.

Xia Yue felt a bit indignant. Why could Amaron from Bangladesh, a woman who wore a headscarf and practiced Islam, get a day off for Ramadan? They claimed that everyone in Canada was equal, but it seemed hypocritical!

As she pushed open the coffee shop door, a blast of cold air instantly fogged up her glasses. She couldn't see anything and had to pull her glasses down to the tip of her nose to vaguely make out a narrow windowsill by the door. She placed her coffee cup on it and removed her glasses with both hands. A thin layer of frost had formed on the lenses in just a few seconds. She gently wiped them with her beloved cashmere scarf, and the frost gradually turned into tiny water droplets.

Suddenly, a faint female voice interrupted her: "Excuse me!"

Xia Yue focused on cleaning her glasses and turned her head abruptly at the sound. She saw a woman in a green cotton jacket standing behind her through the haze.

"Can you spare me some change for a cup of coffee?"

Xia Yue quickly put on her glasses and saw that the woman was about forty. Her dark face was rough and cracked with wrinkles, seemingly never having been treated with any skincare products. She wore a hat that covered her ears, with two thin braids peeking out from under the brim. Although the brim was low enough to almost cover her eyes, it couldn't hide the long scar from her right eyebrow to her nose. She wore dirty sweatpants that sagged so much it seemed the crotch would fall to her knees, and the pants were so long that the heels were being stepped on by a pair of unidentifiable sneakers. The woman stood before Xia Yue with her shoulders hunched, hands tucked into her sleeves, and smiled at her, two puffs of white breath escaping her mouth.

Their eyes met briefly, and Xia Yue saw a longing look in the woman's murky eyes. She hesitated for a few seconds, then suddenly remembered it was New Year's Day.

"Let's consider it a good omen," she thought and reached into her handbag for her wallet.

Unexpectedly, a stack of red envelopes came out with it, scattering onto the ground. Two landed at the woman's feet, and another was blown to the roadside by the wind.

Embarrassed, Xia Yue bent down to pick them up while the woman ran to the roadside, squatted down, and handed the envelope back to her. Feeling awkward, Xia Yue thanked her and handed her a red envelope.

To her surprise, the woman's response stunned her: "We are brothers and sisters. Happy Chinese New Year!"

Xia Yue stood in a daze, watching the woman open the coffee shop door and disappear inside.

## II

January in Canada is truly cold; you can see your breath instantly condense into mist. Xia Yue looked up at the electronic billboard across the street, which showed today's temperature as -27°C, with a wind chill of -31°C. A few days ago, she had called her parents in Hunan, who were happily preparing cured meats and sausages for their New Year's Eve family reunion and celebrating her mother's birthday. They had sent her pictures of the smoked sausages and cured meats, which only made Xia Yue crave them more. Fortunately, her husband's sister in Vancouver had invited them to bring their child over for a New Year's celebration. They had a four p.m. flight, which would get them to Vancouver an hour later.

The snow had stopped falling, but the biting cold wind blew the snow on the ground like smoke. Occasionally, snow too heavy for the tree branches would slide off, and if you were unlucky, it would land on your shoulder as you walked beneath. Few pedestrians were on the street and those who were out hurried along with hunched shoulders and lowered heads. A homeless man pushing a shopping cart full of belongings walked towards her. As Xia Yue passed him, she noticed a small, shivering dog in the cart, which barked at her twice.

Moving to Canada, Xia Yue's first visual shock was the numerous homeless people in the city, but unlike back home, none of them were disabled. Some carried bags or pushed shopping carts filled with their belongings, moving around freely. In the summer, they would set up tents in secluded corners of the streets, basking in the sun, drinking, or smoking marijuana, which was quite an eyesore.

Xia Yue had no fondness for these people. Canada was where one could easily support oneself with a job, so these people must be lazy. Today was the first time she had given money to a homeless person, and she was surprised that the woman knew about the Chinese New Year and even said that indigenous people and Chinese were brothers and sisters. Oh, she remembered hearing that the ancestors of Native Americans had crossed the Bering Strait from Asia about 40,000 years ago, possibly Chinese people who had crossed the frozen strait.

**III**

Xia Yue saw her company's building from a distance. The thought of the warm office with a potted succulent and the fragrant hyacinth in bloom made her feel warmer. She quickened her pace but almost slipped. Fortunately, she only waved her hand in panic, causing the coffee cup lid to fall off and spill most of the coffee.

Xia Yue worked at an insurance company located in the tallest commercial building in the city center. Pushing open the heavy glass door, she was greeted by a wall with the golden words "Maple Leaf Insurance Company" and a reception desk in front of it. She had arrived early to complete her tasks as soon as possible, and the entire floor was empty except for her. She quickly organized yesterday's report, called the client as scheduled, and finished everything by ten a.m.

As usual, she had prepared a stack of red envelopes filled with crisp one-yuan RMB notes to distribute to her close colleagues in their cubicles. Holding the red envelopes, her colleagues clasped their hands and wished her *"gong xi fa cai!"* (may you be happy and prosperous) in their accented Chinese.

With some time to spare, Xia Yue walked through the corridor between buildings to the adjacent commercial building. The central area of this building had an escalator that allowed you to see the glass roof from the ground floor. She habitually entered the flower shop on the first floor, inhaling the fragrance of the roses as if she wanted to absorb the flowers into her lungs.

The young shop assistant, Minhee, from Korea, was already familiar with Xia Yue.

She smiled while trimming the flower stems and said, "These flowers just arrived this morning."

After indulging in the fragrance, Xia Yue bought a bouquet of mixed flowers, including roses, lilies, chrysanthemums, sunflowers, and green branches, to give to her neighbor, Dairy, who had promised to help shovel snow while they were in Vancouver. Westerners loved receiving fresh flowers as gifts. After paying, she left the bouquet in the shop, saying she would pick it up after a visit to the restroom.

In the restroom, she saw a woman at the far end of the sink applying makeup in front of the mirror. When the woman noticed someone entering, she turned and smiled at Xia Yue.

Xia Yue washed her hands and looked for paper towels, only to find the dispenser empty.

Seeing the woman had some paper towels, she quickly grabbed two sheets and handed them to her, saying, "Sorry, the rest are with me. The cleaner hasn't refilled the dispenser yet."

Xia Yue politely thanked her and, while drying her hands, observed the woman in the mirror. Despite winter, the woman wore a very revealing red dress and a pair of seemingly cheap high heels, with long black hair draped over her chest. She looked about thirty.

The woman seemed to sense Xia Yue's gaze.

She turned her head, applied powder to her face with a compact, and asked, "Do you work nearby?"

Xia Yue replied, "I work at the insurance company in the adjacent building. And you? Do you work nearby, too?" Xia Yue asked out of courtesy.

"I'm a prostitute," the woman replied nonchalantly.

"A prostitute?" Xia Yue's heart skipped a beat as she repeated the word to herself, unable to believe that a woman would openly admit to being a prostitute without any shame.

"I'm a prostitute. I work at the hotel next door," the woman added, pointing her thumb toward the hotel as if worried Xia Yue hadn't understood.

Feeling awkward, Xia Yue quickly left the restroom.

**IV**

The eagerly awaited Chinese New Year passed in a flash. On her first day back at work, Xia Yue found her email inbox flooded with over a hundred messages. After selectively addressing the most urgent matters, she realized her colleagues had already gone for lunch.

In Canada, there is usually no lunch break, just an hour for lunch. Western colleagues liked to chat after eating, but Xia Yue wasn't interested in their conversations about hockey, movies, or comedy shows. After lunch, she habitually walked to the adjacent commercial building, where she liked to visit the flower shop to smell the flowers and help digest her food.

The flower shop didn't have Minhee but an approximately fifty-year-old Indian woman.

Xia Yue walked in and took a deep breath near the roses: "They smell wonderful!"

The Indian woman asked if she needed to buy flowers. Xia Yue shook her head and said she worked in the building next door and usually came here during her lunch break to smell the flowers and recharge for the rest of the day.

"Why isn't Minhee working today?" Xia Yue asked casually.

"You don't know? Minhee has been on leave for almost a week."

It was normal for employees to take leave, but the Indian woman seemed surprised that Xia Yue, who liked to come here every day, didn't know about Minhee's leave.

"Oh, I went to Vancouver for the Chinese New Year. The Korean New Year is the same day as the Chinese New Year. Could she be celebrating, too?"

"You really don't know? Two Fridays ago, a woman jumped from the fourth floor and landed at our shop's entrance. Minhee saw it and was scared out of her wits. The boss gave her sick leave for psychological counseling."

Xia Yue's heart tightened, her eyes widened, and she instinctively glanced outside the flower shop as if a blood-soaked corpse was lying there. It seemed as though the scent of all the flowers in the shop was tinged with blood. She suddenly felt her mind and stomach start to churn with the thought, "Oh, how sad. Why did she choose to jump here!?"

**V**

Since Xia Yue heard about the woman who jumped to her death, she hadn't visited the flower shop for a long time. She felt a bit superstitious and scared, and the psychological shadow was hard to shake off. On weekends, she could only buy a flower from another shop to place on her desk. Still, it was never as eye-catching as the variety in the flower shop. Occasionally, when she went to the food corner to buy coffee or lunch, she deliberately avoided the route past the flower shop. Still, she couldn't help but glance at it from afar. The flowers in front of the shop were still vibrant, and customers were coming and going. However, she noticed that there always seemed to be a woman sitting on the ground, leaning against the pillar by the shop's entrance.

Gradually, the incident of the woman jumping to her death began to fade from people's memories, and the shadow in Xia Yue's heart slowly dissipated.

Walking and smelling the flowers was a physical and mental exercise for her. She decided to start visiting the flower shop again after lunch from today. The fragrant roses, serene daisies, and carnations with a lilac scent seemed to pull at her heartstrings.

Xia Yue walked through the passage between the two buildings to the first floor and saw the colorful flowers displayed at the flower shop entrance as usual. She noticed the woman sitting on the ground against the pillar, with a black cloth bag beside her. As she passed by the woman, she was surprised to find that this was the same woman who had asked her for money to buy coffee in the snow a few months ago! Without her hat, the scar on her nose was even more noticeable. The woman had a vacant look in her eyes, appearing numb and indifferent, in stark contrast to the vibrant flowers across from her.

Xia Yue walked straight into the flower shop and bent down to sniff a large bouquet. Minhee was helping a customer wrap a bouquet.

After the customer left, she came out from behind the counter to greet Xia Yue: "Long time no see, Sister Xia."

"Yes, it's been a while. How have you been? Ever since I heard someone fall at the entrance, I didn't dare to come. I hesitated long before mustering the courage to come today."

Hearing Xia Yue's words, Minhee grabbed her hand and whispered, "Keep your voice down. The woman at the entrance is the mother of the deceased."

"Ah!"

Xia Yue instinctively turned to look at the entrance but found that the woman had already left.

Then, Xia Yue heard a tragic story.

On the evening when Xia Yue went to Vancouver for the New Year, a woman, to be precise, a prostitute, jumped from the fourth floor above the flower shop and died instantly.

"A prostitute?! Could it be her?"

Xia Yue's mind flashed with the image of that heavily made-up face.

"What did she look like? Did she have black hair?" Xia Yue asked urgently.

"I don't know. I was arranging flowers at the entrance that day when I heard a loud bang, like a huge sack hitting the ground. I turned around and saw a person lying in a pool of blood and fainted on the spot ...."

Xia Yue gasped, feeling a sharp pain in her heart. Her woman's intuition told her that the jumper was the same woman she had met in the restroom who claimed to be a prostitute.

## VI

Xia Yue didn't dare to go to the flower shop for a long time again, this time because she couldn't bear to see the mournful face at the entrance. However, she strongly desired to know if her intuition was correct. She wanted to confirm if the prostitute who jumped was the same woman she had met in the restroom. She finally mustered the courage to buy two cups of coffee from the coffee shop, one for herself and one for the woman's mother.

The woman was still sitting cross-legged against the pillar, her head down, with two braids hanging in front of her chest, seemingly longer than before. A plastic bucket was in front of her with scattered bills and coins, and a bulging black cloth bag was beside her.

Xia Yue gently approached the woman with the two cups of coffee, squatted down, and handed one to her. The woman seemed to recognize Xia Yue. She pursed her lips, her nostrils flared, and two lines of tears flowed from her cloudy eyes.

"Thank you, sister!"

Xia Yue could feel the grievance and sadness in those tears. She was momentarily speechless, her eyes also becoming a bit moist. She didn't know what to say, so she patted the woman's arm and left.

She didn't want to put money in the bucket before the woman. She felt that giving her coffee was more humane and warmer than dropping a couple of dollars in the bucket. She continued to visit the flower shop daily and bought a cup of coffee for the woman each time. She learned that the woman's name was Maggie, an indigenous Canadian. In the Métis language, Maggie means "leaf." Her parents named her that, signifying their family was like rootless leaves drifting in the wind. Maggie's ancestors lived on the western plains of Canada, relying on hunting and fishing for survival. When European colonizers arrived, they sent indigenous children to boarding schools to make them forget their language and culture and forbade them from returning home. As a result, her ancestors became addicted to drugs and alcohol, leaving emotional scars for the next generation.

However, the mystery in Xia Yue's heart remained unsolved. She didn't dare to ask Maggie, as it was an invisible scar, different from the one on her face, but a permanent pain in her heart.

## VII

One day after lunch, Xia Yue bought two cups of coffee and headed to the flower shop. She saw Maggie sitting on the ground from a distance, with a striking pile of red in front of her. Xia Yue's heart skipped a beat, feeling a sense of foreboding as if she had seen the black-haired prostitute again. She quickly walked closer and found that it was a bright red T-shirt on the ground. A piece of cardboard next to it had a few words written on it: "The Red Dress!!!" Oh, today was May 5th, the "Red Dress Day" for indigenous people, a day to commemorate missing and murdered indigenous women.

Maggie took out a thick stack of photos from the black cloth bag beside her. She showed them to Xia Yue one by one. There were colored photos, but more were black and white. One yellowed black-and-white photo was of her great-grandfather and a Chinese man.

Over 100 years ago, the government relocated the villagers to a designated area when the railway reached Bear Town in western Canada. Maggie's great-grandfather had once used herbs to treat a sick Chinese laborer who had been abandoned. Later, this laborer became a friend of their family, telling them stories about China and giving red envelopes to their children during the Chinese New Year. These stories were passed down through generations in their family.

To avoid discrimination, Maggie's grandmother married a poor white man, but it didn't change her fate. Their child, Maggie's mother, was sent to a boarding school at six. Maggie's father became deaf from beatings after escaping from the boarding school twice, becoming permanently disabled. He successfully escaped the third time and started wandering, learning to drink. After Maggie's parents began cohabiting, they had Maggie and her brother, and the whole family lived on government subsidies, eventually becoming alcoholics and drug addicts. With industrial expansion, factories began to occupy their land in Maggie's hometown, forcing many indigenous people to flee to cities. However, the cities couldn't accommodate them and couldn't adapt to urban life.

At seventeen, Maggie came to the city alone, with little education and no skills, unable to find a job. She wandered around, drinking and smoking marijuana, living on meager government subsidies. At eighteen, she was raped by a man and gave birth to her daughter, Aponi. Two years later, as a single mother, life became too hard, and she had to cohabit with another man, giving birth to her younger daughter, Grass. One day, when Grass was thirteen, she suddenly disappeared and was never heard from again. Although Maggie reported it to the police, they were indifferent. Her elder daughter, Aponi, not only had a drinking problem but also became addicted to drugs and had to work as a prostitute to support herself. A few months ago, on that fateful Friday, Aponi had an appointment at a hotel but was tortured by two perverted men and couldn't get paid. In her rage and sorrow, she jumped from the fourth floor here and died instantly.

"I know how hard her life was," Maggie said, wiping the tears from her face.

Xia Yue saw the same face she had seen in the restroom, almost identical, except that she was smiling brightly among the flowers in the photo. Xia Yue's mind flashed to that face covered in heavy makeup. She instinctively looked up at the flower shop, where the flowers bloomed brightly in pots with nutrient solution. In an instant, she seemed to understand why Maggie's daughter chose to end her life here.

Maggie was never seen at the flower shop entrance again. She left, and no one knew or cared where she went.

Xia Yue never visited that flower shop again.

# That Window, That Girl

## I

Jim has lived in Canada for almost eight years. He goes out for a walk every day, no matter the weather. Ice storms won't stop him, nor the high heat of summer. It's a family tradition. Jim's parents often remind him of the tradition: "If you take a hundred steps after dinner daily, you will live to at least ninety-nine, if not a hundred. Look at your grandma — she's ninety-six already and still healthy."

This is Jim's fifth year researching the differences between Asian and Western cultures at the university. During that time, Jim published three books.

Jim's father has often told him, "Men should marry and have a family first, then start their career."

However, Jim has done the opposite; he has a successful career but no family.

"Not everyone follows traditions exactly," Jim says to himself.

In addition to her insistent advice on walking, his mother always asks when he can bring back a daughter-in-law from Canada. He is the hope of two generations because he is the only son in the family, which is a Chinese tradition, so he can't break the family's legacy.

He was so annoyed by such questions that every time this topic was mentioned, there would be a pause without sound at both ends of the phone. Mother was also annoyed, and finally, she did not ask; all was unspoken.

It's not that he doesn't want to be married; it's that no one he sees suits it. He cannot accept the Cantonese-speaking second-generation Chinese because of the barrier of politics, and even more so, he cannot accept the girls whom he could sleep with after just one meeting. He met a Taiwanese girl, but she only wanted to marry a white guy.

Jim's work needs lots of concentration. That's why he walks after dinner every day. Walking helps him relax. He can think about his studies and look at the trees and the sky. He also enjoys looking at the people passing by. And, of course, walking can help him live until he's one hundred years old, as his dear parents believe.

The sidewalks are paved with square stones. Jim likes to count his steps on the stones. Sometimes, he will find a wildflower stubbornly blooming between the cracks in the stone. The little flower looks so delicate he doesn't allow himself to step on it. Jim also likes to look at his neighbors' gardens as he strolls.

Almost every day, Jim passes an old couple from Eastern Europe. The old gentleman's white hair is untouched, and he wears gold-rimmed glasses with a literary look. When it's cold, he likes to hang a Scottish-style plaid scarf around his neck. The curly silver hair on the old lady's head shines brightly; her white, wrinkled face has a light foundation, and her lips are always delicately smeared with bright lipstick, bright but not vulgar.

The couple is walking along the sidewalk, hand in hand. From time to time, Jim sees them chatting, laughing, and exchanging glances and smiles. Jim can tell that they love each other. He enjoys walking behind them, but they always gently yield the sidewalk for him to go first.

Sometimes, Jim meets them on his way back as well. It's so nice to see them sitting on the roadside bench, the woman's head resting on the man's shoulder. It's such a quiet and sweet picture that Jim immediately thinks of the words to his father's favorite Chinese song, "The Most Romantic Thing," written by Ruolong Yao and Zhengfan Li:

The most romantic thing I could imagine
It is to grow older with you.
All the memories we have been through,
We could talk about them when we are old,
Sitting on the rocking chair.
The most romantic thing I could imagine
It is to grow older with you.
Until we are too old to move anymore
You still treat me like the apple of your eye.

Sometimes, Jim meets another couple from mainland China. The wife smiled and said to him one day: "*Nihao*!" ( 你 好 ) in Chinese while they walked past. This couple also walks no matter what kind of weather it is. But they are different from that old couple. They walk fast, and the wife always falls behind; she never quite catches up with her husband.

**II**

On this late summer or early fall evening, a slight coolness fills the air in the largest oil town in western Canada.

This evening, Jim takes his jacket and steps out the door as usual, heading straight toward the West. He likes to walk facing the sun. He enjoys feeling the warmth of the setting sun directly on his body, even though the beams feel like fine long needles poking his face and arms. The prickling sensation reminds him of an acupuncture session. He can feel his pulse grow stronger, and his blood flows faster. His body hums with energy, like an engine running smoothly after fresh oil and a thorough check-up. Jim can feel the passion and energy. Sometimes, this even allows him to jump up and grab a branch over his head.

Suddenly, Jim notices a giant moving van parked across the sidewalk, with piles of furniture blocking his way. Jim sighs. He has no choice but to turn east.

Jim moved into this neighborhood about three years ago, he has never walked in this direction.

"Isn't this the place I drive by daily?" he wonders. "Why does everything look so strange? A different direction offers a different perspective."

The sidewalk is a wider road called Baiting—a pretty name. Baiting Road connects the east to the west. As Jim goes further east, he finds that the trees and plants have become more luxuriant. The aspens stretch into the sky; their yellowing leaves dance in the wind, gently touching the branches as if they were lovers. A leaf falls from a branch, dropping to the ground with a sigh.

He stops in front of a small house; the house and the fence are pure white. Inside the white fence is a world of flowers. It's September, the beginning of the fall. Chrysanthemums of different colors raise their smiling faces, greeting people passing by. Right next to the fence is a line of white lilies. Several butterflies dance around the petals. Jim looks further into the yard: Pearl-sized red fruit hangs on a tree he doesn't recognize. The fruit looks so tempting that Jim wants to taste it. The small house set inside the yard features a picture window and faces the front of the yard; pink wild roses climb up beside the windowpanes.

This small, pointy, Gothic house reminds Jim of his birdcage from long ago. It used to house his parrot, but one day, as Jim was about to hang the cage on his balcony, the parrot pecked the door open and flew out — toward a world it may have dreamed of all its life.

Jim is enjoying the charming garden and the pretty little house with its lovely window. But as he takes in the view, he suddenly notices a pretty young Chinese girl wearing a cute dress sitting at the window. What an innocent face! Look at those big, clear eyes! Jim cannot move—the picture window, the roses, and the girl make up a stunning oil painting, just like Renoir's beautiful western masterpiece "Kahn, Miss Irene."

When Jim finally returns to his senses and sees the "painting," his face burns red. He guesses the girl must be staring at his silly look and laughing. He then looks down and walks away quickly with a little shyness.

When he gets home, he can't wait to turn on the CD, which comes out with the poet Leonardo Cohen's "Like a Fallen Man."

Then, he fills the bath with water and lies in it. The song dances around him while the "famous painting" appears intuitively to his mind's eye, and his heart jumps a bit inexplicably.

### III

The next evening, he doesn't see the moving van when he walks. Jim could resume his walk to the West as he normally does. However, his legs are driven to walk toward the east ….

In no time, Jim comes to the lovely little white house. He can't help looking into the window; he sees the girl. This time, she's sitting at the window doing something. Some flowers are still blossoming in the yard.

Jim is about to leave home for his walk the second day when his mother calls: "Jim, your grandmother is sick; her mouth is chanting your name, saying that before she dies, she wants to see her great-grandson."

"Please tell grandmother I will visit her after this busy period."

Although he avoided the favorite topic that his mother loves, at this time, the topic didn't seem to bother him as much as it did before.

Putting down the phone, he walks east as usual. Everything is the same, except the bright glass window has a beautiful butterfly paper cutting. The girl has her head down as if she were reading a book.

An inner urge makes him want to go to the doorbell and say hello. But he finally just smiles, shakes his head, and turns back.

Then, the next day, on his walk, he sees the girl standing in front of the window from a distance, with her hands on the clear glass like a cute rag doll. The girl sees him coming and smiles slightly at him. The pure beauty of the girl next door makes his heart beat faster. He grins a little unnaturally in response.

As soon as he passes the window, he curses hard at himself: "How stupid! Why can't I even smile?"

On the fourth day, he goes to the east as if this is his new habit. Everything remains the same except for a beautiful paper cutting of a butterfly on the windowpane. The girl's head is bent down as if she is reading. Jim notices she has black hair.

## IV

One week later, Jim returns from a business trip to the States. Anxious for his walk, he finishes dinner quickly and steps out toward the east. His pace is exciting; the birds in the trees are his cheerleaders.

Autumn has announced its official arrival. Fallen leaves carpet the sidewalk in several layers. The petals of the flowers are no more.

This change of season and color won't stop Jim from visiting the big window and the beautiful girl with innocent eyes and a sweet smile. Jim promises to give her a sunny smile if she smiles at him again—he has practiced in front of the mirror about a thousand times.

Jim quickly walks toward the little house until he can see the window.

His legs are shaking; he can barely stand still. It's as if someone suddenly slammed on the brakes of a speeding train, and the momentum carried the train out of the rails. In a blink, the once-perfect train crashes.

The girl is not at the window. All he can see is a curtain of dark green. Only the red of a butterfly paper cutting on the window tells him this is the same one.

He is thrown into complete darkness. The sadness is so heavy that he can hardly breathe. In despair, he stands on the sidewalk until an old lady from the neighboring house comes outside.

"Excuse me," says Jim. "A girl once lived here, didn't she? Where did she go? Do you know?"

The lady thinks the girl is his friend; she is happy to share what she knows.

"A man with a big beard came and took her away. He's a truck driver who couldn't find a Canadian wife; I heard from the house owner."

Jim's dream girl with innocent eyes and a fairy smile is gone—with a truck driver with a big beard. Jim is thrown again into complete darkness ....

The house remains, the white fence still stands, and the tree is still there, but ... but ... but...

The girl will never again appear at the window.

The window and the girl are the constant pain ironed in Jim's heart.

# About the Author

Manna Liu（嘉妮）, from Sichuan, immigrated to Canada in 2003 and now resides in Edmonton. She is an employee at NorQuest College, a member of the Alberta Writers' Guild and the Edmonton Chinese Writing Club, and a recipient of the Edmonton Arts Council Grant. Manna Liu has published bilingual children's stories in Canada, which have become extracurricular reading materials. Currently, she focuses on writing about the immigrant life of overseas Chinese. Her work "The Comfort of Scallion Pancakes and Coffee" won first prize in a writing contest by Canada's *Guanghua Daily*; "On the Path Forward" won second prize in a writing contest by the magazine Chinese Women; "Jane in Red Dancing Shoes" won third prize in a writing contest by the Magazine *Selected Novels*; and "Mother's Small Bowl of Noodles" won third prize in the national "Piao Mu Cup" writing contest. Her works have been published in *Style*, *Sichuan Prose*, *Jialing River*, *Redwood Forest*, *Shanghai Overseas Chinese Newspaper*, *Chinese Literature* in Canada, and other domestic and international media. Her short story collection, *A Solo Dance and Other Stories*(Chinese version), was published in Canada in 2024.

   *Manna Liu*（嘉妮）

# About the Translators

**Yingrui Gong** is a Professor of English in the School of Foreign Languages at Qingdao University. She studied English writing and translation at Ocean University of China (1991-1995), Shandong University (1996-1999), and Shanghai International Studies University (2006-2009).

**Jicheng Sun** is an Associate Professor of English at the School of Foreign Languages, Shandong University of Technology. He pursued his English studies at the Department of English at Shandong Normal University (1988-1992), the Institute of American Modern Literature at Shandong University (1995-1999), and the Department of English at Peking University (2001-2007). Email: jichengsun@pku.edu.cn.

# About the Editor

Hal Swindall is a native Californian with a Ph.D. in comparative literature from UC Riverside (1994). He is a vagabond English professor around East Asian universities in China, Korea, and Malaysia. His main academic research interests are late nineteenth-century European literature and art. Still, he has become interested in Chinese literature, Korean Buddhist art, and similar studies during his time in East Asia. He has also translated academic and journalistic French articles.

# About the Proofreader

John Drew, [B. A. (New Brunswick); M. A. (Chicago); Ph. D. (Cambridge)] a poet and tutor in Cambridge, UK, has earned his PhD in the English Department at the University of Cambridge. John has taught poetry writing in different universities worldwide with his wife, Rani Drew, who teaches drama writing and performing.